W9-AFP-005

JAKOB'S COLORS

JAKOB'S COLORS

LINDSAY HAWDON

New York • London

Quercus

New York • London

ISBN 978-1-68144-615-8

Library of Congress Control Number: 2015954551

Distributed in the United States and Canada by
Hachette Book Group
1290 Avenue of the Americas
New York, NY 10104

Manufactured in the United States

10 9 8 7 6 5 4 3 2 1

www.quercus.com

For Dow and Orly

Si digo amor,
doy nombre a lo último que he sido
caminando entre el pájaro y la tarde

If I say love I name
the last thing I have been
on my way from lark to twilight.

José Heredia Maya

Part One

This Day

There is a rhythm to his steps, slow, staggered, but nevertheless a rhythm, lest he fall and not rise. Small boy. Barely eight years old. The sheepskin coat that had been given to him in the first village he had run to, when he had all but forgotten kindness, hangs down to his knees—small round caps that he knows can be smashed away from the bone. Knows because he has seen rifle butts held back from the shoulder and then swung against them, cracking the thin skin that hangs like dirty cloth.

Jakob pulls the sheepskin coat around him and smells the scent of the man who gave it to him.

"We live in a time when a coat is one of the most precious things on earth," the man had said. "How did it come to this? I ate my own dog from hunger, and before that I traded all I had. But my coat I would never trade. You cannot stay, but you can take this. My dog would have liked you."

Even at age eight Jakob knows that by now that man, shaven headed and too old for his years, will no longer need his coat.

Jakob coughs. His breath wheezes. His teeth are loose in his gums. His skin is gray. Jakob—a half-blood gypsy child of Roma and

Yenish. He does not recognize his own thumb or the very scent of himself.

"Run if you can," he has been taught. *Te den, xa, te maren, de-nash.* A whispered plea. "Always, if you can," and as young as he is, he still knows what this means, for not to run stirs a longing that is suffocating until sleep saves him. And even then he wakes.

So he runs. With shoes of sackcloth, still stained with another's blood, a stone clutched in one hand, a small wooden box in the other. He runs blindly, full of fear, empty of hope. For hope lies behind him in a green field with a twisted tree that stands gnarled and leafless and shaped like a Y.

Through narrow passes, across the bleakness of snowy slopes, his heart splitting. Through fragrant forests, spruce trees clinging to the top layers of soil. He sleeps during the day, warm under fallen pine needles, and runs at night, the trees collapsing into the darkness behind him.

He gnaws wild garlic, forages for nuts, pulps fennel in the palms of his hands. He knows the kind of berries that he can eat, but three times he has taken a chance and eaten something unknown to him: a mushroom in the grasses, long stalked, like the ones his mother used to dry and cook; a berry red, sour, and unripe, bitter in his mouth; and a leaf—sucked because he is so thirsty.

When he closes his eyes he sees his mother's face.

Zyli wsrod roz, she sings. They lived among the roses. *Nie znali burz.* And they did not know of any storms.

While he sleeps he dreams strange dreams. In them his sister finds a woolen hat, pulling it tight onto her head, and his brother a fur glove that he wears on his right hand, holding his palm over his mouth so his hot breath can warm his face. Neither will take them off, even when their mother, pale with cold, sits beside them, her teeth chattering, sounding out like a tinny drum. But when Jakob says that he is cold his sister draws the hat from her tiny head, his brother the glove from his tiny hand and, without a word, hands each to him on outstretched arms that demand he take them. He wakes weeping, blue lipped with cold and dread.

Dusk falls. He forgets what it is like to stare at the moon. He chews grass. His spit turns green. His head itches, lice infested and full of sores. He waits until it is dark before leaving the woods, creeping down the side slope of a grassy field and smelling the dew. Below him a lake glistens in the half-moon light, a still sheen, honey colored with a promise of tranquility. He turns away from it, no longer able to trust the land itself.

Te na khuchos perdal cho ushalin. He hears his father's voice. "Jump your own shadow, my boy," he whispers.

Back into the woods where the trees lean darkly above him, hiding his silhouette on the ground. Wood moss softens his tread in places, but when his steps can be heard, the wind often blows, drowning out the noise of brittle leaves breaking, so that even then the sound of him disappears and he is as close to invisible as the world dares to make him.

Before

She had been christened Glorious because that was what everyone hoped she would be, but from the very beginning they had called her Lor. Spoken softly, a low note that seemed unfinished and barely audible, but that was appropriate, for it turned out she wasn't the sort of person to light up a room.

She stumbled now in the shadows, not wanting to be seen, pulling her children with her, two boys: Jakob, age seven, Malutki—the Little One, who was barely three, and her girl, Eliza, age five. Sewn into their clothes to the left of their chest, each of them wore a black triangle with the letter Z embroidered into the cloth. Sleep deprived, their ebullience buried, hands clutching hands and gripping them tightly. None of them wanted to be separated from the other. Touch was a necessity for her as much as for them now.

Their feet sounded over the ancient cobbles polished over the years by the many shoes that had scuffed across them. They gleamed like tiny mirrors underfoot. Either side of them the houses rose upward from the narrow street, hiding the sky. They slanted with age and neglect, the paint peeling, the brickwork fissured and cracked with salted air. Lor stepped over the warm vents, scents of baked bread coiling around them, her children's mouths filling with saliva and longing.

"Just a little farther," she assured them. "Just a little." They did not argue as they used to. The fight had all but gone from them.

By the time they reached the bar, their faces and hands were numb with the chilled autumnal air, their coats damp with night mist. She kissed their palms, squeezing them to her lips, like a good luck charm on the dice before it is thrown. The bar was called De Clomp, meaning the Shoe. It sat as such upon the street, unkempt and sunken slightly, worn, like toe-stretched leather. Music seeped from it, out into the night like a sweet smell.

She pulled open the door with a jerk. The sound of a trumpet, the blare of it, blasted from the room, vibrating off the buckled walls. A beast of a man was playing, a mass of curling hair and cheeks pink with exertion. The instrument looked fragile in his hands, and it seemed impossible that such a noise could explode from it with the melody of a lullaby.

Lor pulled her children into the clammy warmth of De Clomp. Felt the heat of it on their faces, on their hands. The oak bar was full of the flicker-light of candle flames. People appeared through a fog of smoke, pallid and lavender colored. A few looked over at them, their eyes lingering on the children with mild inquisitiveness and smiles of nostalgia. Lor pulled them across the room, through the miasma of sweat and heat and the noise of clinking glasses scraping against teeth as shots were knocked back, showing a flash of a swollen mouth that she imagined looked monstrous to her children's eyes.

Alfredo was behind the bar, as rotund and flushed with endless nights of drink as he ever had been, despite all that was passing. He stood pouring out fast shots with well-practiced speed, one hand holding a bottle, the other drumming his fingers on the worn wood in time to the music as simultaneously he joked with a young man across the bar. She stepped toward him and he turned his head.

"Alfredo," she said. Then hesitantly, "Do you remember me?"

His eyes glanced down at the three children who clung to her hands and legs, taking them all in; the badges on their chests, the disheveled look of their clothes, the lost look in their eyes. His face crumpled.

"Lor," he said finally. "Such a long time."

She nodded. The children were almost asleep where they stood. Jakob had picked up Malutki, had heaved him up onto his back, the boy's small hands locked tightly around his older brother's neck. Jakob swayed and fought to keep his eyes open.

"We need a room," Lor said. "The one above the bar. The one that looks over the street?"

"Yes, you are welcome to it."

She searched Alfredo's face for a flicker of expectancy, but he was startled that she was there.

"You want to eat first? Or I take you now?" he asked, nodding toward the children.

"Now. But perhaps some bread and milk to take with us?"

He fetched what she had asked for. Then they followed him out into the street, relieved to leave the noise behind them, and around to the dull-green door at the side, which was still battered and in need of a new coat of paint. Eliza was in Lor's arms now, lolling between sleep and wakefulness. Jakob still carried Malutki. He is so good, she thought. So good, and then she told him so, but the praise he once sought so fervently no longer lit him up as it used to. He had not uttered a single word of protest all the long day. Now he just looked up at her with his wide gray eyes.

"I can take him if you like?" Alfredo offered. But Jakob shook his head, and so Alfredo turned and hurriedly unlocked the door.

"I did not see Elpie down at the bar," Lor said, as they climbed the long battered stairwell, which was dark and narrow and smelled of the wood smoke that seeped up from the bar. "He is well?"

Alfredo shook his head. "He is a Jew. They took him," he said simply.

They used the climb as an excuse not to speak after that.

They reached the first floor and stood outside the room, cramped tightly together on the landing while Alfredo fumbled breathlessly with the key, milk slopping. The latch clicked and he pushed open the door.

The room was in front of them. Empty.

He was not there. Lor breathed in deeply. Then she turned and hugged Alfredo, who squeezed her tightly, his warm soft belly against hers, before she pulled away.

"We'll be fine," she managed. "We'll be fine . . ." her voice breaking.

"You sleep. Tomorrow we can talk."

"It's all right that we are here?" she asked as he turned to go.

"Always." She watched his immense bulk descend the stairwell, listened to the boards creaking.

Then she held her breath, closed the door behind them, and rested her head against the wood. He was not there. Her heart was barely beating. She turned. The light from a streetlamp shone into the room. It was so sparse, she thought, the walls so bare. The furniture was the same. The brass bed was still there with its springs that sagged and sung, and the worn wooden wardrobe with the oval mirror that was oily and rainbow stained with age. The fireplace was still black with soot, and the basin had the same ring of brown scale scarring the white enamel from the many times the town's hard water had swilled down the plughole. But without their belongings none of it looked the same.

Malutki was still asleep. She took him from Jakob, cradled her face into the warmth of his neck and then placed him on the bed, where he lay motionless and exhausted. She kissed his closed eyes. She always wanted to kiss his eyes, at the corner, where his cheekbone met his temple. There was the blue of a shallow vein close to the skin on the bridge of his nose. It came and went, like a small stream in the map of his face that dried up when the flow was not strong enough. She took the pebble he clutched in his hand, a smooth but dull pebble of insignificance that he'd picked up somewhere along the way, stooping in the dirt to retrieve this jewel of ordinariness that must be held and treasured at all times. She placed it on the bedside table next to him.

Then she undressed Eliza, kissed her knees and the knot of each elbow, and laid her down beside her brother, where her breath lengthened and deepened toward slumber.

"Ma," said Jakob.

"Yes, my love?" she asked, drawing the sun-bleached drapes across to dim the lamplight from the street.

"We need a shell, Ma. A big shell, to curl up inside," he said. "Then we can lie there, hearing the sea, falling asleep to the sound of it."

He was untying his small bag from his back, opening it and pulling out the jar that held the two baby snails clinging to the miniature forest of leaves and flower petals that he had found for them, fresh every day for the past week. He put them on the bedside table and then lay down with his thumb to his mouth, became the child he was again.

"Our story?" he mumbled. "Gillum and Valour?"

She lay down beside him, felt the familiar dip of the bedsprings, the angular ridges, like the ribcage of some Jurassic skeleton beneath her. She lay, facing the way she used to, with the view through the window, and stroked the smooth, warm skin on her son's back as she thought of what to tell him. It was a story she had begun weeks ago, when there had been need for it.

"So you are on Gillum and I on Valour, with Malutki behind me and Eliza behind you," she began. " 'Hold tight to your horse's mane,' I say to you and you do so, gripping clumps of his coarse hair in your hands. Sometimes we ride sidesaddle to rest our legs, but you like to ride cowboy style best in this land that is not known by you or me, or anyone before us. In the vessel tied to the underside of your right saddle is the indigo we have found, a thin glass vase that looks as if we have captured the night inside it. And beside this, the malachite green, cut from the azurite we found in the copper caves, cut and welded and ionized with sweet wine. We keep them safe in a leather pouch that holds the five other vessels. Empty for now, but only for now. We are far beyond the Ushalin World. Far beyond that Shadow World, with its deserts of smoke and ash that eddy across the Great Plains."

"But them Ushalin people are fast, Ma. They follow quick on our heels."

"They ride fast, it is true. But we ride faster. They can move only on the horizontal or the vertical, they are all lines and edges, governed by rules they have laid down themselves without thought or reason. And they are often misguided, are easily misled, take one path when they should take another. They are like ponderous merchants, or hapless architects that have only their designs to sell, mere promises of a plan. We are more solid, our venture etched, as in stone."

"So our task is set, Ma?"

"Yes, our task is set. We are well on our way to fulfilling it. Even the woods we have left behind us now, and our horses are walking across the valley floor, which is covered with red rocks and bare trees that slant toward the west and the setting sun."

"Is there no rain?" Jakob asked, his words slurring with sleep.

"There is no rain. There has been no rain for months. Everything is biscuit brown, and there is dust, so much dust."

"I wish I were a camel," he mumbled.

"Why a camel?"

"For the dust. So that my long lashes could trap it from my eyes."

She smiled and loved him more. "In the middle of this valley floor there is a crevasse, no wider than the length of me, no deeper than the length of you. As the sun sets we climb down into it because we will be hidden there and can sleep safely. We set up our camp. We tie Valour and Gillum to a tree and unload our bags, keep safe our vessels, storing them in the cool shade where the light will not dull the pigments within. You collect the wood. You get the thin, dry twigs first, knowing they will burn easily, that they will lap up the flames as you sleep."

She paused and listened. His breath had lengthened. She waited until his thumb fell from his mouth. "My boy," she whispered.

She climbed from the bed, stood in the center of the room, regaining her balance. Outside, from the street, there was the sound of slurred voices and the staggered steps of drinkers heading home. She could still hear the music from the bar, the vibration of it through the age-old floorboards, and the hum of distant chatter.

She gathered up their coats, sat on the edge of the bed, and one by one unpicked the black triangle that was sewn onto each of their breast pockets. Then, slowly, she began to undress, moving across to the sink. She stroked the enamel, circled the edge of the bowl, looked up, and in the mirror above it she saw herself. She had not seen herself for days. She had never looked so colorless, her mouth never so straight, so defined. Her hair was tangled and coiled with three days of rain: soaked and dried, and soaked and dried, and soaked and dried again. She was afraid to brush it and she had always brushed her hair, religiously, thirty strokes each night for "sheen and shine and follicle cure." "Radiant," her mother had said of her hair, "as sleek as an eel." But not this night. This night her hair was dull with grime.

She had nothing with which to wash herself so soaked her cotton shirt with water so cold her fingers ached. She moved the damp cloth over her arms, down the ladder of salmon-pink scars that ran horizontally from the crook of her elbow to her wrists, healed now, sealed like secrets. Her skin tightened as though a needle were pulling a thread beneath the surface. Again she soaked the shirt and wrung it out. Her movements slow and concentrated, as an atonement. She dragged the cotton across her stomach and trembled in the night air. She washed her whole body in this way. Soaked her stale skin, a pool collecting on the wooden boards as she remembered the very first time that she had stood in the center of that room, alone with him, standing face-to-face, raw and self-conscious in the silence that surrounded them. She had stood shivering, her thin arms wrapped around herself, the damp of the past days buried in her bones. Dressed still in his clothes, old clothes that were too big for him, far bigger for her, rolled at the ankles, at the wrists. Worn at the seams, torn in places, and still damp from the two days where they had slept in the reeds, and the three nights where they had rowed the wooden skiff of faded green and red until it could be rowed no more, water leaking through the loose slats, up to their ankles, up to their calves, until in the end they had left it hidden in long grasses, dragging it from the bank to the thick fringes of a moist plowed field, moving on by foot then, following a silty path along the river to the largest town, where they had found De Clomp and this room.

She remembered how he had stood, watching as she shivered with a look of helplessness, before he had fetched the woolen rug that lay across the bed and pulled it around her.

"Don't be afraid," he had whispered.

And she had shaken her head, felt the tears in her eyes. It was not him she had been afraid of. No, for him she had felt only gratitude, that strange boy with his tousled hair and funny talk who had brought her there. Her fears were a residue of the place they had run from.

"You do not know my name," she had said.

"So tell me."

"It is Lor."

"And mine?" he asked.

She already knew it. "You are Yavy."

"Them tears are bright in your eyes, Lor," he had said. "No matter if they spill over. Don't be thinking back," he had told her. "I been long used to not thinking back. Tell me what you want of your life. What you dreaming of in your while-away days."

She stood now in the center of that same room, the sounds of her children, his children, softly sleeping behind her, and only then did she weep. The tears filled and blurred her vision, spilling over. So many she could not dry them with her hands.

"Yavy," she whispered. "Where are you? Please, Yavy, I need you."

This Day

AUSTRIA, 1944

At first Jakob makes himself aware of nothing but the movement of his own limbs; the crease of his cotton shorts, the thud of his own feet, brittle twigs that have fallen a whole long winter before cracking beneath his tread. He squeezes the stone in his hand, holds tight to his box. He runs until the only sounds are forest sounds: the ghost-hoot of an owl, breeze-blown branches, and the creaking of trunks. He leans against the mottled bark to catch his breath. How he longs to be small enough to hide in the crevices.

"The mushroom is the ant's umbrella," his father used to say. How he longs to be a passing ant.

He takes in the rusted ochre from a mossy bough. He runs on. Steely white from the sap of a chestnut tree.

"Lead white," his father would have likened it to. "The white of whites, the cruelest—black at its core. Women dying for this white, paint the soft canvas of their cheeks with the sweet poison of iron oxide, float in clouds of lethargy before it stealing their shine. Before they fainting to the floor."

Jakob sticks to the paths that run from north to south. He knows how to read a path. Knows how to seek out the contrasts of damp and dry that form when the sun shines directly down. He knows how to read the puddles, to read the wind direction from the sediment that collects at the edges, green tinted and murky, and to read the moss that settles on the northern damper sides of rocks and pebbles. He knows which tree to interpret the land by, knows to seek out the giant that stands wider and higher than all the others, or the tree that stands alone, affected only by the elements. Knows to look which way the branches grow, how they will splay toward the highest sun. And, too, that sweet is south facing, that the nuts and berries he finds will be riper on the southerly side. He knows which flowers follow the sun, which lift their heads to face the golden orb in the sky.

"Run if you can," he has been taught. "Always if you can, my boy. With them shadows over your left shoulder at sunset. Run south."

Why south?

"Because south is safe. Closer to the sun."

South to where, then?

But there is no "to where." He runs simply to survive. Moves on from forest to field, from field to forest, forages for mushrooms, dandelions, nettles that he pounds with stones and sucks the juice from. He knows to sleep where the spider webs cling to the nooks and crannies, where the wind won't find them or him as he slumbers beneath their jewel-frosted weaves on a pillow of moss. And he knows how to read the clouds, when to seek shelter, when not. Knows the coming of a storm, the vertical towers that will fill the sky, swelling as the warm air rises rapidly, or the lighter wisps that come with the fairer weather, and the change in their hue: darker where there is open water, lighter where there is snow. He knows how to make a night dial, knows how to join the two points in a crescent moon so that they will lead him south. He has grown up directing himself with the wind and the shadows. This is familiar to him. It is the loneliness that is not. He has never, until this time, been so alone.

He is afraid to sleep. His dreams have him crushed beneath mounds of loam and silt, clogging his mouth with clay, his eyes with darkness. *Pe kokala me sutem.* He sleeps on bones. *Bi jakhengo achilem.* Becomes without eyes. He breathes in grit, stifles his screams, and claws at the warm earth above him. Jakob—a half-blood gypsy child of Roma and Yenish. He scratches the loose soil away, scrapes aside the stones, the splintered roots, soaked with blood, until finally his fingers feel the wind. And then, through a crack in the earth, he catches a glimpse of the blue lapis sky.

He wakes gasping, pulls himself upward, gulping air, choking with memory, as he stumbles to his feet.

"Them shadows moving as the sun commands," his father had told him. "You are the sun, my boy. You are the sun."

Rusted ochre from a mossy bough. Steely white from the sap of a chestnut tree. See that. Only that.

"Don't be afraid, Jakob," his father had said, his voice weak and wavering, his blue-stained fingers faded, a mere memory of the color that most defined him. "*Spourz na kolory*. Tell me what you seeing, Jakob," he had whispered.

There is only day and night and the survival of each. How, he does not know. Why, he does not dare to question. *Te den, xa, te maren, denash*. A whispered plea. There is nothing else but that whispered plea. No longing to live. For he has none. All he has is the instruction to do so. To run is to live. To fight for it. So again he runs on. And on. A ragged density to his breath that wards off tears as the ice of a winter wind freezes the sweat on him.

It is as if the sky has fallen to the earth. *Ceri pe phuv perade*.

He eats only fire. *Jag xalem*.

Drinks only smoke. *Thuv pilem*.

Becomes dust. *Thaj praxo*.

But in the end the hunger of winter forces him from the woods. He hears the toll of a town's heavy bell before he sees the red-tiled roofs of a village that begins where the trees end. He sees a crowd, hears the murmur of voices, a melodic chatter, and finds courage with the sound of it. He creeps out from the shadows and under the cover of leaden clouds finds himself on the thrumming outskirts of a busy market.

He stands by the rusted remains of a truck, the wheels and doors long wrenched from it. A small boy, the same height as he, is siphoning gasoline from the cap, sucking it up through a pipe into his mouth, choking when the liquid spurts through. It gushes momentarily, then slows to a rhythmic drip that lands in a metal bucket, ticking away time like a clock. Another boy, with hair like sedge grass, sits on the ground beside him, struggling to make shoes out of a rubber tire with a blunt knife, his knees so tight you can see the white of bone through his translucent skin.

An old man passes by, jolts against Jakob. He mumbles something Jakob doesn't understand and walks on, his voice gravelly with phlegm that he coughs up at intervals, retching into his grime-clogged sleeve. Jakob watches the old man undo his fly, turn toward a mud brick building, and address it in conversation as he urinates against the guttering pipe that is punctured with bullet holes. His piss is the color of creosote; he himself the color of decay. Jakob walks on, the stench of aged urine on the wind, comforted, despite that, to be in the company of humanity.

The ground is still wet with recent rainfall, but drying as the sun pushes through the clouds. Jakob makes a footprint on the edge of a puddle and wonders if it will still be there at day's end as a mark of his existence. A cart rattles past on loose wheels. He watches the judder and roll of them. He sees an apple glint in the sun. It sits on the edge of a stall, worm ridden, but red and ripe, and aware suddenly of the clenching pain of hunger in his stomach, he reaches out to take it.

The hand that grabs his wrist is rough and calloused.

"If you take it, they will kill you. It means that much to them," says a voice hoarsely. Jakob looks up toward the silhouette of the man who stands over him. His face is stubbled, his two green eyes glinting in the roughness of it. Bright but small, deeply set and overshadowed by thick dark eyebrows that give him the appearance of a permanent frown. "You'll take my advice, yes?" the man says. His stubble moves as he talks. He lets go of Jakob's wrist, leaving fingerprints on his skin. "It is simple. You want to eat; you earn it. I saw you come from the woods, yes? You have been in them long?" he asks. Jakob takes in features that are large, bulbous; a nose that curves outward from the bridge, bent and flattened at the tip as if it has felt the full force of a fist time and time again. His skin is pitted and rough, his hair unwashed, grease scented, and lank upon his scalp with small tufts sprouting from his nostrils and ears. Jakob does not say anything. He is too afraid. The man shrugs.

"As you like. How old are you?"

"Eight," Jakob manages.

"You are small for eight, yes?" Again he shrugs. "And your name? Again as you like. I am Walther. Walther Bauer. I've no qualms in telling you that. I have lived here all my life, like my father and his father before me. Anyone in these parts could tell you my name if you asked them. So, boy, do you know how to make a fire that doesn't smoke?"

Jakob shakes his head.

"Let me show you. Let me save your little life, such as you may or may not need."

He leads him back into the forest and stops in a place where the land dips into a dwelling of red rocks. "If you are to live in the forest, my little friend, then this you must learn to do. If you want to live." Walther kneels and, with his hands, begins to dig. His hands are immense, covered in thick dark hair that coils at the tips. "You need a chimney, you see, but a chimney that will not point up into the sky. Instead, it must go down into the ground. We dig, come."

Jakob kneels beside him and scrapes back the soil from the hole Walther has already made. The dirt pushes down into his nails and he smells the familiar mushroom scent of trapped earth. His breath catches. He feels for his stone. Squeezes it through the fabric of his pocket. Closes his eyes. Reels slightly with the sudden flash of memory that transports him all too easily back to that place, back to that field again, where the Y-shaped tree stands out against the clear sky.

He is there once more, watching it from the hidden depths of the forest. He is crouched down low behind a dense blackness of bracken, his knees upon a soft blanket of moss that holds only a memory of rainfall. His breath comes in shallow bursts, as if to remind him of what has just passed. He knows he should run, knows he should run far and fast. But he cannot bear to leave. Cannot bear to go where the scent of them will not reach him. He peers through the gaps in the bracken, out across the field that is lit with sporadic moonlight, flickering out from behind passing clouds and blue with the long shadows of clumped grasses. He can see the tree, bone white in the moonlight, stark against the velvet sky. But around it there is no movement, no shift or sleight of hand. Not even a wing beat, or scurried dance from a smaller creature. Just an eerie stillness, a silence, as if all else has fled with what has passed.

"Enough," says Walther when the hole reaches the length of his arm. His voice breaks Jakob from his reverie. The tree disappears. The field disappears. There is only the wood in which he now kneels. There is only Walther. "So, you know how to light a fire?" the older man asks.

Jakob nods. Walther hands him a rag and a scattering of flint pieces from the breast pocket of his worn gray suit. One hard, one shimmering with quartz. Jakob has been taught to pick out his fire flint carefully.

"Mostly you'll be wanting a star in your stone," his father had told him from as far back as he can remember. "To see it shine. Second to that, an edge. If not, pick the hardest you can find. If not that, the grayest. And if a stone is wet, you best be discarding it."

Jakob collects paper birch bark that peels off the trunk that has outgrown it easily, a small pile of tinder, picked from higher, drier ground. Then he strikes the two of them together, igniting sparks against the stripped bark. He makes a flame first, then another as the wood catches and lights.

"So you can," says Walther, impressed. "So you can," and he shows him then how to cover the smoke, how to trap it and direct it down into the tunnel that they have dug, their chimney beneath the ground.

Jakob is warm for the first time in weeks. The flames lick up under the cover of the canopy, white at their core. They dance smokelessly.

"You have lice," Walther says. "Best get rid of them."

He tells him to undress, to hold his clothes over the fire and Jakob does as he is told, layer by layer, holding the fabric as close to the heat as he can bear. The lice drop from it, singeing in the flames. He redresses, the cloth no longer scratching. Next Walther cuts his hair, cuts it short and coarsely with the blade of his knife. "They will drive you mad with their itching. Better to put an end to it," he tells him.

Afterward they sit a while, easily silent in each other's company.

"So," says Walther eventually, and he holds up the apple that Jakob had reached to take. "You have earned your apple."

He throws it across to him. Hands him his knife. Jakob looks up. Wants to lean against the warmth of the older man, but instead takes the knife, uses it to cut thin slivers that his loose teeth can chew. The sour sweetness spurts up into the ridge of his mouth, stinging his ulcerated gums.

"You can sleep at the market for now. Work, eat. I will show you how it can be done."

Before

In the early morning De Clomp was lit with shafts of sunlight that warmed gold squares on the oak floorboards. Malutki and Eliza sat upon these squares, rolling marbles across the floor. Jakob sat with his snails that he'd taken from their box, setting them down to move across the shadows. It was too early for the bar to have opened, and Alfredo assured them they would be safe, that they would have the place to themselves, empty tables and empty chairs and an echo of their own voices. Alfredo had given them bread and slices of cheese to eat, with glasses of milk that had arrived on a cart at first light, sloshing in metal jugs that clanked bell-like against each other.

Jakob lifted up a snail, looked at the underside of it. "Drying up in the sunlight, Ma," he said.

Lor was barely listening. To the right of where they were sitting was the place she had once regarded as "her place," or "his place," sometimes "their place." Either way, it was where she and Yavy had once known to look for the other. In the far corner, beneath a bookshelf stacked and cramped with old books, leather covered with hearty browns, mahoganies, and greens. It was so familiar, even after all these years. She could remember clearly how it had been to enter

De Clomp and see him there, slumped and reading or pushing away the contents of his plate, a last small mouthful resting in its center, which he would unconsciously leave. Unlike the Romans, she used to think, who vomited in bowls so they could consume more, but deliberately left a morsel to inform their host that they were full. For Yavy it was something deeper than that. A need to know that, should he need it, there was food enough for him to eat. That he would not starve.

"De Clomp. The Shoe," he had said the very first time they had sat in that place, before it had become their own. "If you had to, would you go choosing them shoes over your winter coat?"

"Yes," she said.

"Yes. Water first. Food. Then shoes. If that was the choice."

He had gone on to tell her a story about shoes, a pile of shoes in a village where he had once lived.

"So high it reached the rooftops of them houses," he had told her. "We piled it for a month of Sundays. Gathered in the village square after church, an' when that bell rang out we took off our shoes, children and adults, flinging them into the center of that square." He used his hands when he spoke, gesticulated for emphasis. She loved to watch him, listen to him, a bright light in a room.

"And when every one of us was shoeless an' that bell sounding out again," he said, "as quickly as we discarded them, we found them, clambering through that pyramid of shoes for our single pair, seeking out our friends' instead, our mothers' or our brothers', throwing it to them, again seeking out our own. An' at the end of it all, when that mound of shoes was no more, if all of us had found our pair, then we'd won the game. If not, we had lost."

She smiled with the memory. When it came, war had not been such a shock to him as it had to her. He had lived with the fight for survival long before it.

Behind the bar Alfredo was clinking glasses and bottles together. From time to time he looked across at Lor, his face questioning, but never asking. She could study his face in the morning light. Certainly it had aged since the last time she had seen him, but aged merrily. His was a giant of a face; the splayed expanse of his nose, the round shelf of his chin. The local children laid coins across it, and made him chew tough hunks of meat, awed that the coins stayed balanced. Of Italian descent, his parents had fled Italy in the diaspora of the 1860s, fleeing poverty and a cholera epidemic that had wiped out fifty-five thousand Italians living in the south. Like his father, and his father before him, Alfredo was a tower of a man, a bulk of bone and flesh. His size was something he'd had to plead forgiveness for all his life, and the clumsiness that came with it, forever knocking against the world around him. He had ventured outside his hometown only once and that was to see the bear pit in Bern, where he'd stared down into the dry-eyed silence of two cramped beasts and felt akin to their bulk in a way he had never felt with any other human being before. Up above, the electric lines had spanned from house to house, lighting up the bears' dumb suffering beneath, and he'd longed to take them back with him to the dark of his own sky. At night with his wife, he slept shallowly, afraid that he might roll and squash her small frame. He had never found a wedding ring to fit his fourth finger. The muscle bulged there like a walrus.

"I have something special for you," he said, seeing Lor looking at him. He disappeared out into the back and returned with something hidden in his giant hand. "For you and the children." In his palm lay a lemon that he placed upon the bar as if it were made of glass. It was rough, the outer skin shriveled somewhat, but the yellow of it stood out against the night-brown of the wood surface, like a small star.

"We couldn't," Lor said. "You must have it."

Alfredo shook his head. "They grow them here. Most are taken, but a few . . ." and his eyes shone. "Here," he said, bringing out a knife and cutting her a waxy slice, an inch thick. "Eat it all, skin and everything. It will change something. It will begin something."

She did as he said, crunched into the pith, the citrus sharpness making her eyes water. She had not tasted anything like it for months.

"You're crying, Ma?" Jakob asked, his eyes forever watchful.

"No. It's the lemon. It is sharp."

"I can try it?"

"You can. Or we can dilute it with water."

But he wanted to taste it as she had tasted it, and his eyes filled like her own and he laughed because of that, and she thought how long it had been since she'd seen him laugh and how she'd forgotten how beautiful he was.

"I love you," she told him.

"Yes," he replied simply. He sucked the sourness down to the skin. Ate the skin, then licked his fingers.

"What did it change?" Alfredo asked him.

"Made me like a bell, my whole self ringing," Jakob replied.

Alfredo watched them as he continued to polish his rows of glasses.

"I will do all I can to hide you," he said at length.

"I know." She reached for his hand. "But he is not here."

"No."

"I thought . . ."

"I know."

"Have you heard anything?"

Alfredo shook his head. "I will ask around."

Lor smiled sadly. "We need to sleep and eat well. That is all. Is that possible?"

"Yes, that's possible. I can feed you."

She watched him, aching for the normality of polished glass, and wondered if her life had ever been that way.

"Don't be afraid no more," Yavy had told her. "We'll be safe here awhile. No one will be finding us."

Then he had pulled from the pocket of his oversized coat a small book, navy blue and leather bound with gold embroidered along the spine, small enough to hold in the palm of one hand.

"I don't know what it reads. It's in your language," he told her. "But I thought you'd like it to run your eyes over."

She had picked it up, had traced her hand down the length of the spine, opened the brittle pages, and smelled the musty scent of a book that had not been read in a long while. It was a book of old English folk stories.

"You like it?" he had asked, and for the first time she had heard a nervousness in his voice.

"I like it," she had assured him.

"Very much?"

"Yes, very much. Thank you for it," she had said, and when she looked his face was lit up with pleasure, as if she had given him something, not received it.

"Do you think I would feel it if he were dead?" she asked Alfredo now, quietly.

He did not answer. Lor looked away. Outside the sun had risen over the rooftops and was flooding in through the windows of De Clomp. They should not stay down in the bar for much longer. Already there was a scattering of people out on the streets.

"I will find him," she said.

This Day

Jakob is curled up on sacks of cabbage that stink and ferment beneath the warmth of his sleeping self. Still unwashed, still covered with another's blood, his breath is shallow and scratching in his chest from so many nights of cold air. He sleeps deeply, after a day's toil, as the market packs up around him, a clatter of wooden boards and metal frames, dismantled with the precision of habit. He sleeps so deeply that he does not stir, not a single limb or sleepy shudder, and so he does not experience the gradual shift from sound to silence as the sellers leave, the disappearing trundle of cartwheels, the ebb of voices heading for a place they can call home. He does not experience the shift from company to solitude, the cooling of a sunlit day to a honey-colored dusk. The shadows lengthen, hang like sleeping phantoms. The light fades. The night wraps around him, camouflaging him on his soft makeshift bed. He hugs his box to him. The stone in his pocket presses into his skin, imprinting a mauve bruise of time passing.

He sleeps dreamlessly, and then, as the sun slips back up over the hilltops and the dawn shadows creep finger-like over him, there is motion once again. People return to start another market day; the clip-clop of horses' hooves, the steamy blow from velvet nostrils, the unpacking of carts, the opening of shutters, the clatter of metal and wood, the clank and grind and the tap, tap, tap of a hammer, all transforming the empty space back into the market of the previous day, back into the maze of cluttered stores; silver trinkets, teapots, incense, and jewelry that drip like water drops from wooden brackets as scents of sandalwood, sun-warmed leather from the trappings of old saddles, and the blue smoke of cigarettes fill the air—all of it overladen, to hide the fact that this is a wartime market, striving to live as it did before, despite the lack of fresh produce, despite the overriding stench of decay and sweet fermenting fruit that seeps up from the almost-empty food stalls.

Laughter sounds as the sun slips out from behind a cloud, sending shafts of pinholed light down through the gray sheets above them, and everyone believes in that moment that "There is a heaven after all," a sign at last amidst the wreckage of the present day. And it is then that Jakob moves for the first time, shifting in his premorning sleep, with the mention of the word heaven. He rolls onto his back, blinking back the fog of sleep, oblivious at first to his whereabouts. Then he's alert, upright once more, as if to be caught sleeping were a crime. He buries his box beneath the cabbages, climbs down off his mound, his clothes stiff with congealed mud and grime. He sticks out in the crowd with his shoes of sackcloth; a sad clown of a boy. The loss that he feels lies beneath his skin like a pool below the finest layer of silk. The slightest tear and it flows over and around, the weight of water above him. His hands are jammed into his trouser pockets to save his fingers from the chilling wind. He hovers beside a pile of bruised cucumbers, longing to lick the skins, then moves on to the next stall, where a toothless woman hooks a rat onto a rack already heavy with pink-skinned rabbits, broken necks lolling their heads against their spines.

He turns, accepts the cup of goat's milk she hands him, and lingers, drawn toward the warmth of human touch, with a longing, a memory, for something more. *Me kamav tu.* I love you, and a hand tender across his brow. He longs to lean his head against the woman's stained apron, but instead he walks away, on past the man in the next

stall, who is shoving two live chickens into a wooden crate so small
they can hardly breathe.

Jakob searches the ground, stooping again and again, picking the
butts of heel-trodden cigarettes from the mud. Later he will stead-
fastly unravel each of them, collecting the tobacco in tiny mounds
and rerolling them back into cigarettes; a ratio of ten butts to one new
cigarette. He collects the discarded apples, too, the half-rotten ones,
will separate the bad from the not so bad, selling them at a fifth of the
price of the fresh green and scarlet apples in the stalls.

Now, though, as he crouches down, his face close enough to smell
the earth, his hands stained with rancid fruit, he feels the vibrations
beneath his feet, the heavy rumble and grind of something that is
machine, not alive, and with this sound the dread sweeps through
him, as sudden as hot to cold, dark to light. He drops his knees to
the damp ground, curls his spine inwards, small as an egg. Only his
head he lifts, and through the legs of wooden stall tables he sees the
line of trucks approaching from the gravel road toward the market
square, spitting up stones and grit in the deep tread of their wheels,
engines hammering through fumed clouds. They fill the gray slate
sky, the fractured light that had seeped from heaven. They block out
all other noise as if the very world itself were hushed by their arrival.
They come to a stop in a well-practiced line, and beneath the sound
of engines left running, growling like dogs, fifty soldiers, maybe sixty,
he cannot say, climb down into the mud.

"Do you have papers?" Walther is asking, standing behind his stall
of discarded junk that in certain lights shines like some metallic jewel.
"If you have none, you should go now."

But Jakob cannot move. From his place beside the cabbages he is
watching the officer who has climbed from the third truck in the line,
the eagle and the swastika on his shoulder hand embroidered with
white silk and tiny nuggets of aluminum wire. This man whom he
has witnessed with his head in his hands. This man, who had built a
fire, who had collected the wood himself, teased the flames, and who,
when the tears in his eyes had spilled down his cheeks, had not wiped
them away.

Jakob is back in that field, looking up once again at the tree. He sees it upon that green mound. Leafless, twisted and shaped like a Y. Sees it bone white in the moonlight, silver against the sun. And his brother's sweet face. Malutki, his eyes wide, fleetingly fearful. Hot hands . . . hot breath, despite the dawn cold . . . and that look that cut between trust and uncertainty. "It's all right, Malutki. It's all right," Jakob had assured him.

Jakob crouches lower, unable to draw his eyes from the face of this man, who is fingering his stubbled jaw as if to reset it from a journey's slumber. It takes only the distance from the truck to the nearest stall for the officer's body to awaken; for the faint military flourish, the straightness of his spine, the frenetic activity that seems to accompany his every move, to return. His eyes slide over the scene before him, minatory suddenly with an alertness that seems to take in everything and anything. The soldiers around him are stocking up, filling wooden crates with whatever they choose at random. The stalls are ravaged, one by one, emptied with a rough efficiency that leaves behind a mess of the discarded; the old, the bruised, the battered, a debris of the unwanted.

"You work here, boy?" The voice sounds above him, a golden voice, husky and resonant as honey.

Jakob keeps his head down, pushes his quivering fingers into his pockets, and nods.

"You work here with whom?"

Jakob cannot find his voice. There is only silence inside him.

"He is here with me," Walther says, standing tall behind his stall, and from his breast pocket he pulls out his papers. The officer takes them, looks over each word. His skin smells of cologne, his breath of licorice. Finally he lifts his head and stares at Jakob. He hardly blinks.

"You are afraid?" the officer asks eventually, handing Walther back his papers. Jakob still says nothing. He cannot.

"You are afraid?" the officer asks again, sterner, determined of a response.

"Yes," Jakob whispers. Tears spill from his eyes, run hot down his filthy cheeks.

The officer shakes his head. He looks almost sad. "Men are never afraid. You're a man, aren't you? Aren't you? So then. Stand up. Stand up and show me your papers."

Behind him the soldiers are clambering back onto the trucks that are weighted down now with what they have taken. The market is coming back to life. There is the chatter of dismay. Fears, tenuously voiced. The toothless woman is weeping loudly for the loss of her rabbits. The officer turns, irritated by her sobs, moves angrily up the aisle toward her.

"You must go," Walther whispers. "Without papers? You must run. Don't worry. I will find you. Wait for me in the woods. You know how to make a smokeless fire. You can survive anything with a smokeless fire. Now go."

Up ahead the woman has ceased her crying and the officer with his hand-embroidered white silk and his nuggets of aluminum wire has stopped in the center of the path. He stands with his back to Jakob, unmoving, as if he has stopped to consider something.

"Go," Walther whispers. Jakob drops down onto his stomach, lays his cheek against the cold earth. He crawls forward, pushes with his elbows along the sodden ground, the skin on his knees scraping with grazes that he won't feel until much later, as behind him the trucks are circling in clouds of grit, the ground once again vibrating.

Only the officer still stands in the market, turning now, his eyes searching, questioning, perhaps remembering. Jakob crawls to his cabbages, forages for his wooden box, moves on past the makeshift tables, the earth fungal scented and full of orange, a Cremona orange, that hides a miniature world of insects that know nothing of the world above them. He longs again to be an ant. For insignificance to save him.

"The best violins in the world, they come from a town in Italy," his father had told him once. "Cremona, they calling it. Varnish, the color of a tiger's pelt, a shimmering orange, the recipe for it gone, lost centuries back. People of that town been searching for it ever since."

"To paint their violins with?" Jakob had asked.

"Yes. Because it don't just make them violins shine, this Cremona. It makes them sing, too, an' the locals, they believing that once they discover the secret of their instrument's color, they can find the soul of any song."

"The boy?" he hears the officer shout, still honey voiced. "Where is the boy?"

Jakob keeps on crawling across the orange soil.

"The boy?" he hears again. *Wo ist der Junge?*

Then there is a shout and a whistle that splits the air with its shrillness, and once again soldiers are clambering down from their trucks. There are cries and the rush of moving feet. People are fleeing, broken from their ordered lines, jarring and knocking against tables, against stalls, heading, like Jakob, for the dark of the woods.

Jakob crawls on, faster now, dragging the earth with him, thick pads of it collecting on his knees, on his elbows, on the scuff of his sack shoes.

"So you on Gillum, and I on Valour," he whispers to himself. "With Malutki behind me and Eliza behind you. 'Hold tight to your horse's mane,' she says to me. 'Grip clumps of his coarse hair in your hands. You are brave and strong in this land that is not known by you or me, or anyone before us.' 'Keep safe that vas of indigo,' he tells himself. 'Keep safe that vas of malachite green. Head on toward the west and that setting sun that'll shine the life back into you.'" As shouts sound behind him that he blocks out with his words.

Then he hears the gunshots. The echo cracking against the air. His screams die inside him. He turns his head to the earth. He cannot bear the sound of them. He keeps on crawling across the soil that eventually changes to grass, the brightest green, growing thicker the closer he gets to the woods. He is no longer sure which forest he is heading for, or which field he is in. This field or the one he left behind him. He looks for the Y-shaped tree on the mound. Sees no such tree. There is only the market and the sight of others fleeing behind him. But it is that field he returns to now. That field. That forest.

Back and forth, back and forth, he had run, from the woods to the grass fringes, several times, seeking out *their* scent on the wind. Could he smell it? Could he? He was not sure. Was no longer sure of anything. When did solidity leave him? When did the sky fall down?

Step by step, yard by yard, he felt the distance between him and them opening up, the fallen leaves etching out the space between them. A lone bird flew above, crossed his path, and then flew back, low across the blood-wet grass, a flash of metallic green on his open wing. All my heart's there, he had whispered into the night. All my life. He did not shed tears. He could not. Only the wind cut into his eyes and blinded him as he sought to head onward, strangely to nowhere other than a place that would put more distance between him and the one place he could not bear to be distanced from. Malutki, he sobbed. Is it the worst? The very worst?

Behind him more gunshots sound. And with that the woods disappear. The field. That place. He crawls onward, the market behind him once again, and Walther, waiting somewhere in the cluttered stalls.

You must run, he tells himself. You need to leave. You cannot linger.

"Zyli wsrod roz," he whispers. "They lived amongst the roses. Nie znali burz. And they did not know of any storms."

Finally the trees hide him once again, until he is but a shadow beneath the leaf-blown branches. He lies still, his breath rasping. His heart fissured. He cannot bear to think of the man whose last words to him had been full of the fight for survival and the promise of hope. He cannot bear to wait for the man whom he had known only for his apple and his kindness. Cannot bear for him not to come.

Te den, xa, te maren, de-nash. Run if you can. Always if you can. So in the safety of the forest darkness, once again Jakob, a half-blood gypsy boy of Roma and Yenish, pushes his weak-limbed body up from the ground and, with his wooden box clutched in his hand, a stone in his pocket, begins to run.

Before

AUSTRIA, 1943

That night, after they had climbed the stairs from De Clomp before it became too crowded, after they had spent the day moving with the squares of sun-warmed light that fell through the window of their room, Lor lay in bed looking up at the ceiling that was covered with mold dots. Below she could hear the musicians in the bar, smell the wood smoke from the fire that seeped up through the floorboards, permeating their clothes, their hair, their skin. The bed still smelled of the someone who had occupied the room before them. A smell of stale beer and garlic sweated out in the night.

Jakob lay beside her, not quite asleep.

"Gillum and Valour," he mumbled. She stroked back the hair from his face, looked down at the soft curve of his wind-burned cheeks.

"In the morning, the dust has settled," she began. "So you have no need to be a camel any longer. It is warm, but not too warm, the wind strokes all the burning heat from the air. We rest for we are weary. We sleep long past sunrise and wake only when the rays burst from behind the shade of the trees around us. We break up the bread ration we have for that morning and share it out."

"Is there jam?" Jakob asked.

"Do you want there to be jam?"

"Yes. Something sweet."

"There would be no jam, but there might be honey if we can find bees in the Forest of the Light-Footed."

"Why Light-Footed?"

"Because there are no sounds in the Forest of the Light-Footed. Not from creatures anyhow. Just leaves in the trees and maybe the occasional wingbeat from a bird passing over, but they are barely perceptible."

"There are bears in this forest?"

"There are bears, but they are silent bears. Only the air gives them away, the sudden gust of their hot breath as they roar with rage. If we feel that we must ride, ride like we've never ridden before. Can you do that? Are you afraid to do that?"

Jakob shook his head. "No, Ma. I am not afraid at all," he told her, and all she could see was the fear in his eyes.

"We are faster," she told him. "Faster than the bears. Faster than the Ushalin. They who linger on the lines and crosses and who must stop for their Worship Ceremonies that without fail or pardon they have to partake in. They must find the exact moments between day and night, between dark and light, to say their prayers. For they venerate neither. It is the void of things that they worship. A nothingness that moves like a great wave of black ink rolling in from sea to shore, washing over everything in its path with the color of disintegration. At the hours of worship they stand in their ranks, a crowd so vast it fills the slope of the highest hill. They wear robes made out of wind, headdresses of rain, boots of ice. At the hour of dawn, when they look at the sun they are blinded to the day. At the hour of dusk, when they look to the moon they are blinded to the night. It keeps their will resolute. Keeps them unseeing. They see the world only in monochrome.

"After the dark cloud of their worshipping has passed, the flowers come out crumpled in the Ushalin Lands, ragged and withered. They bloom without color. If you look at them against the clouded sky you cannot see them. If you water them they wither more. The wan, gray sun there burns them to cinders. The wind strips the stamens away. Then the Ushalin make their sacrifices of dry leaves and the carcasses of dead insects to a God who cannot see or hear or speak. Who makes known his feelings with roars and grunts and by thumping his fists down hard upon a bed of rock, his left for pleasure, his right for wrath, again and again until the whole of Ushalin reverberates with the sound, and those worshipping him will feel the pounding deep inside their skulls. Their heads will be full of the pain of it for weeks, for years.

"That is why we are faster. Because to sustain such bleakness takes great effort. Our task is easier than theirs. Far simpler, because what we seek was there from the very beginning. What we seek is, without effort or restraint, present before our very eyes."

"Yes," Jakob whispered, almost asleep now. "Before our very eyes."

"But we will be riding against the wind in this forest," she told him. "And this wind, though it is slight, can drive you mad if you let it. So close your ears. Put your hand over your nose and mouth. Don't let the wind drive inside you and it will not touch us. It will not harm us if we do that. There are always ways to stay safe—you know this? Always if you learn them and seek them out, then there is no reason to be afraid." He did not answer her after this, and she knew she had lost him a while back, that he had not heard about the wind as he slept.

She turned toward him, curled her body against the warmth of his back and tasted the brine of dried tears on her own lips. They would move on soon, she knew that. Tomorrow? The day after? There seemed to be no place safer than the next. To stay was to be found. To run was to be captured. There was no ending to any of it. To find him. That was all that there was.

"Yavy," she whispered, just to hear his name. "Yavy."

Over and over she went through the last moments of seeing him, rewrote them, redreamed them. But always in the end when she opened her eyes, nothing was changed. He was still gone.

She lay on the bed and listened to the music downstairs in the bar, tried to ward off the soporific drone that was filling her ears.

"Can take you from here, if you wish it," he had told her all those years ago, in that place they had first run from. The scent of him;

wood smoke and something other: grass, soil, both rain drenched and sun dried, lake water, both deep and shallow. "Been here long enough to know they gonna knock the life out of you if you stay."

"How? How can you?" she had asked.

"I can. If you wish it."

"I am afraid of you," she had told him.

He had bowed his head. When he had looked up again, he was smiling. "Remember," he had said. "Nothing staying the same. You not knowing it yet, but you can trust me."

"You are Yavy," she had said.

"Yes. I am he."

And then he had gone, defiantly striding out from the shadows and out across the moonlit lawn of that place, and she was left knowing that her life was broken either way, and that if he had the will for it she would go with him. Strange what life became. She was not who she had set out to be. Was not then who she was now. There was cotton where there had been silk, braids where there had been silver clasps and diamond bands. Mint and lavender, which she picked, softened and rubbed across her skin, where once there had been perfumes compounded with expensive vanillin and coumarin. She dried her children's eyes with an apron she'd sewn with her own hand, and wore an amulet around her ankle that she could not take off for the half belief of what would become of them all if she did not wear it. She knew how to read the signs left along the road, the arrows and the lints from tree to tree. Could recognize the *speras*: a straw band tied to a branch or post, its narrower side pointing toward a road that was safe, its thicker end to one that was not. Four grooves—four carts. A circle carved in the wood of a welcoming door. A rag tied to a branch of a telegraph pole, a bone wedged into a crack of tree bark, a broom left on the ground. Signs of safety, where gypsy folk might pass.

All three of her children had been born in a wagon, had been lulled to sleep from the earliest age by the rock of Borromini's hooves. At night they fell asleep to the wind whistling through the wooden slats. At day they woke to scents of horsehide and wild garlic. Lor had made beads and strung them around her children's necks, told them if they became invisible, that way, she'd always find them. She learned how to twist and break a chicken's neck, was both sickened and full of self-congratulation. She wore skirts that flared, wore beaded bracelets on her wrist, braided flowers into her hair. She was like a photograph that had been taken twice, one negative casting its shadow over the other, blurred, each picture not quite correlating to the other. Who was she now?

She grappled for understanding. There were words missing. She could not remember the name of any English tree. There were vast holes in her story like moth bites in a tapestry, and the moments of clarity that she had, the threads of memory that drew her onward to the next, moved like a snail's silk trail, unraveling too slowly.

Part Two

Long Before

ENGLAND, 1929

Her house lay in a Somerset valley that on fresh summer mornings was covered with a blanket of mist. It was a high Georgian building, three stories, with a whitewashed facade and a mass of wisteria that each spring bloomed purple flowers over the large ground-floor windows, blocking out the morning sunlight and casting a ghostly lilac hue throughout the ground floor. Only the back of the house showed the paint peeling, the exposed stone bruised with age, rivulets of rust running down from roof to ground. Not for the lack of money, but rather for the indulgent foreboding that this lack might one day arrive.

Inside, the house was decorated grandly, too grandly some would say, for the size of the interior, which was not as vast as the imposing furniture implied. There was so much of it; a mahogany breakfront bookcase dwarfed the living room doorway. It held no books, instead a collection of Wedgwood miniatures, a gift passed down through the generations, admired and vaguely fondled. A dining room table, a George IV oaken slab, fumed but too long. The chairs sat cramped against the wall around it. Surreptitiously, the thinner guests were seated upon them. A Liberty washstand, one of a kind designed by

Archibald Knox, sat redundant in the marble-floored hallway, scarred with cigarette burns, a scattering of silver, daily polished picture frames of family long perished smiling up from the marble surface. Persian rugs covered the oak floorboards. Indian shawls draped across worn leather ottoman chairs. Elaborate tapestries hung from the walls above reams of glossy magazines that lay unfingered, unread. Everywhere there was too much clutter, crowded trinkets that no one was allowed to move, bought with a compulsion, the easy delight of spending, that could take hold weekly, daily even.

By the time Lor was eleven years old, she was used to finding her mother, Vivienne, standing amongst these possessions, poised in the center of a room as if she were one of them. She would be silent, her neck bare, her head slightly bent, staring at a place where the floor met the baseboard as her long fingers toyed with the silk of her dress. Still young enough for her dreams to cling to her, unchallenged, unrealized. Her ambitions lay in art, vast canvases that she streaked with brilliant color but struggled to fill, alternating between bouts of intense activity that were driven and frenzied and this dreamy languor that held her locked in thoughtfulness in the center of a room. Watching from doorways, Lor felt in those moments that her mother was lost to them, that if her name were called out, she would not hear it. But then, as swiftly as they had come, the reveries would break. Her mother's hand would drop, and she would wander the room, manicured fingertips caressing the smoother objects, a high hum of a tune absentmindedly resonating from her lips as she returned to her surroundings.

There was this, this blissful inertia of youthful ambition, before age threatened to make her regretful, but then there was the other. Days, sometimes weeks, spent coiled up on the bed in her room. A shadowy obliqueness, a void, where the world was dark, as if already life had left her stale and wanting.

"Her father was killed in the war, you know? Her mother was Polish. An heiress, apparently. She drowned herself," Lor had heard people say in hushed tones into their cocktail glasses as if that explained something. Lor had found her once in the river, standing with the water lapping against her thighs, her coat pockets full of stones.

"It's beautiful," Vivienne said. "This moment before. Exquisitely so."

"Before what?" Lor had asked.

"Before after."

Lor had looked out at the ripples and the currents that circled in wide slow pools.

"Will you swim?" she asked.

"No, I won't swim. I shan't swim a single stroke." Vivienne let her fingers rest on the surface, let the water rush between them. "My mother always told me there was a family of kingfishers who lived here. I've never seen them. In all the years I've been here, from childhood to now, I've never seen them. Not once. What do you suppose that says about me?"

Lor took off her shoes, waded across the currents to her mother, linked her arm through hers.

"It's not so very strong," she said. "The current. We shan't be swept away."

"No, perhaps not," her mother had said vaguely. *"Zyli wsrod roz,"* she whispered. *"Nie znali burz."*

"What are you saying, Mother?"

"We live amongst roses, darling. Know of no storms." And with that they had made their way back to the shore.

"You are good, you know that, Vivienne, don't you?" they said of her half-finished paintings. "You could be great if you were more prolific. If you weren't so afraid of mediocrity."

Often she would take Lor to the antique market in town that, now that the Great War had ended, was overflowing with lost and unclaimed objects, with widow's wares. They never came home empty-handed. The house was filled with silver spoons, Worcester china, George III silver-shelled ladles, a baluster coffeepot, boxes of war memorabilia, a dead soldier's medals. They bought sketches in gilded frames and faded photographs of people they had never known: a group of scholars in top hat and tails, standing on the steps outside St. Paul's Cathedral; a crowd of Welsh rugby fans, cheering beneath newspapers held over their heads in the rain. There was an African pot in the hallway that still smelled of the sour cheese that had fed a nameless village; an oriental rug lay by the fireside still stained with soil from Kerala; a portrait of someone's beloved family horse. Vivienne said she had a tale for each and every object, that war was the best time for stories, but somewhere, deep in the tone of telling this, there was the sad half-acknowledged truth that they weren't her stories. That she had simply found them in a town hall that smelled of the rain brought in on the soles of other people's shoes. Of her own story there was very little. Such was the glossy monotony of her life.

Lor's father, Andrew, listened to his wife in silence. A heavy silence that could last for days. Like Vivienne, he was tall, broad, with dark, almost black hair, slicked back with a defined right parting that he combed meticulously into place each morning. He had a way of standing that exuded confidence rather than arrogance, a quiet authority that was unchallenged, unassailable. And though it was Vivienne who filled the chatter of a room, though it was she who delivered the stories that entertained, there was about him an unconscious shine that had him stand out amongst a crowd as if he were made of some other metal. People fell silent when he spoke, fell silent simply when he appeared. He ignored Vivienne's reveries. Chose not to witness her bouts of decline. They were a tall, graceful couple who locked arms when people were watching.

At the end of the summer, they planned a party in the hope of prolonging the frivolity that came with the warmer weather.

Vivienne took Lor to buy new wineglasses from the market, five different sets: Waterford glass, Baccarat glass, Boston Crown, Steuben, and Bohemian crystal, a mishmash of double- or single-footed rims and baluster stems. Some were perfectly intact; others were chipped.

"It isn't the done thing," she had said. "But let's start a trend. Pretend it's some new fad from America."

On the day of the party the skies were clear and filled with birdsong. Vivienne wore an ivory chemise that was matte in the shadows but which shone in the light. The garden was full of orange blossoms that did not smell of oranges. The new glasses gleamed, filled to the brim with white wine the color of her mother's dress. Lor and her mother picked handfuls of honeysuckle and sat on the lawn together, their legs tucked up beneath them, sucking up the sugar water that came in such tiny quantities they were left always wanting for more.

"Nature's sweets," Vivienne said. Her dark hair was cut sharply around her face, bobbed just below her cheekbones. She wore lilac eye shadow that flashed when she blinked. Her lipstick was so red it looked as if it hurt. "Stay close," she whispered in Lor's ear. "Stay close." Then she tipped back her head and laughed at nothing at all. Her laugh was something that should be discarded. Like a veil. But Lor did not know that yet.

"So I walk a little too fast," Vivienne sang. "So I laugh a little too loud. But what else can you do, at the end of . . ."

Andrew stood by the rose garden that was due its second bloom. He stood tall, his dark hair shining. The woman he was now talking to wore a blue dress, pleated just below the knee. Her calves were long. Her ankles slender. She was almost as tall as he. They stood side by side, she touching his sleeve, just a forefinger on the cuff, the nail manicured and sharp. They were both smiling.

"Don't stare, darling," Vivienne said, smoothing down her dress. "Why don't you get Mommy another drink? Gin, please." She held out her glass and cocked her head playfully. Lor took it, wove waist high through the chatter and the lacquered air. There were a multitude of shoes, stilettos that punctured the grass and soiled brogues. The man in a dinner jacket who exchanged the wineglass for a crystal tumbler, which he half filled with gin, half with lemon bitters, smelled of the oranges the orange blossoms should have smelled of.

Lor took in the faces around her. She was familiar with them all. They came and went from one another's parties, a vision of solidarity against whatever it was they were against. Conversation amongst them was like a story. It strove to be intellectual, but their intelligence was something that was sought out, muddled together and hoped for, rather than something they had been naturally blessed with. Quietly they competed with one another, each victory of erudition rejoiced over behind smiles of platitude. But within the confines of their group they remained obliviously unchallenged, and the superiority with which they spoke was merited only by the fact that they were wealthy—moneyed up, jazzed up, boozed up, "fabulous" as long as they believed it. Not one of them lived fully the life that they had. They spent their waking hours dreaming of living an entirely different one, one not filled with the legacy of war and the quiet guilt that accompanied having survived it unscathed.

When Lor returned with the glass of gin and lemon bitters, her mother's eyes were full of tears.

"Thank you, my love," she said as she tipped back her head and took a large loud gulp, a single ice cube clanking. Lor reached for her hand. "They liked the glasses. Remember, darling, you can sway anyone to believe anything if you speak with enough conviction."

A shadow fell across them. It was John, a man with a handlebar mustache, whom Lor had not seen amongst their crowd before. Her mother seemed to know him already. He was slightly older than Lor's father, his hair tinged with gray, and immaculately dressed. Uncreased and polished. His navy suit was so dark it was almost black.

"You look well, Vivienne," he said, standing tall above them.

"I am well, John. The summer suits me. How is Maggie?"

"Much better, thank you." He was softly spoken, a look in his eye that held a quiet weariness, an ambivalence almost about wanting to be present at all. "Been told to rest. Excitement best avoided," he added.

"Oh, and our house is simply spilling with it."

They both fell silent. John cleared his throat self-consciously. Then momentarily he and Vivienne stared at each other, a moment that almost openly acknowledged the failure of their conversation.

"Nice to see you again, Vivienne," he said quietly. It was only as he walked away, vanishing into the crowd, that Lor saw the twisted gait to his left leg, the slight drag to it as he moved.

"He was shot, two days before the war ended," Vivienne said as though it was something vague and distant. Lor sucked at the honeysuckle. "Mommy's pretty, isn't she, darling?"

"Yes, very pretty."

"He brought lilies. A huge white bouquet of them." She sighed. "Tell me a story. I need a horse, a blue-black horse of a story."

"Othagos?"

"From the hunting accident?"

"Yes, the stray arrow that came from a bow no one had fired."

"Yes, I remember him. He'll do just fine." She lay back on the lawn, her ivory dress grass stained where her shoulder blades met the ground.

"Everyone knew that Othagos had a glass eye," Lor began. "But no one knew that he could see through it, that he could see into the heart and mind of anyone who rode him and could judge therefore whether to go fast or slow, to go left or right, be lost or found, before he was told to do so."

"Never bring lilies to a party, darling," Vivienne said quietly. "That's what the dead smell of—they are the flowers left to rot on the lid of some beloved's coffin, for God's sake. Stay close to Mommy, won't you? Stay close."

People left in dribs and drabs. Bottles emptied. Discarded glasses, lipstick stained, glinting in the tender heat of the late sun.

"To the survivors," Larry, one of their oldest friends, drawled, swaying in the center of the lawn. "To the ones who made it rich while all around them tumbled down. Are they all in this garden?" He laughed, lurching forward. "All's fair in love and war," he slurred.

Gini, his wife, dressed in a cream trouser suit that looked as if she were naked in certain lights, started pulling on his arm.

"Larry, shut up. No one wants to hear your lamenting. Vivienne, I'm taking the child home," she said. "Can't hold his damn drink."

Vivienne wasn't listening. She was looking across at Andrew. Lor caught the light in her eyes, a glint of tears welling again at each corner. He was talking to John. Both of them stood in a cloud of cigar smoke, puffing it from the side of their mouths with the exaggeration of two people in stilted conversation. The woman in the blue pleated dress had disappeared. Lor had not seen her go.

"Cigarette, darling?" Vivienne asked brightly, swinging her hips as she approached them. She reached out, touched Andrew's arm. He endured it. Her nails were not as long as the woman's in the blue pleated dress. He pulled out his cigarette case, silver and discreetly initialed, and turned briefly to light the cigarette in Vivienne's mouth. She leaned forward and looked up at him. Her lips twitched with a smile. Andrew did not see it. He turned away, put his hand back in his pocket, and continued talking. She flinched, was wise, almost wise to it.

They were discussing tobacco. Lor's father owned the Trimborne Tobacco Company in the West Country's Tobacco Valley, and several tobacco shops around London, York, Bath. Now they were branching out toward the Continent with a new establishment in Paris.

"Oak-paneled shelves, mahogany floors. Anything you can touch in them, you can smoke," her father was saying.

He had taken Lor to the factory for the first time that spring. She'd stood beneath the dark vastness of it, watching black smoke billowing from the towering chimneys above, and then had peered through the iron bars of the elevator, which clanked and creaked, the floor beneath her vibrating as the shaking cables heaved it up the shaft. Down below lay the cavity of the factory—a Dickensian cave of crumbling stone, the machinery rattling with ancient decay.

"Some of this stuff is nearly a hundred years old," her father had said, his voice echoing around the walls. He sounded younger than he normally did, oddly eager, alert.

Lor remembered how he had heaved back the metal doors and how she'd breathed in, tobacco fumes stinging her eyes. The back of her throat had burned. The room in front of them was huge. Workbenches that ran from one end of it to the other, rows and rows of hunched backs working in the summer heat. He had led her onward and upward, to giant machines that rolled out cigarettes in their thousands, to pasting floors, sorting floors. He had wandered down the aisles of each, straight backed. She'd never seen him look so tall.

"Ah, tobacco, a subject Andrew never fucking tires of," Vivienne was saying to John, rolling her eyes in despair, half-mocking, half-resentful. Her cigarette was now a line of ash, unsmoked and smoldering. John was swilling his drink around in his glass. In the garden the light was changing.

Vivienne dragged finally on her cigarette, then turned away, the smile struggling on her lips as she searched the throng. When she found Lor her face broke with relief and she stumbled toward her. The honeysuckle that hung from the high back wall flattened in a pocket of wind. Lor watched a woman's hat flutter from her head. Auburn locks fell down her back. Her father's head turned.

"Want to run away?" Vivienne asked, leaning against the trestle table and crossing one foot over the other. Her cream shoes were grass stained like her back. Lor did not reply. "I want them all to go now. Need some peace," she said, stroking the hair from her daughter's face, but more as a show of resilience than as a gesture of affection.

The garden emptied. Bethany, their housekeeper, was clearing away plates of discarded food, her hair tightly twisted with the narrow rollers that she wore every night, removed every morning. The man in the black dinner jacket was collecting glasses. Five o'clock. The light like melting butter. Andrew turned around in a patch of it, alone now.

"Well, that wasn't so bad," he said, his face lit up. He shines, Lor thought. No one left to see it but she and her mother. Vivienne couldn't take her eyes off him.

"Wind's changing," she said finally. "I'm cold." She moved closer to Andrew. "Lor and I have dined on honeysuckle. We shan't want a thing for dinner."

He looked at her then. Seemed about to say something as his eyes wandered over her face. His hand shifted. Seemed almost about to reach out to her. But then he stared back down at his empty glass, let his hand rest on the stem. The shadows on the lawn lengthened. Starlings were descending, pecking at discarded crumbs, their wings tucked by their sides like folded handkerchiefs.

"I'd better get on," he said eventually. "Got some things to clear up before tomorrow." He flicked his cigarette stub onto the grass, ground it out with his shoe, and walked briskly across the lawn and into the house.

"Mommy's pretty, yes, darling?" Vivienne whispered.

"Yes," Lor replied.

"Oops, too much to drink," her mother mumbled. "Everything's giddy. Come on, let's make tea, sober the old gal up a bit," and she pulled Lor by the hand across the lawn and into the house.

This Day

As he runs, his tears cut against the cold wind. Jakob—a half-blood gypsy boy of Roma and Yenish. Barely eight years old. He moves fast, pushed by fear that keeps him running, night after night. Pushed by loss that slips into the raw meat of him, into the pulsing of blue veins, the slab of his liver, the sponge of his right lung, stabbing there with a pain that is the only thing he recognizes. He can smell the woody scent of fallen pine needles seeping up from under his feet, and the stale heat of past days released from the soil's dampness. Forest moss softens his steps in places and cloves of garlic spit scents upward with his tread, stinging his eyes. He runs through a blur of tears and hears the sound of his own breath in his ears.

When he rests he makes his smokeless fires, warms his hands and feet and heart, and sleeps under layers of leaves. Dreams again of clawing at the warm earth, his mouth clogged with clay, his eyes with darkness. He never sleeps long. Fear wakes him. Loss wakes him. At intervals he hears the trickle of a shallow stream, the song of water rushing over smooth pebbles that is familiar, soothing. He tries to keep the sound of it in his right ear, for want of some direction, for the certainty that he can quench his thirst should he need to. All streams lead to the river. All rivers to the sea. Would the sea save him? Could he walk forth into the choppy waters, until his eyes filled and blinded? Would he be forgiven if that was his choice? To run and not stop until the waters found him?

Not yet. Not yet. In the past they had buried their dead in these forests, buried them along the way, laid loaves of bread upon their chests, sprinkled berries over their heads. People grew old beneath the ancient trees. They said prayers and heaped earth upon them.

When you burying the people you love, the earth changes, his father had taught him. You could hold, in a single handful of soil, sun warmed, damp with precipitation or silver with frosted ice, all the love you ever felt for that person. There were scattered pieces of so many lives beneath the turf. He should not be so afraid. He sees the shine of two eyes glinting out of the blackness; a hare perhaps, a bullfrog?

He listens for the croak and sporadic whine. Hears something indecipherable. A cry. Strange forest noises that will remain nameless in the black of night. Stay with me, he wants to cry. Stay by my side. Simply the light of another's eyes, the companionship of it, even if the only existence shared is the experience of sight. Is there comfort in that? If not, then what? Then what?

"*Nie lekaj sie*—Don't be afraid, Jakob," his father had said, his voice weak and wavering. "See the colors. Tell me what you see, Jakob, my boy?" he had whispered.

Jakob looks, seeing movement everywhere, shadows where there are no shadows, shapes where there are no shapes. Even the crack of his own feet over brittle twigs punctures him with the conviction that he is caught, and every moment that passes he imagines iron-boned hands grabbing him.

But night after night they do not find him. He succeeds at least in this single task. And then finally, from sheer exhaustion, he finds a dwelling in the ground, a crack of rock and soil. He falls into it, stumbles down and lays his head on the still sun-warmed rocks, the gold dust of lichen sticking to his cheek. Forest slugs slither over him, moist like his sister's kisses. He licks the salt from his stone. He sucks the cold out of it and imagines it is water.

"Mamo?" he hears his own voice pleading, claustrophobic with longing. "Mamo?" And the answer. Always silence.

"What do you see?" she had once asked as he closed his eyes and tilted his face to the sun. "It does not have to be darkness. It does not have to be cold." She was talking of death as she held him in her arms.

For two nights and a day he lies in the dampness of the dwelling, clutching his box, his stone, hiding in the darkness and the fog of his own sleep, racked with dreams of nostalgia, waking always with the pain of recognition that the nightmare is the life he is now living. *Ceri pe phuv perade.* As if the sky has fallen to the earth. *Jag xalem.* He eats fire. *Thuv pilem.* Drinks smoke. *Thaj praxo.* Becomes dust.

But on the second morning a voice wakes him.

"Are you alive?" a man asks softly, and when he looks up a pale lilac-veined hand is reaching out for his. Jakob shrinks back. His voice is lost in the earth. His hands hold clumps of it. In that moment he feels that he has lived long enough, that he should like to stay as he is, curled up against the dewy morning cold, in a ball of damp leaves, waiting till the blood dries up inside him. There is nothing left. Even the fear has withered, like desert grass.

May I die now? he thinks to himself.

"Don't be afraid," the man says. "You must not be afraid." He pulls Jakob up, the grip on his arm so firm Jakob is unable to resist. He looks up to a face that seems unused to smiling, a face made gentle with years of melancholy. He is a gray old man under the silver stubble of his shaven head. As if the colors have left with his smiles. "You are all right," the man says, seeing the tremor in Jakob's limbs. "Everything will be all right. I promise you that."

Too weak to resist, Jakob lets himself be led out of the dark woods, the dirty light of dawn creeping through the breeze-blown leaves, a sky of chrome blue in the east that seems too blue for their lives. They move across a field, keeping to the shadows and a dip in the eastern hedges. They stumble down a slope to the broken-tiled roof of a small, low farmhouse, the land long since taken from it on a day when soldiers had arrived and claimed it as their own. The old man tells him that they had eaten all the livestock, feasting off the herd of long-lashed cows. They had taken eggs, still warm, from beneath the feathers of roosting hens, stripped unripe vegetables from the ground, ravaged time as carelessly they ripped open the earth. They now used the farm and the pillaged village beyond it as a stopover from one valley to the next.

The German border lay a day's journey north from here. The Swiss a day's journey south. And there were rumors of a work camp a day's journey farther west, where slivers of people, ghost remnants, hollow eyed and hollow hearted, dug earth behind high barbed wire fences. The farmhouse and the nearby village lie between all three of these, the old man explains. Passing trucks, filled with passing soldiers use the barn as a place of refuge. Soldiers sleep there, on makeshift beds to break their daylong journeys. Their trucks made by convicts. Bolts and cogs, wheel clamps, suspension cables, hammered into place with the intention of disintegration. Regularly they break down. Regularly they need to be mended. And so the barn is full of tools and spare parts and lingering soldiers who lie lazy in patches of sunlight, smelling of grease and gunpowder and hay.

They come on a weekly basis, first to pillage what little food the old man has foraged, then to question, to seek out the pathway from the camp to the border, where people still flee to escape.

"I tell you this not to scare you," the man says, seeing that Jakob has stopped. "But so that there is only truth between us. Then you can come to trust me. Come, please, there is no one here. There have been no visitors for the past two days. Come, I can take care of you." Again, he takes Jakob by the hand and pulls him toward the farmhouse. "How old are you?" he asks, as he leads him through a loose-hinged door that swings open too easily to keep the fear at bay. They enter the woodstove warmth of his stone house.

"Eight," Jakob replies, finding his voice in the rawness of his throat, spitting out bits of peat and moss. He is pushed gently down onto a small stool that hides his head from window height. The man pours him a cup of water. His eyes watch nervously as his hands move hurriedly from object to object, despite their geriatric awkwardness.

"My name is Markus," he says eventually. "And yours?"

Jakob can hardly bear to say it. "Please," the old man says. "Be brave. Tell me your name so that I can help you exist again."

"I am Jakob," he says finally, and Markus nods approvingly.

Jakob drinks quickly, taking in great gulps.

"Slow," Markus warns him.

After he has finished, the empty mug is refilled with a thin soup of potato roots and seeds, barely more flavored than the water, but hot inside him.

"You have a destination you are heading for?"

Jakob shakes his head.

"There is someone who can take care of you?"

Again Jakob shakes his head.

Markus shrugs. "You will not live through a winter in the forest. Once the snow sets in."

He fills a metal bowl from a tank outside and he washes him with a piece of rough linen. Jakob lets the old man wipe the dirt and another's dried blood from his face, his hands, up and down the length of his skinny arms and across his chest, his ribs a wiry birdcage for his fragile heart. Markus does so tenderly, silently, stilling the tremors with his touch, and when he has finished the water in the bowl is dark and murky, but full of things Jakob cannot bear to throw away. Gently Markus pours it over the earth outside.

"Back to where it came from," he says softly. And afterward, "You will have to hide. I can keep you safe if you hide. You can rest until you are strong again. It is cramped, but it is warm."

Jakob is given one of three cupboards beneath the stairs, the lowest in the row, a small tight triangle of a space where wedges of light slash through the cracks in the door. But he can be a triangle; the hug of his arms around him, the scent of his knees against his nostrils, scratched and scarred; his eyes, mole-like now, blinking back the dim light. He finds a way of sleeping, legs curled up into his chest, and come morning there is a way of stretching every part of himself, one limb after the other, his feet slipping into the lowest cavity of the stairs. His eyelashes scrape against the closeted walls. He can smell the wood chippings on which he sleeps. He holds handfuls and smells the locked-awayness of them, wondering if he, too, will smell that way soon.

He is used to scents of grass and soil, scents of the wind before rain, rain before sun, sun before dark. He is used to horse scents, dusty hides, hot oated breath in the palm of his hand, and the feel of their soft downy pelt against his knuckles. Of feathers and the yolk of cooked eggs. Of lemongrass and the lavender that his mother rubbed in her hair. He has never known four walls. Never bricks and mortar. He closes his eyes. Breathes in splinters. Breathes out his past.

It is then that he hears a shifting of fabric behind the highest wall of his cupboard. That and then farther away, more muffled, a sudden cough that gives rise to a spasmodic eruption of phlegm-filled chokes. Jakob does not move. Engulfed once more, fear, like floodwater, filling his triangle.

"Jakob," the voice closest says, softly spoken. "That is your name?" Jakob stays silent, dares not answer. "It is all right. You will see it is all right?" the voice says, intruding into his only space. Jakob curls up, longing for silence and darkness. These are the only places of life for him now. He feels he can exist only inside them.

A long night draws on, full of moon shadows that slide past the gap beneath his cupboard door, lengthening, then shortening with the arctic light of dawn. He sleeps, sleeps deeply for the first time in a long time, and strangely, when he wakes, what he feels first is the warmth of his cupboard, the solace that there is no more running to be done, no more food to be foraged, paths to be followed. He has found a place now that in the very constriction of its size offers a sanctuary from the world outside.

He feels for his box, pushed down into the lowest corner of his cupboard. The wood is smooth, warm, the metal clasp a crescent of silver beneath his touch. He opens it, finds a flat, lake-smoothed circle of glass, pale as cloud when he holds it up against the crack of light beneath his door. He presses it between his thumb and forefinger. Strokes it back and forth around the curved edges. Holds it to his lips. To his cheek, against the lids of his eyes. He thinks he hears the lake in his ear, as if the pebble had lain for so long on the silty bottom that the sound of it had somehow penetrated through and remained.

"Jakob," the voice next to his says again, slight and shaky, hesitating on the harder consonants as if to expel them from his mouth takes effort. "Jakob, that is your name, yes?"

Jakob replaces the glass and closes the lid of his box.

"Yes," he whispers, finally able to speak. "That is my name."

"And Cherub is mine."

In the end it turns out that there are two others in the adjoining cupboards. The voice closest to his belongs to Cherub, and the voice next to Cherub's belongs to a man called Loslow. Both of them are Jewish.

"Jakob, have you ever tasted Swiss chocolate?" Cherub asks.

"No," Jakob whispers, and because he cannot see Cherub's face he imagines what it might look like, matching the voice to someone he has once known and liked: the tall and wiry twenty-something boy on the rusty black bike who used to bring his family news, wind chased and avian with the flight of his wheels, and whose wide, smiling mouth exuded contentment.

"Jakob, it's the most wonderful taste in all the world. It's like the creamiest, sweetest milk you've ever tried, and then it's more than that. It's like café crème, honey, and bitter cocoa all together. That is what Swiss chocolate is like."

"I most long for cheese." Loslow speaks then, whose voice in contrast is aristocratically clipped and hoarse, an older man, Jakob imagines, with cheekbones of distinction and polished silver hair that shines like quartz. "The strongest, bluest cheese," Loslow says. "The kind you can smell through walls."

Jakob comes to recognize the tips of Cherub's fingers through a tiny hole in the partition between their two spaces. It begins with a game that is unspoken, a silent dance between their hands. Jakob has to guess which of Cherub's fingers is pressing into the hole. He does it by the feel and size of each tip, the roughness of Cherub's forefinger and thumb, the smallness of his fifth.

At these times there is a sound that Jakob becomes aware of, when he and Cherub are playing and Loslow is silent. A pitter-patter of something back and forth across the floor.

"What is that sounding, Cherub?" he eventually asks. "Mice?"

"No, that is Loslow. He is playing his piano."

They wait until the sound of nimble fingers upon the floor stops.

"You are a pianist, Loslow?" Jakob asks.

"Yes. I have owned a piano since I was six years old. I began to play when I was five, and for my next birthday my parents knocked through the wall of their kitchen to fit a grand beech-veneered Weinbach into our home. As a consequence of their sacrifice, I practiced hard. Now I play for the Vienna Philharmonic, twice as a soloist. You must not let a war stop you practicing the one thing you have worked so hard for. My imagination demanded that I brought my piano with me," Loslow tells him. "Can you bow, Jakob? I don't suppose you've ever had the opportunity."

"No, I never need to be bowing."

"Well, that is something we must see to when we get out of here. To bow well is to make a gentleman of you. And to be a gentleman is one of the most useful tools a man can learn." He pauses. "Hear this," he continues. "I saw a thing in my hometown. A bomb had exploded in the main street, beside a breadline of thirty men and women. They'd been waiting in the cold for over three hours for their bread, and in the end they never got any. But the next day, this old man he comes with a violin and he sits on this fire-charred chair, outside where the breadline had been, dressed in his formal black evening clothes, and he plays. He plays terribly, a screeching sad song that is painful to everyone's ears. But nevertheless, without fail, every day after this he plays as artillery gunfire explodes around him. And every day, after he has played, he bows, as if an audience were applauding him. I love that he does this. He is no longer afraid, you see, and because of that I like to think he is still playing. Do you not think so, Jakob? Do you not think that old man is still playing his tuneless song?"

But the yes sticks in Jakob's throat and will not sound. He leans his head against the cupboard darkness, hearing the wooden planks contract with the coming cold of night, and watches the light beneath his door lengthen and slowly ebb.

That night he wakes to the sound of sobbing, a retching, haunting sound, full of tears and mucus. It is Loslow. All the clipped aristocracy rubbed from him, in the rawness of distress.

"Please, no?" he cries. "Don't hurt him. Please no."

And behind that he hears Cherub. "It is okay, my friend," he is whispering, his voice calm and clear. "It has passed now. It has passed."

"What is this world we live in?" Loslow is asking. "I cannot bear it."

To which Cherub replies the same thing, over and over again, like a lament. "It has passed. I am here now. I am right here."

Curled in his cupboard, Jakob listens to the endless sobs that rack the night, and the continuous stream of Cherub's comforting words, on and on until eventually the sobbing stills. Until eventually Loslow goes back to his precious piano, to his past of vinegar and newspaper with which his mother used to polish the ivory keys. Back to the place where he would play and play, until there was only the music.

For Loslow does not know if he was born with it or not. He's read Proust and Helmholtz, from the biomusicology manuals he once ordered in abundance. And neither one of them can really explain why he can recognize a perfect middle C on the piano, or the E of a passing bicycle bell. Or how when he plays in D major he hears also a tractor outside droning in E-flat, so that sometimes he struggles to follow his own tune, such is the other a part of it. He knows what key birds are singing in, knows the chink of a crunching pebble, the smack of a lake wave, even what pitch the wind is making as it blows through the sails of a boat. He is one in ten thousand, the manuals tell him— he and his perfect pitch.

But when he plays he forgets all of this. All that exists is the rise and fall of his heels and the intake of a breath. When he touches the notes upon the wooden floor, he hears the sound of Brahms, Rachmaninov, Horowitz, and Gilels. Sounding out into a tiny space that hardly holds him.

In the morning nothing is said of the night before. Loslow is talking about cheese. Cherub is talking about names.

"My real name is Sergei," he tells Jakob. "But no one has ever called me by that name and I have never liked it. You should like your name. It is who you are, what you stand for in the world. Jakob is a good name?"

"It is my da's name," Jakob replies.

"So there you go, then."

In the darkness Jakob nods, the tip of his fifth finger on Cherub's thumb. He does not tell him then that he owns two names. Of the secret name that was whispered, only once, into his ear as he screamed himself into the world, to confuse the demons in their vengeful hours. But for then, this name has not been uttered since.

"How is it that Markus found you, Cherub?" he asks eventually.

"It was I who found him. He is the uncle of a friend of my father's. I was at the library when they took my family. When I got home, only my father's friend was there to greet me. He gave me Markus's address along with a bag of bread and sausages. And I left my home and did not look behind me because I wanted to believe it was not the last time I would see it."

"I will wish for that, too, wish for it not to be the last time."

"Thank you, Jakob."

Occasionally there is the sound of a not so distant train clacking over the tracks. The rattle of it rings in Jakob's ears, bleakly familiar. Tuchun tuchun tuchun. Metal on metal. A hot spark and the cradle-rock back-and-forth motion.

"A goods train," Loslow will say. "Simply a goods train."

But Jakob does not hear him. Already he is back inside the cattle cart, cramped against the metal walls. He feels his brother's heel in his ribs, bare toes in the crease behind his knees. He smells the grease of his sister's hair next to his own, feels her hot breath on his cheeks. The sweat crusts on their bodies. The stale stench of urine seeps into their skin. Nothing to do but sleep and fear. When it rains, the air smells of mushrooms. When it doesn't, it smells of blood.

"You," the guard is calling from the open door on the other side of the carriage. "Gypsy scum. *Habt ihr verstanden?* I said sit down." He is talking to the man who stands, staring at the sky, at the Y-shaped tree that breaks the flat of the horizon, his face luminous with nostalgia. "SIT DOWN. *Sich setzen. Sich setzen,*" the guard yells.

"Jakob," Loslow is calling. "It is just a goods train, just a goods train."

But Jakob sees the tree, sees the crowd of children rounded up beneath it, who sit upon damp earth, dirt smeared and sucking their fingers, choking on their own tears. He sees the sun, white on the horizon, the shadow of a Y cast over the green grass. The man and the almost-smile that crosses his lips.

"Jakob," Loslow calls, bringing him back to the cupboard darkness. "A goods train, simply a goods train."

"You can squeeze that cochineal beetle between your fingers," Jakob hears his father's voice telling him. "You can pop it dead, so that its blood staining your palms. The reddest dye in the world, this blood. The treasure of the Aztecs and the Incas."

Jakob runs his fingers over the walls of his cupboard. Holds sawdust in his hands. Presses it to his face, inhales palmfuls of it. Becomes a triangle once more. Yes, he tells himself—it is a goods train. Just a goods train.

But at other times throughout the week the army trucks arrive, dropping off one group and picking up another, and then there is no escaping from remembering the fragility of the place in which they hide. They hear them trundling down the track to the house. The wood rattles with the weight and speed. The ground vibrates. They hear voices outside behind the stone yard, and occasionally in the kitchen. At these times they will not move, trying to ascertain whether they are village voices or accent stained. Jakob holds his breath. He presses his palms down hard on the floor to stop his hands from trembling, and after the voices disappear his joints ache.

Every afternoon Markus's steps sound in the hallway. Jakob recognizes them by the low shuffle of his feet that never really leave the ground and the ratchet-click of his knees when he bends to open the cupboard door.

"Were they here, Markus? Were they here?" Loslow asks.

"They came for my leeks," he will tell them. His leeks, his apples, his beans. "My precious leeks. As if they had sniffed them out like dogs."

When he gets to Jakob's cupboard the boy will see the crimson marks that he wears like a bracelet on his right wrist, or his left, the slight tremor of his hand, a bruise on his face that in the oncoming days will change from mauve, to violet, to dull viridian green.

"They hurt you, Markus," Jakob says over and over, a boy again, weeping with the sight of him.

Markus shrugs. "A firm handshake," he always answers. "A mere slap. Simply bravado. That is all." And then, "Jakob, my boy, you are going to be such a handsome man when you grow up," as if this were his way of building Jakob's strength. Then he allows Jakob to rush swiftly to the latrine, a bucket placed at the opening of the doorway to the cellar stairs, where he rids himself of twenty-four hours of confinement, and fleetingly catches a small chink of the sky in the hallway window: blue, gray, mauve in the earliest hours, peach in the latest, clear or cloud covered. He spies it through the dirt-smeared glass. Sometimes lingers.

"Move on, Jakob. Move on," Markus urges him. And reluctantly he does so.

Markus hands him a hot cup of watery soup on his return, nervous and eager for him to be hidden once more. And Jakob crawls back into his cupboard, catches through the cracks in his door a glimpse of Cherub passing: white cloth, white limbs, thin as thread, and clamps his eyes shut so as not to see more.

There are small hunks of bread to be had, and an occasional potato that he sucks and gnaws, and always this one cup that Jakob holds to warm his hands first. Clover he thinks, mallow, sometimes nettle. He will take a gulp, when it is still too hot, feeling the sting on his lips and at the back of his throat, the deep throb as it swills into his chest. And this is a pain he looks forward to, such is it an event in the hours and days that pass so slowly. He longs for a lemon. For the citrus sharpness to come after the heat, as his gums bleed.

"You'll get to have the girl of your dreams," Markus says, and Jakob catches the flash of his granite-eyed smile before the door closes and once more there is only cupboard darkness. "The world is your clam."

"Oyster. You surely mean the world is his oyster," Loslow says with a gritty chuckle, as he in turn hobbles back from the latrine, the sound of his bare feet padding on the wooden boards.

"Oyster, clam, what does it matter?"

"I am a much more handsome man in this cupboard," Loslow continues, his voice muffled once again in his confined space. "Without a mirror, I feel like a real looker of an individual indeed. With one, I always found that the reflection staring back at me was such a disappointment. I am much more content in my own skin now that I cannot see it."

"The whole world is charmed by beauty," Markus says. "Never be ashamed to use your good looks to your advantage, Loslow. You, too, Jakob."

He leaves then. Three doors open. Three doors close. A warm cup in three pairs of hands. And that is all for the day.

At night Loslow dreams of his piano and his cheese, while Cherub gnaws hunks of milk chocolate. Jakob dreams of stones. When he cannot sleep, he will play a game. He will walk his way through his family's home, a horse-drawn home, their wagon of chipped green wood pulled by a mare they'd called Borromini. He will close his eyes and see things he never noticed when he lived there. If he forces the memory, it will blur before him and he can't quite grasp it, but if he simply imagines walking up the two wooden steps, he suddenly sees the darkened interior, light spilling in squares from the two carriage windows. He sees the roughly embroidered patterns of the rugs that cover the seats by day, the beds by night, crimson and orange and warm in color, even when the outside air is cold enough to mist his breath. And, too, the smoke of the stove, the memory of its scent in his nostrils and in his hair, wood smoke boy that he is. He will see the knots in the wooden floor and the worn green drapes that over the years the sun has bleached. A floorboard creaks by the bed he shares with his sister and his brother, a tiny bed for tiny people, set on a shelf above where his parents sleep. The three of them squeezed

into it during the winter months, skin against skin, keeping the cold
out. He will climb up the rungs of a small ladder, duck under the covers, warm where Malutki and Eliza are already waiting with a gap in
the middle that is his space.

"Jakob, your feet," Eliza will squeal. "Your feet, they so cold," and
she and Malutki will shriek with laughter as he dabs at them with his
icy toes. Then under the flimsy blankets he smells their milky scent,
muggy with days of unwashed clothes, as stupendous snores sound
from their parents, who sleep beneath them.

And in the comfort of this memory Jakob, a half-blood gypsy child
of Roma and Yenish, falls asleep in his triangle cupboard, his stone
warm in his hand.

Long Before

ENGLAND, 1930

The vicar had said there was a scattering of four-leaf clovers in the garden, and if the children could find just one, he would make a treacle dessert that would be so sweet as to make sleep impossible for the entire night. The other children were searching. Lor was not. She stood behind a tall laburnum tree, blossoming with citron-colored flowers.

"Poisonous, darling, laburnum. Touch it and it can kill you," her mother had told her, omniscient with a morbidity that seemed to verge on delight. Later, Lor had ventured back there alone, tantalized by that "strangely exquisite line that puts life so clearly in one's own hands." These, her mother's words—"tiptoes over the edge of a cliff; a handful of pills cupped and held to the mouth; the leaning of one's weight against cast-iron railings that might give way to rushing waters below. Just a single line, my love, between life and death."

Lor took herself back to this hazardous spot of dabbled light, cast down by the leaves above, that was the perfect combination of sun and shade. She lingered in the shadows and watched from a place that was in between. The breeze brought scents of rattle and sweet peas on it, was leaf and wood scented. She rested her head against the bark, which was cool and smooth. Thought about what it would be like to pick and chew and swallow one of the luminous flowers. To sleep. To have earth heaped upon her.

From where she stood, she could see the adults at the table. She could hear their murmured chatter, the odd shrill laugh. There were eleven of them—all of them familiar—Larry and Gini, John, no Maggie, who as usual was absent. The woman in the blue pleated dress was sitting beside Andrew, locked in closeted conversation, she leaning more toward him than he to her, as if she understood him entirely. Lor wondered if she only had one dress. Vivienne sat at the other end of the table dressed in mauve, which gave her a ghostly waif-like look, as if she were only half there.

The conversation was stilted, forced slightly. It was the second party in two days, and they had said all there was to say at the first. Vivienne was already loose on gin and humming quietly at the end of the table, indulging her own drunkenness with a look that seemed to slur as she glanced over too frequently at the woman in the blue dress.

"So I walk a little too fast," she murmured. "And I talk a little too much, and I'm reckless, it's true, but what else can you do . . . at the end of a love affair."

"I'm learning the tambourine," announced Gini.

"Can you learn the tambourine?" Vivienne asked.

"Yes, apparently you can. I have a teacher, an actual teacher who specializes in it. He says it's all about the rhythm."

"Don't you have any?"

"Apparently not. I fall over a lot. The doctor prescribed this to me, literally, scribbled down 'music lessons' on one of his official prescriptions, and signed it."

"How very modern."

"Yes, very."

Before they left, Andrew had made a point of fetching a bottle of red wine from the cellar, where a film of dust made the bottle look older and worth more than it probably was. It sat unopened on the table, amidst the many bottles of homemade drinks that the vicar had made: elderflower wine, dandelion and pear, jugs of sloe gin and glacier punch, which sloshed in blue-bottled glasses in a haphazard combination of bizarre new tastes.

"They are all from the garden," the vicar was boasting, nodding toward the flowers that lay scattered across their plates. "And you can eat each and every one of them." He was wearing a sombrero hat, slanted on his head, hiding the mop of thinning gray hair that hung down from his scalp in sweaty strands. He looked older than he really was because of years spent traveling to the colonies, where he slept rough and preached hard. He liked to hold sermons at dawn on the top of a hill overlooking the river and the countryside beyond. His sermons were about life, rarely about God. He could just as easily have been a politician, an actor, a showman with a philosophy he longed to share. All he needed was a stage, but the pulpit had offered itself to him first. That was how it seemed, at any rate, to his closest friends, and probably to the crowds who attended his sermons and loved them despite the lack of religious piety.

Heads turned to see the sloping flower bed that he was now pointing to with an exuberance that verged on hysteria. The bed was bursting with pastel-pink daylilies, planted without order or symmetry.

"One should pick them in the sunshine to get the full flavor. They taste quite different on a day that is overcast." The entire meal was about the flowers. Even the honey that threatened to sweeten the sticky toffee pudding was dandelion honey, with lemon slices and vanilla bean. Eventually Lor's father leaned across the table, picked up his bottle of red wine, and opened it with a small pop that filled a pause in the conversation. He poured himself a large glass.

"And the smile on my face isn't really a smile at all," Vivienne murmured, watching him.

When finally a little later there was a lull in the conversation, she began a series of stories, all of which Lor, and probably the others, had heard before, with a tendency to laugh before each punch line, as if the tale were so funny she could barely voice it. Each laugh built up an expectation that the story could never match, as if Vivienne were deliberately setting herself up to fall. She filled up her own glass, finished the wine, and made no attempt to hide how quickly she downed it. She looked across at Andrew as she drank, her eyes staring at him over the rim. The wine bottle stood on the table, drained to the color of emptiness.

"Is this what you wanted, darling?" she said when she'd finished, indiscreet now.

Lor shrank back, pushed her forehead into the bark till it hurt, and thought of the laburnum flowers once again.

Her father had not responded to her mother's question. "A life of swell parties?" Vivienne continued.

"You sound like an American." Gini laughed, blinded by her own intoxication.

"Pure Hollywood, darling." Vivienne's voice broke slightly. "I'll do anything for you," she said, looking back at Andrew. He looked down.

"Cigarette?" Larry offered too eagerly. Vivienne snorted and got up. She made a show of balancing herself. John reached out a hand, rested it on the small of her back.

"Steady there," he said.

She moved around the table, stopped at a corner, and held onto it.

"Give him the choice, one of his cigarettes or me?" she said, her words half mocking, half spat out with a precise derision that wavered almost as a plea. "No contest." The glass in her hand shook.

Please, Lor, thought. Please hush the things you are going to say. But there was no silencing her now. She was in full swing. Unstoppable.

"Don't mistake it for pride in his product," Vivienne ranted on, bright now, lustrous with clarity. "No, it's guilt. It's guilt that drives Andrew Hullingham Trimborne. Because you know, everyone, not only was he excused from fighting for his King and Country, for the mildest of nearsightedness, he was also given the one damn thing he might be proud of. He was handed his tobacco company on a china plate with not a single chip in the enamel. Didn't have to fight for the damn thing like most people."

"Shut up, Vivienne," Andrew said from his chair.

"But charity comes at a cost, doesn't it, my darling? Tell them what you did for this glorious empire." She looked around the table. When no answer came, she laughed again, as if it were funny. "Oh, for goodness sake, don't pretend you're not all dying to know. What on earth is wrong with the Trimbornes, you want to ask? Well, nothing as it turns out . . . we just had to take on a name. That's all. Just the one. Some cousin of a distant cousin gave Andrew the entire Trimborne Tobacco Company and Sons. Because you see, there never were any sons, only poor childless Trimborne, who found Andrew, his closest living relative, and then all Andrew had to do was adopt a simple god-forsaken name and continue the family line. But oh, don't you know how it rattles him not to have his own name up there in lights. Want to be a star, darling? To shine brightly? So fucking Hollywood."

"Jesus," said Andrew quietly.

"I imagine that's a private matter between you and . . . ," John muttered.

"Is it? Is it really, John?" And she looked directly at the woman in the blue dress when she said this. The woman didn't look away, and for a long moment they both stared at each other. Lor looked, too. Felt in that moment that there was little contest. Her mother was a drunk. The woman in the blue pleated dress was not.

"When I met him, he was such a star," Vivienne said quietly, her eyes glistening now. "Weren't you, my sweet love? Such a star. So much potential. We used to drive around the countryside in his Bentley. One of only seven, he told me. Unique, as I thought we were. Of course, it wasn't at all. He'd lied. Embellished, if you'd rather. Just a regular old thing he'd fixed up and polished until it shone.

"I met his family for the first time only after I'd agreed to marry him. And that was when I knew. Knew that he embellished. We drove up to Newcastle, squeezed into their tiny terraced house that stank of meat. There were smears of butcher's blood on the kitchen floor. How aristocratic. I was marrying a damn butcher's son. A simple Geordie boy. 'Are you likin' it, luv?' they kept asking me. 'Likin' what?' I asked. 'Us,' they replied."

Lor's father stood up and walked around to her.

"And I did. I always did," she murmured as her tears spilled over, smudged the kohl around her eyes.

"Please, Vivienne," Andrew whispered. "Please, that's enough."

"I love you," she sobbed.

"I know," he said. "I know."

"We're drowning. Why are we drowning?"

Andrew said nothing. A hand against the table as if to steady himself. A hand in his pocket.

"Why?" She pushed again.

"Because you relentlessly want of me," he said suddenly, his face full of blood, his voice, like hers, breaking. "Want me always to fill the space and vacuity that is you. I cannot. I am as empty as you are."

"Is that true?" Vivienne wept. "Is it?"

"Yes," he told her. "Yes, it's true. We are the cowards of a nation."

"Is that what you feel you are?"

"It's what I feel we all are. You, me. The whole horrible gang of us."

"But I love you."

"So you say, Vivienne. So you say. Over and over."

And then he left, walked out of the grounds, one hand in his trouser pocket, the other clutching his lapel, down the single-track country road, leaving John to take home Lor and Vivienne, who by now was silent, spent with gin and tears.

This Day

AUSTRIA, 1944

On the first day of his second week, the door to Jakob's cupboard opens earlier than usual, and Markus stands grinning in front of him, unable to contain his excitement as he holds out a bowl steaming with a familiar smell that Jakob hardly dares to recognize. His mouth fills with saliva.

"It is rabbit," says Markus. "It was in the backyard. Can you believe it? Right there in front of me. I spied it through the window." He hands Jakob the bowl of stew, strips of meat bobbing in the steaming liquid. "I thought they had all fled with the end of this world. I got it with my slingshot. Eat it slowly. Make sure you chew it. Your stomach will not be used to the richness."

Jakob nods wordlessly. Rabbit is something he has dreamt of.

Loslow squeals from his cupboard next door, words of elation already muffled as he speaks through mouthfuls. Jakob takes his first bite, savoring the flavor and the texture. He chews hard. Chomps down gently on his tender teeth. He swallows. Bites and chews again. He feels his stomach swell. Feels the warmth of it, and the sudden surge of something in his limbs. They quiver. His hands shake. He takes a second mouthful, a third, then devours it thoroughly. When finally he lays down the spoon with an empty clank, his jaw aches.

He slumps back against the stair wall as a memory surfaces.

"Like peeling an apple," his father had taught him, as he laid the rabbit out gently on the table, its white stomach still warm, its eyes wan and glinting. "You skin it whole. Slowly. Tear it, you ruin it."

Jakob had used his own knife. He had pressed into the center of the rabbit's throat and brought the knife down toward its stomach.

"Cut it like it were a suit to be undone," his father had told him. "Straight down the middle. An' for the arms and legs, where you having the seams."

It had cut easily, the silver sharpness of the knife slicing through the flesh, red and raw and sticky with warm blood. He continued, hearing his father's steady breathing beside him. When he was done, he looked up.

"Now undress it, as you undressing yourself," his father said with a satisfied nod, and Jakob had peeled away the skin. Later he washed, dried, and prepared it with care. His mother had made him mittens from the skin of that first rabbit. Jakob had given them to his younger brother after he had squealed and choked with envy. Jakob had knelt down and pulled them onto Malutki's tiny hands, hot in the summer sun, and watched him totter off, clapping his new rabbit-skinned mittens together. He had worn them all that day and all that night though his palms grew pink and clammy.

Fleetingly he sees his brother's face, bright, luminous, full of contentment. Rushing toward him as he had on that day. But then there is the tree again. Up on the mound, leafless, twisted and shaped like a Y. He sees it as he first saw it, bone white in the moonlight, later silver against the sun, and his brother's face beyond, eyes wide. There seems to no longer be one memory without the other.

"Now you are a man," the officer with his nuggets of aluminum wire had told him. That officer who only moments before had held his own head in his hands and wept. "All men hold secrets from their mothers."

Jakob squeezes his eyes shut, holds tight to his knees. Waits for the pain to pass, the haunting of it to cease. Malutki. Malutki. Tiny hands that cup and squeeze his face when Jakob holds him. Is it the worst? Again he asks. Is it the very worst?

His sister had lifted her foot up from the ground, asked if the grass felt pain.

"No," he told her. "That grass never feels no pain."

Two doors down, Loslow's voice is sounding out in the meat-scented air, jarring him back to his cupboard space. To the comforting warmth and the company beyond the plasterboard wall.

"My family life used to revolve around food," he is saying. "It used to be part of the delight of living. Now it is the only thing that separates us from the dead."

Listen to him, Jakob tells himself. Listen to Loslow telling his tales.

"Stay cheerful tonight, my friend," pleads Cherub. "We have just feasted."

For a time there is silence from Loslow's cupboard, but for the pitter-patter of his fingers back and forth upon the floor, and Jakob dreads that this will be it for the night, that the chatter he now finds such a comfort has ceased and that they have lost him to his piano.

But then Loslow's voice comes out of the darkness once again. "I once knew a man who was addicted to plaster," he says, his tone decisively lighter. "We lived together in Verona for a brief time. He was a strange fellow. He was the accountant for a firm of accountants, all suited and stripe tied. Left for work at seven, lunched at midday, returned at six. No surprises. No secrets. Except for this addiction, which he only admitted to when the hole in his living room wall became too large to hide."

Jakob listens, loosens his clasped hands.

"His room was next to mine. I could hear the scraping through the walls. He used to chip at the plaster with his nails. He had the hands of a stonemason, not of an accountant. At night he'd crave the plaster like a smoker craves cigarettes. He'd wake at hourly intervals. He used to collect the dust and lick it from his palms, lapping it up like a dog.

"I tried it once," Loslow admits. "To see the appeal. It was so dry, it stuck in my throat. I lay awake all night waiting for the craving to begin, but it never came. He said it was just as well. That it ate away at your stomach lining. But even knowing this, he couldn't stop. In the end I had to move out. The scraping, I couldn't stand it. Perhaps we, too, are now unwittingly addicted to the stone dust of this house. We must have inhaled sackfuls of it."

"There are worse things to be addicted to," Cherub says.

Jakob curls up in his cupboard and wonders if he has become addicted to darkness. He has seen little light for weeks. He has not seen his own face for months. He wonders if his skin has dulled, if beneath it he is as black as the cupboard dark, the air inside his lungs thick with wood dust as he breathes in splinters.

Again, he reaches for his box, finds a leaf, pressed and dried, an autumnal red, he knows, burned and streaked with maroon. He closes his eyes. "There you are," he whispers to himself. "Just have to find you. Just have to look harder. *Spourz na kolory,* Jakob. Tell me what you seeing." His father, his face all in earnest as he speaks.

"What is it?" Jakob had asked him once, his head table-height, as he watched the man he most loved in the world kneading a dough of finely powdered resin, of wax, gum, and linseed oil.

"Lapis lazuli," his father had whispered.

"Lapis lazuli," Jakob repeated. "Lapis lazuli."

"Listen. A lullaby of sounds. Can fall asleep to it."

"What will it look like when you are done?"

"You remember the sea of the Mediterranean? Like that. A color without edges, without end. Italians call it *oltramarino*—from beyond the seas."

"And does it come from there, Da?" Jakob asked, shifting so that he leaned his weight against his father's right arm.

"Comes from a country they calling Afghanistan, from the valley of Sar-e-sang," his father told him. "That is where those gem mines are. Where those painters of the past finding their seas."

"You ever been there?"

"No. Most difficult place to find on earth. Surrounded by mountain peaks and valleys filled with roaring rivers, it is. Mine shafts, two
hundred an' seventy yards long, dug horizontally into the mountain.
Those miners lit their fires beneath the rocks where the soot blackened their skin. Threw icy water from the rivers 'cross it, watched that
rock cracking with the change of temperature. There, they finding
their lapis lazuli."

His father had kneaded that dough for three days. Only then did
he begin the process of extracting the color, soaking it in a bowl of
wood ash, squeezing and pressing it for hours until the liquid was
saturated, until his fingers were stained blue, for weeks, for months,
for years afterward. He dried that mound in the sunlight until all that
remained was a powdery pigment of bright shimmering lapis lazuli
that was indeed the color of the deepest bluest sea.

Long Before

No one spoke on the journey home. John drove his steel-blue Aston Martin steadily, two hands on the polished walnut wheel that slid easily between his manicured fingers as he rounded corners at a safer-than-safe speed. Vivienne fell asleep on the backseat, her head in Lor's lap, her hair splayed out like a lacquered fan across her daughter's knees. Lor sat silently staring out at fields of swaying corn, sporadic pools of poppies clumped on the outer fringes as if they were aware of their brightness and wary of intruding. At intervals she rested her hand on her mother's head, held fistfuls of her glossy hair.

When they got home, John helped Vivienne out of the car. She let him, leaned her body against his and smiled at everything he said. He took charge, seemed to visibly expand, ordering strong coffee to be made and for the chaise longue to be moved away from the window to a darker corner of the front room. John with his too-slick mustache, his sickly wife who never seemed close to recovering from whatever it was she needed to recover from, and that veil of some unspoken horror of history past that left his leg to drag behind him. He seemed to regard it with disgust as if it were something pathetic that crawled in his wake. Occasionally his lips quivered. Occasionally his fists clamped. Now, though, standing against the mantelpiece, he looked like a robust and magnificent male.

Vivienne looked up at him and slipped off her shoes, curling her legs beneath her.

"You're an angel, John. Truly you are."

Lor was sent to her room. It was late. Dark. Supper would be brought to her. She sat on her bed and for a while tried to recount the roads from the vicar's house to her own home. Would her father walk, she wondered? Would he know the way, blindly fumbling cross-country through bracken fronds and shrubbery, no moonlight on this cloud-covered night? Or would he stick to the roads, risk a passing drunkard behind the wheel, who might swerve at the sight of him lumbering ahead in the darkness, swerve but not miss the man on the road lost too deeply in his own thoughts. She closed her eyes. Tried not to imagine the horror that might unfold.

Much later, she heard a sound, the breaking of something: glass, china. Was he home? She opened her door and listened. She crept down the wide staircase, dimly aware that what she was doing might be wrong, but urged on by the violent shifting of a piece of furniture back and forth, back and forth.

Tentatively she sat down upon the middle step of the stairs, looking down through the polished banisters, and from there eventually witnessed John slip silently from their house, closing the front door with barely a click of the latch. It was his face that struck her. There was a look of fury upon it, there clearly visible in his pale eyes, in his pallid face that seemed in those moments to be full of bleakness and regret. Lor heard his car start out on the drive, heard the slight spin of the wheels as they caught on the gravel, and then the slow ebb of the engine as it hummed down the lane, faster than when he had arrived.

From the living room there was no sound. She walked to the threshold of the door. The lights were off, the moon shining in through the open drapes.

Vivienne was sitting on the floor in a patch of cold light. Lor could see only her back, exposed in the mauve dress, the knot of her spine, the skin taut as if the bone might puncture through. Lor walked around to face her, saw how she held clumps of silk in her hands, clutched them to her chest. She seemed dazed, lost in some distant spot upon the wall. Her hands were stained with lily stamens, like brush strokes of rust.

"What is it, Mother?" Lor asked.

Vivienne looked up. "Darling," she said. Then looked back down. "I'm fine. Really, I'm very fine. Go back to bed." She closed her eyes, ending the conversation.

Lor returned to her room, wavered between fretful sleep and wakefulness.

Much later the covers shifted, and she felt her mother's cold body slip into the bed beside her. They lay there in the darkness until the gray dawn light crept through the cracks in the curtains and then through the gap beneath the door. Then, as silently as she had come, Vivienne stole from the bed and disappeared down the corridor to her own room, leaving Lor alone again with the stillness of the house.

Andrew did not come home at all that night. Nor the next. Her mother glanced out of windows as she passed them, opened and closed the front door, swooned from one empty room to another, picked up trinkets and put them down again.

Three days later Lor found Vivienne in her room, studying herself in the full-length mirror.

"Which one, darling?" her mother asked, holding up two dresses, one of sky-blue silk that covered her shoulders, the other a decorous black halter neck of chiffon studded with tiny silver beads. "Day or night?"

"Day," said Lor quickly.

"Day it is, then." Vivienne slipped into the blue dress. Her skin smelled of lemons. Her breath of gin. "Do me up?" She pulled her stomach in. Lor slid the zipper up her back. The silk clung to her. "Pretty?" she asked, stepping back.

"Very."

"Wish me luck, darling. Bethany's here. I shan't be later than eleven."

"Where are you going?" Lor asked.

"Out for dinner."

They sat on the stairs together, clutching their knees, waiting for the bell to ring. When it did, Bethany answered it, pulling back the heavy front door to reveal John. He had shaved off his mustache. The exposed skin looked paler than the rest of his face. It made him look younger, but less elegant.

"Hello, John," her mother said, standing.

"Vivienne, Lor," John replied with a nod. He looked nervous, was playing with a pair of brown leather gloves as if he couldn't decide which hand to hold them in. Bethany welcomed him in and disappeared. Her shoes sounded on the kitchen tiles. The hallway felt empty without her.

Lor's mother swayed leisurely down each step toward him.

"You're lovely," he said, but looked away as he spoke.

Vivienne turned back to Lor.

"You'll miss me?" she asked as they reached the front door. She looked vulnerable suddenly, apprehensive.

"Yes," Lor replied, and then they were gone, muffled voices sounding outside. Lor listened to their steps across the gravel. Heard the slamming of car doors, the engine starting, revving, and then the wheels crunching stones before gradually all sounds disappeared and they had gone.

Lor went back upstairs, climbed out of her bedroom window onto a flat section of the roof, and sat amongst the chimney pots and the stone turrets, watching the white moon rising. It was that tranquil hour when it felt not quite night. When the light was mallow, almost transparent. High up there, above the house, excluded from the happenings that went on inside, she felt safe from their intrusion. Down below, she watched rabbits grazing on the freshly mown lawn, imagining they were alone. The lead guttering was littered with the carcasses of bees that, she fancied, might have died in fruitless search for a sprouting flower up there among the turrets.

She waited until it was dark and too cold to remain outdoors any longer before finally taking herself to bed. The house lay still beneath her. She could not hear Bethany or the kitchen help. She fell asleep to the familiar silence.

Hours later, the sound of bath water gushing from the taps woke her. She pulled off the covers, felt the rush of night air, and crept up the landing. The floorboards in her mother's bedroom creaked. The bed covers were rumpled and thrown back. She knocked softly on the bathroom door. When there was no answer she opened it.

Her mother was sitting in the tub, in a shallow puddle of rose-colored water. She held a sponge between her thighs, absent-minded in the washing of herself. The kohl was smudged around her eyes. The whites of them were pink, rose tinted like the water. When the sponge dropped from her hands Lor saw the bruising on her thighs, noticed too the marks on her arms, laced fingers across her wrists.

Her mother looked up, her face tense, as if she were seeking to comprehend something. "It's late, darling. You should be asleep."

"I heard you running the bath."

"Please go to bed." Then to herself, rather than Lor, "He feels it, the aloneness. I expect he puts his anger into it." She looked back up at her daughter, her eyes, the flecks of pebbled gray around her pupils, clear suddenly. "Don't fret. I like it. It is quite something to be female, you know," she told her. "The unfathomable power we have, the unfathomable lack of it."

"I don't know what you mean, Mother," Lor said.

"No, my love. I don't suppose you do. Now go back to sleep. You'll suffer for it in the morning if you don't."

Lor did as she said but woke in the night to find her mother curled at the foot of her bed, smelling of something sour.

The next day was spent in distant abstraction. Vivienne drifted restlessly from her canvases to outside, a watchful eye always on the driveway, her head tipped to listen for the arrival of Andrew's car. She sang and stroked her belongings. Tied and untied her hair. But he did not come home until the very end of that week.

When finally his wheels did sound on the gravel drive, coming to a halt with a slight spin, he clambered out with a forced air that all was usual, that nothing was remotely untoward. He greeted them with well-practiced ease, poured himself and Vivienne a drink, briefly rested his hand upon Lor's shoulder, talked vaguely about work, about Paris, which was where he claimed to have been. He did not mention John. He did not mention the woman in the blue pleated dress. Vivienne smiled through her tears and did her best not to cling to him.

Throughout the following week he drifted in and out of the house. Monosyllabic when he did speak. Vague and absent when he did not. Vivienne danced around him.

"Do you know what to boondoggle is?" she asked, trying to be comical. But he hadn't heard her. He was lost too far inside himself to hear anything she said.

"It's to waste time," she told him. He managed a smile and then left the room.

For a month they limped through the passing days and nights. There was the act of hopefulness because to live without it would have been unbearable. There was politeness, her mother and father passing each other in hallways, corridors, dark musty corners of the house. Occasionally they found themselves in the same room, were forced to witness what they saw in each other's eyes. There might then be a rare reaching out, the touch of a hand upon a hand when the witnessed grief became too hard to bear. But there was no natural sufficiency to survive whatever it was they were trying to survive. Mostly there was an awareness that they were building toward something; that this deadening state of limbo would not last. And in the end it didn't.

"Are we drowned yet?" Vivienne asked him one evening.

"Almost," he replied. "Almost," and again he left the room.

She took to standing in the river again with her pockets full of stones. Lor found the stones. Took them from her. But Vivienne found more.

And later in her workroom, crouched amongst spilled paint, beneath a canvas awash with streaks of lurid color, Lor found her holding a palette knife in her hand.

"Mother," Lor whispered when she saw her. "Mother, are you hurt?"

"Always," her mother screamed. "I am always hurt."

Lor knelt on the ground, let her mother cling to her, weep upon her dark stains of kohl that bled out across the collar of her blouse.

"Zyli wsrod roz," her mother whispered. *"Nie znali burz."* Over and over to herself like a lament.

When a week later Lor found her once again in that room, lying in a square of polished light, surrounded by paint tubes that had been opened, spread out onto her canvases and the floor around her, she asked again, quietly from the doorway, if she was hurt. This time though, there was no reply. Vivienne looked like she was sleeping, her face set in blissful repose as if at any moment she might open her eyes. Her expression gave nothing away. She faced the window and the pale sky that had not held a single cloud for days. She was dressed as if she'd planned to go dancing. It was only when Lor stepped forward that she saw the pool of blood that spread out beneath her mother's still body. Already it had darkened from red to deepest indigo.

Lor rushed to her, held her mother's bloody wrists in the air, held them to her chest as if the thumping of her own heart might stir Vivienne to wake.

"Mother," she cried. "Mother." She lifted Vivienne's weighted head up from the ground, held it in her lap, hushed her, told her all would be well. All would be well. Why the threat of stones, when in the end the choice was so much bloodier? There had been no sign that this day would be her mother's last. She had not talked to Lor differently, had not reached out to touch her more frequently. There was nothing that could be interpreted as a farewell. It was as if death, when finally it did come, had arrived in a fleeting moment of decisiveness, startled and abrupt.

Lor called for her father, called for Bethany, tried to steady the tremor in her voice. Rushing steps sounded down the corridor. Her mother in her arms, eyes still closed, face still sleeping. People looked younger when they slept, Lor thought. Even younger when they slept not to wake. As if the child they once were had come to take their hand and draw them away.

Andrew fell to the floor beside them. There was a twisted expression on his face. A confusion that looked like it might never leave him.

"Get her out," he shouted. "Get her out." By her he meant Lor, and soon Bethany's arms were upon her, pulling her away, down corridors to the kitchen and the warmth of the stove, where the older woman fussed and chattered and tried to hide her shaking hands.

Hours later Andrew himself confirmed unnecessarily to Lor that her mother was dead. He stood at one end of a room, she at the other, hid at first both his distress and his tears, before he stumbled in his delivery, before he choked and bent his head.

"You mustn't fret," he whispered. "I will take care of you. I will." But he seemed more lost than she had ever seen him. A frightened boy, barely older than herself.

It was the only time he showed her shed tears. In all her young years. But he recovered himself quickly. She watched, standing still at the far end of the room, trembling slightly with a hand on the back of a leather chair, as he stood tall, the stolidity that would accompany him from then onward setting over his face. He fell silent. Stayed that way. She wanted to shout, to shock the silence back out of him. Instead she told him that she would not fret, that she knew he would take care of her, and when he then left the room and returned to his study and the comfort of his dark wood-paneled walls, she found herself tramping across the lawn from the house to the field, then to the river, where she stumbled down the muddy banks and filled her pockets with stones. She waded out through the waters, in up to her thighs. She let her hands rest on the surface, the cold of it rushing against her fingertips. She moved one way, then the other. Afraid of the depths. Back to the shore, back to the river. Squeezed her hands, stroked back her own hair. Scoured the banks for kingfishers.

"No, I shan't swim. I shan't swim a single stroke," she heard her mother say.

The wind grew restless. A strong northerly wind that held in it the ice of the winter to come. It blew the leaves from the trees, then blew where they had fallen, picking them up and depositing them in the currents, where they drifted past her, too swift to catch. Each one left her behind, flashed a farewell of green, then silver. When she could no longer feel her feet she filled her hands with river water and drank it till her head ached.

Finally she gave in, let what courage she had mustered slip from her, turned and waded back to the damp, silted banks, where she climbed up across the field, her dress waterlogged. She dragged her feet through the moist green grasses. Felt a great lethargy fall about her. She tipped her head up to the low gray sky. It was the lowest she had known it, a baleful sky of wax white, sickly almost, as if, were she to reach out and touch it, her hands would be filmed with a mist of illness. A great darkness was building up behind the fringe of woodland that filled the hill, a surge of black rain that, when it came, would be torrential, would thrash from the sky and quickly swell the river to the upper banks, perhaps flood the lower fields.

She walked toward the house. It loomed against the horizon. There was no desire to be anywhere. The light had gone, deserted her.

She entered the house through the back door, peeled off her clothes, leaving them in a puddle heaped upon the pantry floor, her shoes full of dank river water. Then she lay down naked in the small nook by the fire, curled into a small ball, listless, inert, upon the rug that was still stained with soil from Kerala. She lay there and heard the door to that room open, saw the shadow of her father linger, hesitate on the threshold.

"Lor," she heard his voice, questioning, alarmed. She turned, covered her nakedness with her arms, her hands.

"Yes, Father," she replied, her voice so low she was not sure he heard it. He stood staring down at her for a long time. She lay looking up at him. Then she reached out her hand, held it out into the air. There was a brief moment when he looked as if he might move toward her, a hesitation, a want. But in the end he withdrew, shrank back into the distant familiar. Then he stepped over the threshold and closed the door softly behind him. Lor turned back to face the fire. Later she found someone had removed the stones from her coat pockets and crudely sewn up the openings.

This Day

AUSTRIA, 1944

His is a life of warm confinement, broken only by the daily trip to the bucket at the foot of the stairs and a view of the sky through a grime-smeared window. Jakob longs for the sight through this window. Aches for the moment when Markus will open his cupboard door and free him for a few minutes only. In time the old man lets him linger. Lets him peer upward from beneath the ledge, his hand reaching out as if he might touch the sky.

"It is bright today, Markus," Jakob will say. "So bright."

"It is, my boy," the old man will confirm. "It is a bright winter's day."

Sometimes there is snow fringing the four corners of the glass. Other times there is rain, rattling against the pane from a sky of rubbed chrome, but even that merely smears the dirt, never washes it away.

"I am afraid to clean it," Markus tells him. "Afraid to make it stand out."

"It's of no matter," Jakob tells him. "No matter. I see all that I need."

It is at night that they suffer cramps and at night when each of them lets the tears come, as if the darkness were a sanctuary for pain. When the cramps tear at his limbs Jakob learns to stretch into them, pushes his heels, his toes, the length of his calves, against the pain, so that at first it intensifies and sharpens and then just when he thinks he can bear it no more, the pain will ebb with a sudden clarity, like the ending of a loud noise, or the sudden stopping of rainfall. Cherub holds his pain silently. Loslow screams. His chilblains sting him. At night he binds them tightly in cloth.

Yet despite the cramps and the confinement and the dark, Jakob is not often afraid in this triangle of a space. The wood is warm and the closest thing to being held that he has felt in a long time. Sometimes the darkness around him feels infinite, as if behind him the space opens out and he is as insignificant as a mollusk. He cups his foot in his hand, rests the heel in his palm.

"Jakob," he whispers on occasion. "Jakob," just to hear his own name. He strokes a lock of hair from his face. He kisses his own arm. And presses his thumbs against his toes. He no longer knows who he is on the earth. What defines him.

"We existing in the eyes of another," his father had told him once. "That is why we seeking them out." Jakob no longer knows in whose eyes he exists. But for a gray-eyed old man, he is not seen by anyone. He is a boy in the darkness. He lives in the void. Without light. Without color.

He wakes. He sleeps. He dreams of his mother. Dreams of a day in late September when maple leaves were turning burned and gold, but when the warmth of summer was still in the air and in the ground. They had waded out downstream, the cold water lapping at their shins, too strong for his sister and his brother to join them, so it had been just the two of them. Just the two of them beneath the dappled light, the water's surface tinged with the dark green of the canopy above, and he had asked if she had ever done this when she was a child. Were a river, and a stony riverbed and her bare feet things of her past? For it seemed to him, of the few things he knew about her then, that this would not be so. That his childhood and hers were not familiar to each other in any way, and he was always seeking to find ways in which the two might meet.

"Yes," she had told him. "Yes, this is something I remember as a child. Bare feet and wading through water. My family, they had a house with a river running right through their land."

"A river and a house, where we have neither?"

"Yes."

He had thought about this for a while.

"We have no photographs on the walls of our wagon, Ma?" he had said eventually. "Everyone we know has photographs on the walls of their wagons. Why so?"

"Sometimes you leave a place too quickly. You take yourself, but little else. Perhaps our photographs still hang on walls. They are just not our walls."

"But we will never see them?"

"I don't know. Perhaps, one day we might see them."

He'd been pleased about the river, about the wading through it, been pleased to have found a memory they could share, and she'd seen that, and had cupped her hand over his knee and held it there until they were both dry. And in the warmth of that dream Jakob sleeps deeply.

Mostly, though, the nights are broken with the creaks and shifting of the ancient floorboards above their heads, or with the wind that seems to swell in the night like an incoming tide, whistling through the cracks and crevices. And if not that, then the sound of Loslow sobbing will pull Jakob from a sleeping slumber. A guttural sob that resonates from somewhere low down inside the older man.

"You could not have saved him," Cherub is saying one night. "You could not. Please, Loslow. Try to let it go. Grieve for him, yes, but try to let this go."

"I have seen the places they will take us, Cherub. I have seen them. I have looked for him, looked and not recognized his face among the crowds within them. I have stood behind this high fence, day after day for a whole week. Watched shaven-headed men and women grapple on the ground to fight a child for a piece of moldy bread, watched them lick their steel bowls clean. Day after day, until I could bear it no longer, until I would stare into their eyes and see not a trace of thought cross them. We are right to be afraid, Cherub. We should be more than afraid. Man is not man anymore. Or worse than that, man is the very essence of all that he should be. When I came upon this place it was death I had surrendered myself to, not a sanctuary. I had obliterated all hope of a sanctuary ever existing in this world again."

"But it does exist, Loslow. Everything that ever did exist, still does."

"I know, Cherub. I know," Loslow sobs. "Just at night. At night in the darkness, when all I can hear is my own breath, my own heart, then I cannot find the belief of that."

Jakob does not speak during these spells, and he does not speak of them afterward. Instead he opens his box, runs his fingers over the contents: a stone, a petal, a piece of colored fabric in the palm of his hand. Jakob closes his eyes. Small boy, barely eight years old— a half-blood gypsy child of Roma and Yenish. Rusted ochre from a mossy bough. Steely white from the sap of a chestnut tree. A Cremona orange that can make a violin sing.

See the colors, Jakob. See them.

He is standing in a blue field of saffron flowers that are opening as the sun sets. He is barely five years old. They have traveled for weeks to get there for the end of October, the peak of the harvest, across the Pyrenees, through northern Spain where bulls with horns the size of tusks run down cobbled streets and big-breasted women knock back dirt-smeared glasses of sangria, down toward the south where it grows hotter and sparser until they find themselves standing on the torrid plains of Castilla–La Mancha, looking out across a desert of dust.

"Nothing here," Jakob cries. "All this way an' nothing here, Da."

"Wait," whispers his father. "You be patient. Wait for that bright sun to go down. Then some magic happening before your eyes."

They sit watching as the opaque skies fill with black-winged kites that circle and hover on the air currents. They hear the call of warbler birds, the hammer of a lone woodpecker, a flash of green as it flits from one stark tree to another. The sun drops lower, sinks like a hot metal spoon over the horizon, streaks of vermilion cutting across the skies. And then, and only then, as the first stars begin to shine, do the thousands upon thousands of crocuses begin to open their petals and bloom. By morning the desert floor is carpeted in a sea of blue: mallow in the shadows, violet in the light.

"Why blue, Da?" Jakob asks. "Why not yellow?"

"The flower is blue. The stigmas scarlet. Only the dye's yellow," his father tells him.

They would bloom for just one morning. By the day's end they would be gone. They have only until noon to harvest them. Until noon to gather each of the three stamens from the center of each flower.

"And yet . . . and yet, we cannot rush. We best be delicate, exact in our gathering, for if we handle them flowers too roughly, even if the wind blows too strong, that color will start fading away, disappear like a mist. We must collect them tenderly, carry them in straw baskets that we hang from our arms and do not swing. We best be steady, like we're dancing, a fluid movement that we must repeat over and over again."

"Like we are dancing," Jakob repeats. "Like that."

The memory feels tentative, distant suddenly. He tries to grasp it, to hold it close. But it disappears as transiently as it had come, and once again there is only the cupboard darkness and the remnants of Loslow's laments.

If at night, though, Loslow is capable of plunging them all into the depths of despair, in the day he lifts their spirits, brings laughter and a world not of this time to their space beneath the stairs. The daylight hours bring a thoughtful frivolity to his state of mind.

"Loslow, what are you hearing," Jakob asks, when the drumming of Loslow's fingers sounds across the floor. "When you play? You hear your piano?"

"Yes, Jakob, I can hear it."

"Does it fill your ears, like you are there with the very sound of it?"

"Yes, only that. I hear only that."

Jakob closes his eyes. Sees his colors. "Yes," he tells him. "Yes, I know that of you."

At intervals along the passing months Markus comes to cut their hair, because of the lice, but Loslow refuses to be shaved, "to be shorn like a sheep," as he puts it, so he insists that Markus cut his hair in a style that makes him laugh.

"That is the only criterion," he tells him. "It has to entertain you. It has to make you smile."

So Markus does, and through the cracks in the door Jakob can hear him chuckling at his own creations, at the quiffs and curls he leaves on the top of Loslow's skull, describing the end results to them as best he can.

"He has a monk's cropped top," he tells them. "Devil horns, a clown with a smile upon its brow. Loslow, you look like a girl."

"You are rich, Loslow?" Jakob asks him afterward. "In your life before this one?"

"Comfortable mostly, but never rich. A pianist is never rich. I used to teach when I wasn't playing. I loved to teach. Like searching for a shell you love on the shore. You never know when a student will surprise you, when they will burst forth and excel your deepest expectation."

"They say all Jews have gold. Do you have gold?"

"No, no gold," Loslow laughs. "You know there was a time, several centuries back, when tulip bulbs were more valuable than gold. Imagine that. A time when flowers were the most expensive things on the earth. And so . . ."

"And so?"

"We should remember that."

Long Before

The summerhouse had not been used in years. In fact Lor could not remember an occasion when it had been. Perhaps not in her lifetime, but there were photographs, worn and faded, sepia in tone, that suggested it might once have been more than just a relic of decoration in the far corner of the top lawn. That there had at one stage been dancing and merriment behind the stone walls. The polka, the mazurka, the galop, the waltz, the cotillion—had they been danced there? Had her mother and her father swung each other around in this long rectangular room? It was beautiful, magnificent, more like an orangery with its long floor-to-ceiling windows, and its roof that sat like some slick-brimmed hat. Ivy hugged and wove around the crevices, cut back each year, growing more vigorously the next. In the past it had been a subject of much speculation that despite the windows being locked, never opened, the roof sealed and boastfully leak proof, leaves mysteriously seemed to find their way into the interior, to blow somehow across the cold stone floor, where they were found months later, dried and crumpled, bleached of all color, alongside the carcasses of gauze-winged butterflies and long-abandoned cobwebs.

It was here that her father moved her mother's paintings; emptying out the room she had used in the house, singlehandedly carrying her paints, her brushes, her half-finished canvases, her unrealized dreams. So it was here that Lor went, waiting until the main house was still, before creeping out under cover of darkness to venture up the ornamental stone steps, past the smiling cherubs, the pruned privet hedges that this summer had been shaped like bizarre birds in flight, geese perhaps, not quite graceful enough to be swans, wildly wingspanned and open beaked as if fleeing in fright. She reached the summerhouse, the stone moonlit, ghostly, like some otherworldly apparition, the windows reflecting back the black abyss of clear sky. The door handle rattled, loose in the socket when she turned it. The door needed a firm shove to open, but then she was there, amongst the debris of neglect, and the bright half-imagined worlds of her mother's canvases stacked upon one another. Paints covered most of the floor. Pots that had never seen the light of day, tubes immaculately labeled: vermilion, fuchsia, teal. Untouched brushes of horsehair and sable. Now mere scintillations that there had been at least the hope of some brilliance.

"Mother," Lor called. "Mother, where are you?"

And from out of the cobwebs and the shadows she came, dressed in gray, in silk brocade.

"I am here, my love, don't shout. Don't shout."

Lor wept. "I miss you."

"Don't fret so. I'll make it go away. It is easy." And she took a palette knife from a wooden box that was engraved with the letters V and A, sharpened it purposefully, first with a whetstone, holding it in the palm of her hand as if it were something delicate and precious.

"Like this," she said, gently pulling up Lor's sleeve and dragging the blade across her flesh.

Lor looked down, watched a line of blood seeping like jeweled beads across her arm. She didn't flinch. Instead, something else washed over her: a stilling peace. Her mother stroked back a strand of her hair.

"My beautiful girl," she said. "Is it not so that the most tender things in life come after pain? Kindness after brutality. Peace after war. Love after loss."

Yes, thought Lor. The tender things. There had been so much noise in the world. So much metal. So much stone. So much scraping of it, the endless chatter, the words that said one thing but meant something else entirely, the sound of laughter when it seemed more appropriate that there should be the shedding of tears; the split between two wants; the coarse pleading of someone to "Stop," to "Not stop," because . . . because . . . ; the grind of water in the radiators as a scalding bath was filled; bruised skin burning—all of it, like the screech of chalk on a blackboard to Lor's ears. An endless stream of bewilderment that left her with sudden bouts of fury, wanting to march through all of them, to clear them all away.

The parties had not stopped. They had glided seamlessly from one to another as if nothing of consequence had happened. The same conversations, desultory and full of strained cheerfulness. Mumbled apologies for her loss, the odd hand upon her shoulder, on the small of her back, but there was no time to pause, to sit in the dark of grief. The woman in the blue dress had vanished like her mother. So had John. His wife's illness had worsened, they said. He was tending to her more vigilantly. Other than that, everything else stayed the same. The chatter, the demented frivolity as they guzzled bottle after bottle of wine. But now, in the quiet solace of this forgotten place, there was this peace, this stilling pain that was sweetly exquisite.

It was as if her mother stayed with her for days after that. She could hear her voice, a murmur that filled the background of everything. When it quieted and eventually silenced, and when the missing of her again became claustrophobic with longing, Lor went once more to the summerhouse and simply found her there again. Gradually this act of a blade slicing through skin, once endured, led to a stillness like none other she had felt before. Like the rush of steam just before the boil and whistle of a kettle. Or the settling of windblown leaves after a breeze had passed through and left. A softening of limbs, a focusing on the sound of silence.

To begin with she could still herself this way for minutes. Afterward, when it became more of a ritual, she could still herself for hours. Later still, for days. Strange passages of time when she seemed

unable to speak, stupefied in her own quiet inertia. It was a disappearance of self, like her name; a low note that seemed unfinished and
barely audible.

Standing on the threshold of the garden and the timeless, half-
forgotten house, she would stare up at the growing moon, lost beneath
the crescent glow of it, as her blood dripped to the earth onto stiff
sprouts of freshly cut grass.

There you are, she said to herself. There you are. I just have to
find you.

She lived this way for months. Hid in the shadows, unseen,
unnoticed.

But then perhaps because he knew he had been avoiding her, perhaps because he too missed Vivienne with a longing ache; either way,
one day Andrew took Lor up to the far wall on the upper lawn to see
something. A hidden family emblem buried under cascades of over-
grown ivy. He swept back the layered stems, a cigarette in one hand,
to show, engraved in the mottled stonework, a crest with the words
Um Rexum Avioli circling around it.

"What does it mean?" she asked, content simply to be in his
company.

"Something about honor," he told her. "Always about honor.
Whatever that is."

It was a seemingly languid interaction on his part. On hers the very
opposite, the seeking for some sort of affirmation when he looked at
her, a shine in his eyes that perhaps betrayed more depth of feeling than
he showed. Or at the very least that he found her presence welcome.
Strangely, it was as she turned, hopeful of seeing this, that he carelessly
flicked the ash from his cigarette. It landed above her wrist line, singed
a tiny circle of skin there. He began a somewhat comical exploration
of the damage he had done, almost relieved for the distraction, and it
was then, in the pulling up of her shirtsleeve, that he saw the raw criss-
cross scarring that ran like a broken ladder from her wrist to her elbow.

He stilled. The air seemed to sink around them.

And though he had then caressed one of the less tender marks
with his thumb, though he had lingered to examine them, before

momentarily looking up into Lor's eyes, it was the embarrassment
of such an intimate discovery rather than the cuts themselves that
seemed to distress him most. For afterward he had walked away, dazed
it seemed, inertly stricken, clutching his head as if he'd knocked it on
some overhanging branch.

His cigarette was left smoldering on the grass. A line of yellow
smoke coiled into the air and dispersed somewhere. She picked up
the stub between her thumb and index finger, rolled it between them,
before taking it to her lips and inhaling deeply.

The vicar was called in the next day. He arrived with pity in his
eyes, syrup in his voice, as if he believed he could soothe Lor's grief
with his tone. In one hand he carried a brown paper bag filled with
vanilla beans, in the other a bottle of elderflower wine. The beans
were for Lor; the wine for her father. Whispered discussions took
place beside the musty bookshelves. A comforting hand patted against
her father's back. The cupping of her own knees. Low spoken questions, which were asked, but not answered. Her mother's doctor was
called. Again more whispers beside the bookshelves. Lor listened to
the smattering of their words, as she lay in the sunlight that spread
out over the chaise longue.

It was decided that the matter best be dealt with immediately, so
as "to avoid further decline," that "new treatments in Austria were
proving remarkably effective" and that perhaps Lor, and her father,
would "benefit from the privacy of distance," being from a family of
local repute. Three days later a black car arrived. Men in white coats
held Lor down and sedated the tears from her, while the vicar and
the doctor told her that everything would be fine, that she should not
be afraid. While her father put his head in his hands, and wept, calling
out his wife's name over and over again.

"Forgive me," he whispered as Lor's eyes closed and lost all sight,
all sound of England.

Part Three

Before

AUSTRIA, 1943

Lor knew if they stayed much longer it would be too hard to leave De Clomp. Already they were settling into the warmth of the place, already her children were letting down the barriers of the last few weeks. She felt their resilience diminishing; a sense of quiet inertia settling in her own bones, a trick of the senses that left her feeling that Yavy was close; that he was here. But he was not here. He was far from here. She had witnessed the very tearing of him from her.

They had collected in one of the city's smaller squares, a gathering of gypsies, three hundred or so, adults and their youngest, those not of school age. They had stood beneath a clear sky, beneath the slanting shadows of tall city buildings that cast ship shapes across the stone paving. Some stood with the bright sun in their eyes longing for shade. Others stood in the chilled shade longing for sunlight. But mostly they were content, heads down in the act of listening to the gypsy chief, Marli Louard, a tall man, all lengths and angles, whose hands and feet seemed at odds with his limbs. Despite this, he carried about him an air of optimism, his cheeks rubicund with the outdoors, as if he had rubbed across them all things rough, bark and brittle leaves, as a celebration of the ruddiness by which his life was navigated. His speech invested hope in a future that up until that moment had seemed cut with only bleakness. The crowds listened to him, smiled with delight, pleased that they were still capable of creasing the corners of their lips up to the corners of their eyes, however tentative their optimism. For in recent years the light from them had dimmed, and it had taken much courage to come to that square. There had been much rousing of spirits, as if they could no longer sit in the shrunken shadows of who they had become and had now the opportunity to dine on a feast of hope, to rally resolution. However transiently they knew it might last.

Yavy stood listening, his face full of rapture. Lor had not seen that look of his in a long while and she squeezed his arm, stroked her fingers down the length of his back. Eliza stood between them, jittery and moving from foot to foot. Jakob sat on the stone flags, stiller than she, calm and listening, with Malutki beside him. All was well in those moments when Marli Louard filled the square with words of hope.

So the commotion, when it came, was all the more shocking, for where in one moment they were rich with expectation, a light in their eyes that seemed brighter after the slow months that had passed, in the next they felt the current of menace that surged up from nowhere, a shift from peace to chaos, that spilled along the cramped quarters of the market square like floodwater. Then a baby's cry sounded, a haunting sound, the very worst. And next a whistle that cut through the air.

That was when chaos broke out. People began running, before their minds had even grasped the notion of danger and escape. Running blind, before questions could form on their lips.

Marli Louard hesitated. He stopped, then started, then stopped again, silenced eventually as he tried to understand the swell of movement around him. He did not run. He did not leave his stand. Stood instead in gawky disbelief that this moment, when all was well with the world, could have broken.

A single bullet hit him in the center of his chest. He swayed slightly, paused before his long angular body crumpled to the ground. His limbs collapsed in on themselves. He lay with his legs in the square, his head on the platform, his face lit with surprise and incomprehension, eyes blinking as he watched the scene unfolding around him. As slowly his life ebbed away.

Lor grabbed Eliza's hand and screamed for Jakob to follow. Yavy was being pushed in the swell away from her. She saw his face only once, looking back, searching for her, his skin grayest in the mass of gray faces around them. His eyes found hers, briefly. Stared at her with a look of abject dismay, bewildered that she could be so far from him. He grasped at the air. Fought to be near her.

But the crowd surged, pushing him one way, she another, the swell carrying her and the children, stumbling forward on unsteady feet, treading blindly over fallen bodies, already damaged beneath the trampling of boots. She saw a boy in a green coat screaming for his mother. A headscarf that had unraveled, daisy strewn with yellow, spiraling up over their heads before it sank into the crowds, was trampled underfoot. A silver button, on the collar of a fleeing man, caught the light, twinkled ahead of them like some small beacon. It seemed everyone was heading toward it, following this lone individual who ran up ahead of them, following a tiny light as if it might guide them to safety. A woman beside her was weeping. As if already she had decided the worst was to come.

"The schoolhouse," she sobbed, grabbing onto Lor's arm, pulling at her wrist. "Will they have taken the children in the schoolhouse?"

Lor did not know. Her own children were not old enough for the schoolhouse, a slanted wooden structure that let in the rain, situated on the *kampania* itself, now that the local schools were closed to gypsy children. She looked down at the cracks in the pavement, held onto her footing so as not to fall, with the weight of the woman who was almost leaning herself upon her now, as if she could no longer stand with the fear of what she was imagining.

"Will they have taken the children in the schoolhouse?" she shrieked again.

"I do not know," Lor told her. "I do not know," and gently she lifted the woman's grasp off her, and moved on, her hands clasping her children's, studying the ground as they ran, the guttering alongside the buildings. The clutter of cigarette ends, where beneath the eaves of the central office building, on a more usual day, people stood to smoke as if there was still leisure in the day. A can of tooth powder that was being kicked alongside the ground on which they ran, rolling from foot to foot.

She looked up, checked where they were, caught again that silver button still glinting in the light and stumbled on, toward it, because sometimes one just needed to blindly follow a light. Any light. Away from Yavy. His face in that crowd, being pulled farther from her. Away from the calling of her name. Over and over, shouted hoarsely, desperately, until she was too far from him to hear it. Until he was gone. Until he was only an image behind her closed eyes.

Downstairs in De Clomp, she could hear the music starting. Outside it was already dark. She closed her eyes, as if to check that she could still see Yavy there. Standing with his hand raised in the air, as he would always do, a last turn before he rounded a corner for a day's work, a morning's errand, an evening's task. Always, after he had kissed her good-bye, a last look, a last farewell.

And yet, before that, there had been a time where he had had to say good-bye twice, when he would bid farewell and then return to bid farewell again, as if the act of separation itself was too much to bear, as if he did not trust that he would see her again. But slowly, day by day, he had been reassured, with all the times when she had still been there on his return, waiting with a meal, a home made clean, and gradually, in time, he had let go of that second good-bye.

Yes, they must leave De Clomp now. They must set off for the one place left where she felt she might find him, while she still had the resolve. For what else was there but that?

Long Before

AUSTRIA, 1931

In that room, that white room with its exact square of blinding light, the girl was tied down. Her bones were so slight beneath the thick leather straps, the metal buckles weighed against her flesh, leaving imprints. Her shrieks, her sobs of confusion at being trapped in this way, had brought the swiftness of running feet over cold stone floors; two men, two women in crisp white coats who smothered her with their immense weight; firm gloved hands, a mix of hot breath on her face; garlic scented, sweet, sour, sleep stale, and the stench of ammonia, that stung her eyes and burned the back of her throat.

Thirteen years old, her small legs and arms restrained against the hard board beneath her, leaving gray bruises upon the knot of her wrists and ankles. Her screams rang wildly. But once expelled they seemed to dissolve against the dense walls, as if the ancient stone were swallowing them up, silencing her like the thousand others who'd been silenced before.

She kicked out, thrashed her legs, punched, spat. Became the underside of all things smooth, raw and rough and full of edges. Something cold and metallic was forced into her mouth, pushed between her teeth. She retched, tasted her own bile, her own blood. Her tongue lay fat against her teeth. A needle was jabbed into the flesh of her arm. A cold stream of liquid pulsed into her, chemical and cloying.

Then there was a moment when the fight went from her. Fled, like her screams. She waited, was as a boot, laid open and unlaced, anticipating the kick of intrusion. The light glared off the metal instruments that lay upon white tables. A foot shifted its weight, a black-laced shoe, polished, immaculate. She studied the shadow of evening stubble upon the cheek of the man whose face was closest. Saw the color of his eye, the green hazel tinge, the small stain of reddish brown in the center of his left iris as if someone had dabbed at it with a fine-tipped brush. He was looking at the distant wall, seemed distracted, as if his mind were not where his body now resided but had taken him off to some more trivial reflection.

Then it began. The spasm of her limbs. The uncontrollable jolting of her legs. The wrenching of her spine that twisted and made ugly her genteel past. Her feet kicked out on the hard bed. Saliva filled her mouth, ran down her chin. Her eyes rolled back and then too quickly the world went from white to black. The last thing the girl remembered was the sound of her own breathing, the sharp fight for air, as if she were drowning, and above her head, the view of a tea-stained map of the world: *La Carte du Monde,* where the brown of the deserts met the green of the hills.

When the girl awoke, the man, the doctor with the small brown stain in his eye, was there, filling in notes at the end of her bed with his small hands. He looked down at her, above the rim of his glasses, which were perched at the very end of his long nose. He was a slight man, who seemed to suppress the natural agility with which his body wished to move. As if he had been brought up with the belief that to move quickly was to move wrongly, that it implied a brashness of character or, worse, a nervous disposition, the too-eager admission of something untoward. He seemed to quell his natural speed with a studied flow of languorous motion. The girl watched him now, her vision flitting between blurred distortion and moments of too-bright clarity.

"You are back with us, Glorious," Dr. Itzhak said. "You are back with us."

These the words she became accustomed to hearing in those moments when she first came to, as the hours bled into days, the days into weeks. Dr. Itzhak would linger after her eyes had opened, after she accustomed herself to the light, and when she was fully awake, he talked to her of places she had not heard of.

"In Kigali," he said, as he changed the saline drip in her arm, rhythmically, as if he were keeping time to his own words. "When you ask for directions they stoop down by the roadside and draw maps in the dust."

Lor hid the tremor of her hands from him, afraid of what he would do if he saw them. She could feel the needle being withdrawn, the jolt as it left the vein. Then there was only the familiar tightness of the scabs on her wrists and the weight of the sheets upon her.

"You have to memorize them. I do not have a good memory, but in Kigali I always remember the maps that they draw in the dust."

He told her these things to gain her confidence. She saw his stolen glances to check that she was listening. And she did listen, to every word, fearful of the consequences if she did not. But it was too late for confidences. For where in one moment he might be gentle, warm even, she had experienced how he could flit from kind to seemingly brutal in an unexplained instant. How with the shift of his head he could instruct a new ordeal, move her to some other room where they administered their methods of restoration and salvation. A new needle punctured her skin and she sucked in her breath.

"Everything will turn out all right, Glorious my dear," Dr. Itzhak said. "Fear not. We will soon untrouble you." His voice was clipped, betrayed his captious nature, his tone nasal and pinched.

Sometimes, depending on the wind, she could smell the wisteria that grew beneath the window. Other times she could smell only the dust in the room, which had dampened and dried a thousand times over. Outside it never seemed to rain. Most days sunlight slanted onto the floor. When the wedge of light reached the foot of her bed and she felt the warmth of it on her toes, she knew it was around midday.

The institute lay by the lake that was covered with mist first thing in the morning and last thing at night. In the dark hours an unnatural silence blanketed the corridors, too silent for the hundred or so inmates who slept behind the bolted doors. She lay awake listening to it. It trembled against her, seemed to vibrate in her head like an actual sound. But if silence was what she fell asleep to, it was screaming to which she awoke. The daylight hours were filled with the sounds of shrieking, distant cries that brought with them the echo of running steps down the bleached corridors, followed by an abrupt and disquieting silence.

She had been placed in a dormitory to begin with, a great barren room with wood-paneled walls and sixteen beds, filled with pallid-faced women who rolled their heads back and forth upon their pillows. There was the sound of grinding teeth, a constant murmur of distress; strange songs hummed or sweetly sung, screams that were stifled.

Come evening a wave of restlessness seemed to wash over the room. There was rocking, the rhythmic knocking of heads upon the walls. Bedpans were shaken, upturned, the stench of stale urine slopping onto the floor. The songs became more a lament, the same lines sung over and over again, hoarse, off-key. Limbs shook. Hair was wrenched from scalps. A hand slapped constantly at a bloody ear. Young girls in white aprons appeared who would wipe down the surfaces with worn damp cloths and hand out cigarette rations that for a brief period of time seemed to calm, as a cloud of mustard-colored smoke filled the room.

Lor learned that sound brought consequences with it. And later that silence brought the same. You are ill, Glorious. Very ill, my dear. There it was in its simplicity, a small clean click of a word—*ill*. A sickness, they told her, growing inside her head like some black burgeoning flower.

Later they put her in a room of her own, with no explanation why. The only object in it was a spherical glass toad that sat on an otherwise empty dressing table, unmoving and wide eyed, seemingly startled when the sun slashed light upon it. She was grateful for its presence amidst the starkness. Secretly befriended it, despite its inanimate stillness. The glass glinted with colors, twisting like a kaleidoscope.

In contrast the walls of this room were so white that in the morning she could hardly open her eyes. They, too, were bare, but for a single picture, that framed map of the world, *La Carte du Monde*, from the 1800s that had been the last thing she'd seen when they'd first put her under. It was worn and stained with age, tea colored and creased at the folds, where she could see it had been opened and folded and opened and folded again; five times in all, making thirty-two rectangles of locked-awayness, a hidden world in folded paper, before someone had laid it out in its entirety, mounted it and framed it behind thick, daily polished glass. Now it hung there, the macrocosm of the world, its glass reflecting back a microcosm of the little lives within it.

This was what Dr. Itzhak chose as his tool to communicate with her. He picked places from the map, some he had been to, others he had not, and told her things about them.

"Some of the villages I went to have no name," he was saying. "They have no want for one. No one needs to know they are there. Imagine that, Glorious."

Lor watched as he unraveled the bandages from her wrists. His glasses had slipped, as they always did, back down to the end of his nose. She had watched those who worked in his close proximity, saw how they had come to suspect it to be some sort of psychological test, a device almost to judge a person's character by, for he seemed to arouse in them a strong, sometimes uncontrollable, desire to push the glasses back up onto the bridge of his nose when it became clear that he was not going to. He met their murmured apologies with disdain, and when he walked from the room he moved with a defiance, as if his nose led him, as if scent was the strongest of his senses.

She turned her head away, felt the pull as the gauze detached from the drying scabs. She could smell her own blood, salty, metallic. The memory of its taste filled her mouth. Who was she now? Something that had been disassembled, made sane or insane? She no longer knew which was which, if indeed there was a definition, a line that separated one from the other. It was as if she had been taken apart, piece by painful piece, and reassembled in a clumsy approximation of what she might have been before the seal of insanity had been stamped upon her.

You are ill, Lor. Very ill. That small, clean click of a word, only three letters long.

To begin with she had not heard from her father, but then a letter arrived that oddly mentioned nothing of home, his business, of her welfare or his. He chose as his topic of conversation to talk of the walks he was taking, a direct account of each particular one, pointing out the crest of a limestone hill he had climbed, the dip in a mossy valley, a rushing, cowslip-strewn stream, as if in these written accounts he might take her with him, breathe in fresh air, lift her out of whatever it was he felt she needed to be lifted out of. Two weeks later another letter arrived, a different walk, a different description of the things he saw, the journey ventured.

"The woodland anemones are out," he told her. "The heather, the ferns, tall as a man." She had not known this of her father, that he would have noticed these things.

"You are unhappy, Glorious," Dr. Itzhak was saying. "This saddens me, my dear. I had hoped that by now we might have made you happier."

She chose not to tell him that while it was true she did not feel happiness, she could not feel unhappiness either. It was as if all feelings of distinction had abandoned her. She was numb to them. She turned her head and caught his eye. He was a small man, much smaller than his authority implied. And his eyes watered easily. When his glasses weren't slipping to the end of his nose, he had a habit of removing them and rubbing furiously, his eyelids collapsing in wrinkled folds at the corners. She wondered if he liked to walk. If anemones and tall ferns were things he would notice.

He tried to speak to her in her mother tongue, though she knew her French was better than his English. But he persevered, a show of omniscience that flitted between the two, filling in the gaps when he was lost for a word. His accent was thick. He had told her he was from Mont Saint-Michel, "an ice-cream cone of a town, plunked on the seashore"—describing it to her as if she were a much younger child.

She had never been there. The gray cobbled road to it curved, he'd told her, around and around, like a spiral slide.

"I was in Africa for inoculations," he continued, the stench of iodine filling the room as he dressed her wounds. "I began in Kigali, the capital, on the city outskirts at the soldiers' stations, and from there went out into the villages. In Rwanda everything is green. Especially when the rains come. There is so much of it that the ground can slide away from where one is standing. Houses can disappear down steep slopes— trees, whole forests. The days begin in sunshine. Bright skies that trick everyone into leaving their washing out on a line. The rains come in the afternoon. Drops as large as thumbnails. They hammer against the skin. People are bruised by the rain there."

She imagined bruises on her arms, so big and plum colored that they hid her laddered scars.

"They speak French there," he said, feigning insouciance as slowly he rebandaged her wrists with a crisp white dressing. "You speak French very well, don't you, my dear?"

She nodded. Her family had spent many summers in Antibes. She remembers a house that they had rented there, one that overlooked the sea. What it had felt like to stand on the wide veranda and look out at the ocean that seemed perpetually to be lit in sunlight. There was always music playing in that house: jazz or blues, merry, upbeat songs that defied anyone to feel otherwise. She remembers feeling almost sick with it.

"I have never been as far as Antibes," Dr. Itzhak was saying. "To Africa, yes. But in my own country I have been as far east as Paris, as far south as Toulouse. I have not even seen the Mediterranean. They say it is azure, the sea there, not blue like the Atlantic, not green like the Pacific."

Yes, she thought. The sea is azure there; the sand on the ocean floor is white. Because of that it was the only ocean she did not mind swimming out of her depth in.

"It is a calm sea, yes?" the doctor continued. "Not an angry sea?"

"Yes," she whispered. "It is calm." But how it could roll in. She was remembering the whale that had been beached up on the shore that summer after a storm. The waves had seemed higher than the house, had swept in black and frothing beneath the night sky, crashing splin- · ters of white upon the sand. In the days afterward the whole town had fought to save that whale. People came with buckets, with pots and pans, with metal bowls and metal cups, anything that could hold water. They dug deep into the sand, dredged down, bringing the sea up and around the vast mound of blubber. They worked tirelessly, relentlessly, as the sun set and rose in quiet vermilion. They did this for three days and three nights. But the whale hadn't survived. No one was sure of the moment of its actual passing, just that it had passed while they were scooping water around its flanks. Afterward, a sort of sad relief settled over the dredgers, as if mostly they had expected it, as if the battle had been with time, for it to pass and for death to arrive so they might put down their buckets and their spades and go back to the rhythm of their usual lives. No one had moved that whale. In the days and weeks following, people walking the beach had watched it rot away, the flesh darkening gradually from pink to gray to black. From that house she could smell the stench of rotting blubber.

Imitative: *something that is not quite genuine.* Yes, she thought, that was the right word to describe those songs.

The doctor had stopped what he was doing, stood watching her, his head tilted. Past him, through the window she could see the mountains, their frosted tops arrows to the sky.

"We are finished here then, my dear," he said finally. "You should sleep now."

She did. When they let her. Sometimes she slept for days.

This Day

Then there is an afternoon, when the chill of winter is ceasing and the edges of spring are flickering through the cracks in Jakob's door. The air smells less of rain, more of grass. It is dryer, fresher. It drifts through the gaps in the house, as if carried in on the wings of passing moths. Markus comes to him.

"Jakob," he whispers. "Jakob, I would like you to see the sky."

"I don't know what you mean, Markus?"

"The sun is setting. It is beautiful. I long for you to see it."

"I see it," Jakob says. "I see it every day in that chink of window."

"That is not the sky, Jakob," says Cherub's voice from next door. "You are a boy. You should see the sky once in a while."

Jakob hesitates. "I am afraid, Markus," he says finally.

"There is no one here. The barn is empty. It is safe. We can watch from a hidden place. Cherub is right. You are a boy. Once in a while you must see the sky."

So in the end Jakob lets Markus help him from the cupboard. He feels his limbs crack as he stands his full height, sways, dizzy as he looks downward to the floor that seems farther away than it ever has done.

"Come," says Markus, taking his hand and leading him around to the back door. The old man goes first, clicks the lock and thumps at the door where the wood has expanded after rain.

Jakob hesitates. Stands there on the threshold as light bursts upon him. It is that which takes him back, that square of the outside when it is spied from the confined dark of indoors. Once again he is trapped within the cattle cars, watching the face of the man light up at the sight of that lone tree that had broken the flat of the land. Sees the almost-smile that had crossed his lips. Hears the shouts that followed. *Sich setzen.* Gypsy scum. *Sich hinsetzen.*

"I am afraid," he whispers to Markus again.

"Come," and Markus takes his hand and slowly he leads him from the threshold of inside to out. Jakob has not ventured outdoors for the past four months. He has not seen the raw light of nature or heard the sounds of it.

He closes his eyes to begin with, cannot open his lids against the glare, and therefore what he feels first is the wind, only slight, a breeze of freshness that brings scents of wood anemones and sun-warmed pine needles and the promise of rain.

"It is spring?" he asks.

"Almost, almost," Markus replies.

Markus leads him around the side of the house, keeping to the shadows that are navy with dusk, toward the water tower. Jakob blinks, slowly lets the light into his eyes. It aches to walk. The heels of his feet feel tender.

"Look up," says Markus, and finally Jakob opens his eyes, lifts his head, and for the first time in four months he sees the vault of the sky above him. He sways, reels beneath the space. He crouches down, gasping. It is the palest of blues, barely blue at all, and there is not a single blemish to blot the clearness of the air up there, but for the sickle of a new moon that smiles on its side, faint and silver. In the west the sky is reddening, rays of cinnabar, burned like spice, that seem to stretch and stain the distant horizon, deepening in color as the sun sinks farther below the crest of the skyline. Jakob spies a chevron of birds, skimming the air like torn rags. He cannot fathom the sight of them, the impossibility of something so miraculous existing in blissful oblivion to the turmoil below. He trembles, awed, a boy with a kite, a shudder of something close to hope.

Around them dragonflies mate in the thin evening air, dancing hopefully heel to toe. He sees a trail of ants, busy and oblivious. A flower of deep indigo that is opening before its time. A white petal already lost, already withered; the carcass of a bee that has not survived the winter, its abandoned nest clinging to the eaves above it. He spies buds on the trees, the folded leaves of a copper beech, clenched like fists, streaks of blood red inside waiting to burst open. Everything is luminous before him. As if before his months of darkness he had seen the world through clouded glass.

Markus cups his hand in his and pats the back of it. "It is good, yes. I am so glad that you came to see it."

They sit down on the slate stone steps and Jakob lets himself lean against the old man. He has not felt the warmth of another for such a long time. He feels the heat of him through skin and bone.

"You are alone, Markus. Why?" he asks.

"Is that the way you see me?" Markus is surprised. "I suppose I can see why. That is not the way I see myself. I was not always alone. I was married for forty-six years. No children. That did not happen for us, but I was a husband. Part of a pair. I still see myself as that. My wife died only a few months before the war began. I nursed her through a year of sickness, and was with her when she went. I held her hand, watched her eyes close, heard her last breath."

Jakob looks at the old man's face, at the creases around his eyes, the crumpled jawline, and imagines how easy it would have been for someone to have loved it so long.

"I am glad of that," Markus says in the end.

They stay like that for an age, just a boy and a man again, nothing else in the world as the light from the sun disappears and the night wraps around them.

"Thank God it was I who found you," Markus whispers. "Thank God."

Jakob picks up the fallen copper leaf, a creamy stone that is threaded with veins of orange. Holds them tight in his hand.

Later, when all the light from the sun has gone and the stars blink in the blue-black above, Markus returns Jakob to his cupboard beneath the stairs.

"What was it like?" Loslow asks him. "Tell us exactly what it was like."

Jakob pulls his knees up to his chest with a familiarity that feels like home, and thinks for a long while. "It was like when you are sitting in the dust, near where you are living," he says finally. "And it is just before suppertime, an' while you are waiting for your ma to call, you draw chalk circles 'round them tiny insects on the road, counting how long it takes for them to escape. An' all that there is, is that tree and that road and your family nearby, which is all that you know of anything. That is what it was like, Loslow."

"I think that is the most you've ever said to us, Jakob," Loslow replies, his voice low.

Jakob opens his wooden box, places his leaf and his stone inside, closes the lid with a gentle click. There is no sound from Cherub's cupboard, and Jakob is not sure whether he is still awake.

"Cherub," he whispers in the darkness. "Cherub, you awake?"

"Yes, I am awake. I was beneath your sky."

"I want to know if you rode a bicycle when you were a young 'un?"

"Yes. I used to ride a bicycle with my brothers to school," he tells him, and Jakob can hear the smile of the memory in his voice. "We did this every day of my childhood in the wind and the rain of winter, and the sunshine of spring."

"When I see you, I see you on this bicycle," Jakob says.

"I like that you see that."

"I do see it," Jakob finishes. "I see it."

The next morning when Markus lets them out to use the bucket beneath the stairs Jakob sees that the window in the hallway has been cleaned, the dirt scrubbed from it, the sky faintly turquoise, clear and endless beyond.

Long Before

AUSTRIA, 1931

Again they held Lor down, the buckled straps pinching her skin, the weight of them on her ribs, pushing the air from her lungs so that she could barely breathe. Daily they did this. A ritual that had her weeping with the knowledge of what was to come. When they rolled her down those endless corridors, the rattle of the metal trolley beneath her, the jar of the wheels over the stone flags, she could not help but scream, her sobs disappearing behind the thick wooden door that was bolted behind her. They administered the insulin. Again and again took her down into the depths of a coma. She choked, swallowed her own vomit. Called out her mother's name. Her back arched, spasmed, her skin taut, almost translucent over the white of her bones. Her limbs hammered against the hard wooden bed until great bruises spread over her arms and legs like a map of what had been endured.

"The fight makes it harder for us, Glorious, my dear. Harder for us, harder for you," she could hear Dr. Itzhak's voice from the far side of the room. "I know it is difficult. I know you are afraid, but if you let us, we will make you well again."

Afterward she was brought back to her white room. She lay down on the bed, inert, hardly able to move, the words stripped from her.

She lay there, smelled the fungal scent of winter damp that permeated through the cracks in the walls, trapped inside the cement, like the leaking passage of time.

Outside for the first time in a long time it was raining. Slight at first. It tore at the air. Then heavier, slanting from the night sky and smashing against the barred glass window. It came in surges, like waves that dashed against the pane, ebbing then flowing. She longed to see it, waited for the shutdown of night, for the shifting of locks and the silence of the corridors that followed. Then slowly she lifted herself from the bed. Her legs trembled after weeks of immobility. Her head spun. She held it first in her hands, waited for her sight to steady, for the spherical toad on the desk to be still. The stone flags were cold beneath her feet. A draft blew against the back of her legs from the gap beneath the thick oak door. She longed for the movement of rain.

Slowly she crossed from the bed to the window. She pressed her face up to the cold pane and saw the leaden streaks that fell across the lake, pelleting onto the surface so that the water seemed to dance. She pushed against the lintel, shifted it upward and open until it jammed beneath the fixed bolts above. A small space, no wider than her bandaged arms. She laid her head upon the sill, moved her face up against the glass and smelled the rain and the chilled air from the mountains that were filled with the memory of snow. She pushed her arm outward, opened her palm, felt the splattering of drops, not so cold. Not so very cold. She lay that way, staring up at the clouds and the dark of the sky, until a thread of light bled through them and a crack opened up, exposing the hidden moon. Light streaked onto the lawn, turned the slate-gray rain silver. She could see the silhouette of the trees suddenly, skeletons before spring buds opened, the leafless shrubs, the outline of a rosebush, thorny and waiting to flower.

And it was then that she saw the boy. He stood in the middle of the lawn, like some strange apparition. The rain streamed over him, down his hair, his face. His clothes were soaked, hung heavy and waterlogged from his slender frame. He stood with his hands held palm upward, his head tipped back, his face to the heavens. He stood with his mouth open, drinking the rain.

Lor saw him from behind the glass, her head upon the sill, the view of him tilted, and felt something close to sickness. As if she were falling from a great height. She could not move, watched in stillness, he in movement. The rain lashed down from the skies, lit up his eyes against the dark of his skin. They shone clear, crystalline, as if they had been made with only light in mind. She watched, trapped between the fear and the desire for him to look across and see her. His hands clenched and unclenched. He pushed his feet farther apart, seemed to steady himself against the force of the rain pounding toward him. Then suddenly he took his arms up and over his head, covered his face with them, hid his eyes as if he were sheltering them from the sight above. And in that she saw, too, that, though he was like her, of a similar age and not yet adult, there was a look to him, an otherworldliness almost that separated him from the place in which he stood, so that he seemed not wholly to be there. She recognized this. That he, like her, kept a part of himself hidden.

She shifted on her heels, lifted her head, and it was this slight movement that made the boy drop his own head and look directly at her. She stepped back. He forward. The rain poured. Streaked down his face. He spat it from his mouth. Struggled to breathe in the wet air around him. He walked farther forward still.

When he reached her window, he stopped. She could hear his breath: short, sharp, faintly rasping. She was afraid of him: the rawness that seemed to emanate from his limbs; the lightness of them when they moved, as if he might set off at any moment. His shambolic appearance, the clothes that were too big, hanging loosely from his frame, frayed, worn, his hair unkempt. But mostly it was the way he looked at her, as if he were completely unafraid. No conscious recognition that he was looking. Only that he was seeing. Taking in her every detail.

Then he reached out, put his hand through the iron bars and pressed his palm against the glass. He kept his eyes on hers, bold almost. Defiant.

Out in the corridor a door banged shut. She leapt back. Turned to listen for footfalls. Afraid of them. Afraid of him. And in the end it was this that gave her a reason to move away from the window, to return to her bed, where she burrowed under the cold sheets and lay there in the confusion of what had just taken place.

She lay like that for an age, flitted between restless sleep and wakefulness, but thinking all the while only of those eyes of his, lit up.

It was later, much later, that she eventually crept from under the covers, back to the window, where the rain was still falling heavily. But the boy had gone. Only then did she press her hand against the glass, to the place where his had been.

Long Before

They say I not suffered enough, not thirsted enough, not hungered enough.

"Look, Yavy Boy," they say, "you still have one jacket too many, and one pair of shoes too many." Yet they know this is all I have. Lost all that is cherished to me. Lost all my life. *Sa so sas man-Hasardem.* All my heart.

"Nothing too good for you, Yavy Boy," they say as they scrub me in them cold showers, trying to rub the skin off of me 'cos they say it come up too dark, like I am dirty. "You chava boy. Your pa, he is nothing but a dirty *tshor*, a thieving gypsy scoundrel. Your ma, she is a whore. You are worth nothing."

"This true?" I ask myself. Ten years old, and worth nothing? I been taught that God up high gonna love all us little 'uns down low in the dirt. In my language, we using the same word for heart, same word for love, for God. Call them all *soori*. And that boy Jesus, he says that we come unto him, us suffering little 'uns, an' I reckon they lie when they say I am worth nothing.

With God that we found you—*Devlesa araklam tume*, I say to myself, over an' over, 'cos this what my ma been saying to me ever since I can remember. And I hear her loud an' clear. Even when they have me down in the mud, eating dirt with their laughing. And even when they beat me hard, I hear her. Reckon I am worth something, 'cos why else'd they go to all this trouble?

Dream so often of a space that is black and cold, makes me more lonely than before I was born. Aching an' bewildered still by the loss of them gypsy days of mine. How they come to be vanished, when they was something I could reach out and touch? How in one moment did them days be up close 'gainst my *soori*, an' how in the next, did they disappear, like they been cut, sharp an' quick with an ax?

So once, from the garden of that Home, I pick and eat the poison of a berry. And after that I eat another an' another. Ready to die I am. But they find me, just as a light is pulling me out of the cold of this world and into the warmth of that blue heaven. Flushed right back into them cold halls, smelling of bleach so strong it would kill a rat. But not so strong it'd kill me.

They put me in the *strickapen* for that. Trapping me in the darkness of that room. Saying it's their way of enforcing them rules, 'cos they got to have order in this place of theirs or else us little 'uns gonna leave worse off than when we come in. A cold black room this *strickapen*. I am blinded in it. Same as when I wet them sheets in my sleep. Back they put me in that stone damp room with not a single window to show me a square o' sky, and they keep me there 'til the piss dry and crust on my clothes and I am stinking and so thirsty an' hungry I start seeing things in the darkness. Mostly angels, *martiya*, them spirits of the night, flying white and beautiful with wings all a-fluttering like a breeze on my skin. But sometimes them same angels is snapping back their heads and they are suddenly *mamioros*—devil ghosts that show me their teeth and their mouths a-gaping an' snapping at my heart. If I scream they keep me in that dark hole for longer, so I learn quick to keep the terrors to myself. To keep them angels sweet and them *mamioros* locked away in the corners of those dark quarters.

They beats us after we are let out of that hole. Not a beating of passion, but a cold, hard-hearted beating, with a stick that burns across the back o' my legs so that I can't be laying them down for days.

"*Ka xlia ma pe tute*," they say to me, which is the only Romani words they know—"I am going to shit on you," as they beat me hard an' fast. This my home now, they say, and they gonna teach me how to speak like they do. And also reading an' writing things in books and on paper that I ain't ever had no use for reading before.

We sleeping in bunks, and I can feel them wires beneath me, like the spine of some dead beast. And we are cold an' shivering at night under a flimsy blanket that is the only thing they gives us for a covering. I ache for the sweet scent of my ma and pa and my three sisters, who've slept snug an' softly beside of me every night I ever known.

The food they giving us is like some porridge slop that tastes of wood, or a soup in the evening that there ain't no guessing what lurks beneath that murky water: hunks of meat I never seen the likes of before. We say it is the dead 'uns they killed before us and we half believing it an' afraid of our own words.

Ain't no celebrations for us, neither. No celebration of our birthing days. No Easter eggs for us. Never no Saint Nic, coal faced and laughing down the chimney with a bundle of toys, no bells tinkling silver and merry bright. Like we've fallen off the face o' the earth, it is. Even magic can't be finding us. But I find my own magic. Go seeking out the *dook* that can save me.

I remember that first time I was running, leaving behind them stony-faced eyes and the burning pain of that stick 'cross my back. Climbed over that brick wall they built high to keep us trapped inside. But no wall's too high to climb when you are longing for that road, like your heart's gonna split right through if you don't find it.

"*Te den, xa, te maren, de-nash*. When you are given," I been taught, "eat. When you are beaten, run away."

So I running on cold roads, trampling grass into that blacktop, rainwater seeping through my shoes, too small for my growing toes. Happy to be back on that long road, where I belong. Crawling through wet furrows, twenty miles from that place I meant to be calling home. On I run. Wading knee-high through the rushes of a stream, knowing it flows fast to a blue sea, where maybe a boat can sail me far from this land that is no good for my kind. I go seeking out that *baxt*. That is luck, an' I praying out loud a bit of it follows fast on my heels. Dreaming of a village without dogs. Dreaming of a time when a man can walk without a stick.

I know the *satarmas*, them bright stars, are good to follow. And I know my own star, that my ma give to me when I was seven days old. Spying it always just below that morning star, glinting like it knows I in need of a little light. And I knowing how the forest an' I stay side by side in our looking after each other. Know the bindweed and the kelp and the dog-dirty leaves that can keep a boy alive. Listen to that music that falls between them lemon an' apple trees. Not afraid of the forest dark. Not afraid of the outside dark. Only the dark inside scaring me. Us gypsies, we not knowing the meaning of being alone. We not ever alone. We have the *jekhipe*, a oneness, a unity to us, so we just don't talk to a man before he washes his face in the morning, so he gets to be private before the starting of the day. We learn how to be on our own in the company of others. Don't be seeing someone who's not ready to be seen.

How'd they find me? I was lying sweet in the hay when a farmer he stumbles upon a sleeping boy in his barn. He don't go asking where I come from. Just calls them Authorities, an' before I cotton on to his hiding face beneath his smiling face, big arms are hauling me from that warm, soft hay, back to them stinking dark corridors full of all the things they believing in, an' none of the things I believing in.

"To whom God will reveal his true grace, him will he send into the wide world . . . ," we say over and over 'til we are whispering it in our sleep. When the president of that local community come, he holds a speech about that Christ and that God, and about loving our neighbor, how we need be more thankful for this last chance. Tells us we being the ones that forged them nails that held that boy Jesus to the cross. Says us gypsies got a lot to make up for, and he be wide smiling as he says all of this, like it being a privilege for us to hear him talking this way. I look at his eyes when he speaks and they are hard an' stone cold, like he could be hurting you without touching you.

No more running after that. They watch me night an' day, and in the end they knock the running out o' me and I am good as good can be so they beating me less. But still they calling me "good for nothing." Still they calling me "chava boy" and "gypsy scoundrel." "You are a black nuisance. You are a crow," they shout. "Ga, ga. Your mother flies." An' I stay hush-hush, with my eyes looking at them stone flag floors, and my voice low an' polite. Seeing my ma on her knees, that last time I ever saw her, weeping like she'd not ever stop.

But when they puts me in that *strickapen*, I remember something. Remember it over an' over. My pa. Kneeling beside rows an' rows of nameless white crosses from that stinking killing war he fought in. How he tended to them graves stretching into the faraway, with his soil-stained fingers, letting wildflowers grow between the rows. And I left wondering how a field full of dead men, who were killed with bayonets an' bullets of bloody fighting, ending up to be such a place of peace? That's what I think of in that *strickapen*. And that damp stone room fills up with a loving the likes of which I've not felt before. Like it could lift my ma up off her knees, and like it could stop them heavy falling tears from her eyes.

Before

AUSTRIA, 1941

While their parents and younger siblings were being rounded up in the square during Marli Louard's speech of unity and hope, the children in the schoolhouse heard the thunder of trucks arriving at the *kampania* and caught through the small chipped windows the sight of soldiers clambering down into the camp. Swiftly they crept from the schoolroom to the eastern ditch at the back of the wooden building, a large group of them, between the ages of seven and thirteen. They climbed down the bosky banks of the river into the muddy dried-up bed, fistfuls of cloth in their mouths to stifle their screams. They pressed their faces into the bog as they listened to the rampaging in the camp, the splintering of wood, the frantic neighing from their horses, wide and glassy eyed as they bucked to loosen their binds, the shots and sudden silence as one horse fell, then another. They listened to all of this, to the shooting of their horses, their dogs, the shouts, the rhythmic trampling of boots across the grassland on which only days before they had played ball, had rolled and tumbled in the sun and the rain.

And later, when all was silent, when only bits of debris were left to be picked up by the wind, to be buffeted across the empty field, they watched through the mist the figure of a lone man wander from one end of the camp and back again. They watched him upright a fallen chair, push aside broken glass, stoop to rest his hand upon the brow of a dying horse. There was about him an ethereal light, they thought, the mist, streaked with faint shafts of sunlight, and because of that they believed him to be not of this world, to be of another, sent perhaps to guide them. They watched him and did not approach, and when eventually he disappeared as he had arrived, back through the mist, they stayed in that ditch, hid there for three nights and three days, weeping away the hours as they slowly realized that their parents were not coming back for them. There they waited for the lone figure to return and guide them.

They found the first of his signs when the wind picked up and blew the fronds of an overhanging branch away from the gatepost, exposing the white cloth that had been knotted to the highest bar, its edges pointing down across the field. They waited until darkness, moved in the night, headed down across a field fringed with blackberry hedges, which they picked as they walked, filling their stomachs until they ached with fruit sugars and acids. They followed the signs on from there, left scattered at every twist and turn in the road, at every bridge, at every fallow pass: the white knot on a hanging branch, an arrow at the crest of a hill pointing south, a cross etched on the wall of a bridge.

They traveled first in a group, a large group of seventy, but gradually they dispersed as some fell back, small legs and feet giving way. They walked by night, slept by day, hung their shirts across branches and lay beneath the shade of them. They drank water from the stream they followed, picked berries, both sour and ripe, ate them regardless. They chewed hawthorn leaves, gummed their fingers with sweet sap, captured bugs in the palms of their hands: beetles, worms, hanging larvae grubs. Sometimes they trapped rabbits and roasted them over fires that crackled as the fat spat from them. Each night they walked for miles. Traveled across high passes and frozen streams. Flocks of starlings, bustards, and blue jays sweeping swiftly in invisible skies. Up above the snow line. Rugs of ice, so heavy that branches bowed down, touching ground knee high with the whitest snow. They broke off icicles that hung like opaque pendants, sucked them until their fingers grew numb and their heads pounded with cold. They breathed out white smoke and lost the sound of their own steps beneath cushions of packed snow.

Then back down below the ice line, where they slept in long grasses and thick forest glades, hid under leaves and wrapped their small bodies around one another, a tangled mass of folded arms and folded legs that softened the night's sharp edges. They told one another stories they did not know they remembered. Recited poems and old songs. *Latesh de glak the dgon.* We remembered and we sang. They sang and remembered, wept and held tightly to one other.

They let the signs guide them. They believed in *baxt*. They believed in *dook*. They believed that this angel of the night was leading them. They believed in a oneness, the *jekhipe* that would keep them together, and that if they followed their own *soori* they would be safe. They were old enough to look after themselves, young enough to hope against hope. Their eyes were still bright with it.

Long Before

AUSTRIA, 1931

There was a bird in Lor's room when she woke one morning at the Institution. A small house sparrow of pale brown and gray. It had come down the unused chimney, a layer of soot sprinkled across the slate. It stood on the windowsill and seemed content simply to stare out at the world beyond the glass, to watch it rather than to experience it. She woke to its silence, and yet something in the way it stood must have stirred her: the slight quiver to its green-tinted wing, the sporadic ruffle of its dark-capped head. For a while she simply lay there watching the rhythmic rise and fall of its tiny chest, the click of its black eye, which, in contrast to the rest of its body, moved constantly, nervously, twitching with the sounds of outside: the wind that came and went in long, drawn-out intervals; the chirp of another bird, a whistle that came in four sporadic bursts like an alarm. She wondered if perhaps it was calling, searching for its mate trapped beyond the glass.

It was this that made her rise eventually, with the will to reunite them. She pushed herself up from the bed, springs creaking. At that, the bird on the windowsill broke from its watchful stance, became a sudden flurry of wings: desperation where there had been peace, panic where there had been solicitude, hitting against the hard surfaces of the room with a force that seemed impossible for its tiny form to survive. Lor rushed to the window, tried to force the locks that trapped the air and herself inside that room, but there was no shifting them.

In the end she sat back down on the edge of the bed, stilled herself, willed her thumping heart to steady. The bird was flying into the glass, over and over, a rhythmic smash that must eventually shatter its tiny bones. She sat on her hands, turned her head from the sight of it and listened only to the thud and flutter of wounded wings. Over and over and over. Thump. Thump. Thump. Until it became a white sound, rhythmic and undecipherable.

Eventually, though, the battered flight slowed, and finally, far too finally, the bird lay spent on the sill, against the glossy white that reflected back its image as if it were floating on the surface of water. Lor did not move. The bird lay unmoving. Only its left wing flickered sporadically.

They sat like that together, the bird and she, motionless, lulled eventually by their own silence, as outside the dawn light became morning light. Gray to blue.

The stillness in that room did not break until Dr. Itzhak arrived on his morning rounds, opening the door with his quiet manner, the movement of which sent the bird hurling itself one last time into the glass, as if the green world beyond was taunting flight. Afterward, it fell back and lay motionless on the sill.

Dr. Itzhak took a key from his pocket to unlock the window. A sudden rush of air came into the room. Scents of thistledown and cedar, moth mullein and goat's rue, uncut grass and cut grass. But the bird did not stir.

"It is dead now," he said, and he lingered, his hand resting on the side of the sill, as if marking the moment of its life passing. "Not of your doing, Glorious," he muttered quietly. "Not of your doing."

Afterward he took her pulse, fussed and inspected her wounds, which were healed now, sealed like secrets. She did not take her eyes off the bird. Convinced herself that she could see it still breathing.

It was the boy who had stood in the rain who was shortly sent to collect it. He knocked so quietly that Lor did not hear him the first time, and it was only when he knocked again that she called out, and then lay there waiting in anticipation of something fearful. He entered with that look, still unafraid, still defiant. She pulled the covers up and around her. Her face flushed dark. He walked toward the windowsill, but before he got there he stopped, reached into his pocket, pulled something from it and placed it on the side table by her bed. It was a berry, perfect, sanguine red.

"Growing all over this garden," he said. "You see them, you pick them, eat them. No one be troubling you." He spoke with an odd mix of languages, some French, some German, and then strange words she could not decipher. He seemed to flit sporadically from one to the other as if he did not differentiate between any of them. He nodded toward the berry, and so she picked it up, hesitant, unsure if this was allowed. Slowly she brought the berry up to her lips, then bit into the crunch of white pulp that spurted sweetness into her mouth. He did not take his clear eyes from her. Then suddenly he smiled, a reticent smile; halfway hopeful, halfway unsure. She wavered on the brink of smiling back. She had not smiled for months. Suddenly so much lay in the simplicity of a smile.

She looked at his clothes. He wore an old woolen suit that was too large for him, cut coarsely at the hem to fit, the sleeves rolled up over his wrists. The pants were held up with rope that he'd threaded through the belt loops. The suit was worn and soiled, not like the starched gowns of the patients who wandered the wards.

He leaned over the bird, one hand reaching out, hovering just above its chest. He lowered two fingers onto the line of its breastbone, massaged it in slow circular movements. Then he bent down and gently blew against its face.

"Still warm, this bird," he said.

At length there was a tiny movement, a slight shift of the bird's right wing. Then another. "Heart's beating," he told her. "Coming to now."

"It is not dead?" she asked him.

"Not dead. Just stunned awhile is all."

Gently, he lifted the bird into his hands, held its head against his fingers, cupped it to his chest. Lor saw its eyes blink open, bead black and startled. It lay warm and alive in his hands. She wanted to reach out and touch it, to feel the life of it, but she was embarrassed for him to see her arms. Self-consciously she looked down at them, the pink lurid scars that ran from her wrists to her elbows. It was too late to hide them.

"Someone been hurting you?" he asked, softly.

She lifted her head, thought she caught that distant look in his eyes.

His name was called then, from somewhere outside in the corridor, abrupt and reprimanding. And then he was gone, taking the waking bird with him, and Lor was left with the sweetness of the berry that still lingered in her mouth, and his name: Yavy.

Long Before

SWITZERLAND, 1927

Them Authorities are finding it mighty hard to get a placement for the likes of me, they say. No one wanting a bounder, a boy that runs. So I watch the others coming an' going, some looking like they're heading to a family who might treat 'em with a little loving, while I stay stuck in this dark place being more polite an' low each day.

Mostly to get by, I remember that place I still calling home. Remember our horse, Blesham, how we hitched him up to the front o' our wagon and fed him good oats an' hay. How we traveled with our chickens an' our rabbits, and how I was loving them whether they were clucking an' skipping at my feet, or being chopped up an' steaming in a bowl for my dinner.

My work was filling up our horse's bucket and brushing the sweat from his hot hide, making the grain slick an' silky, and feeding them chickens, and playing with them rabbits. Learned how to whittle wooden nails at a young age, whittling them so sharp they can be hammered down easy. One stroke, two. Like that wood was a slice o' butter. And not ever do I think of hammering them nails into that boy Jesus's feet an' hands. Not ever.

I long for them gypsy nights, when we would light our way with
that huge paraffin lantern that rocked in the wind leaving a trail o'
scent we could smell half a mile away. Long for that sweet-sounding
music, instruments tuned, violins, that cimbalom player knocking
chords out in arpeggio with his cloth hammers as them castanets
sounding out the beat.

Sometimes we roast sweet hedgehog, which we is catching in our
traps. Cook it in a cube o' clay that dries solid. Split it apart, and watch
how them prickles an' skin stick to it quick, so when we open it up there
is a meat so white an' tasty smelling, our mouths are watering before
they've even filled. Or we is roasting stuffed pheasant, or wild boar,
chomping on a can of sardines that we mix up with a sweet lard.

I long for them days when we were making balls out o' our own
jackets. How we stuff them full an' sew 'em up, playing soccer with
trees or shrubs for our goals. Long for our caravan, with its two door
wings, that we would let down to let the light and that clear breeze
in. How we'd lie with our heads on them door wings in the daytime,
feeling that big yellow sun raying down on our cheeks.

Sometimes I go to a school close to our *kampania*. Never a day
being happy there, though. What with them children laughing at my
clogs, tying their satchels in front of their chests as they playing at
being airplanes, flying past me an' knocking me to the ground.

Some of them girls at those schools though, they'd take the edge
off a good beating, with their pink lips an' long lashes. Never kissed one
before. Know their pa'd be mighty mean if I getting near 'em, so that be
enough to stop me doing it, but not enough to stop me dreaming.

Then there's my ma, who wraps me up tight in her apron and
holds me 'til I squeal. Don't know when she gonna grab me, when
not. So mostly I circle out of her reach, but sometimes I is wanting her
arms around me, so I close in, and she catches me quick. Remember,
too, the sight of her, when she has a headache, how she set up some
vinegar on a cloth that she ties around her head. Or when she is wanting to keep that mighty sun off her face, how she ties a rhubarb leaf
over her crown, and no matter how hard we laughing at her, or how
many times we asking her to take it down quick, she sits proud an'

straight backed and gets on with the work she got about her. And if we laughing too long, she makes us a rhubarb hat of our own, forces us to wear it, and we half hating her for that, half loving her, despite the others mocking.

Free an' easy in our playing, we are, knowing our ma and pa be close by, and supper coming soon enough, and come that bright moon shining we gonna be wrapped up tight in our beds, hearing the people we love most in the world snoring down below.

But even then, I know my ma and pa don't sleep so softly as me. Got them troubles of the world on their shoulders. Ain't long in a gypsy boy's childhood before he knows the world's not walking by his side, that it's gonna give him a fight each day he got to stand up to.

My pa, he's a Roma gypsy boy. Been hearing taunts an' cruel words all his life. From folks who stand safe steps away as they recite their limericks and their slanging insults, so that if he swings at them, they can duck an' dive and run away with their cowardly hearts. His great-great-grandfather was a slave of the Danubian provinces. Bought and sold by princes, "advertised like furniture in a newspaper," my ma told me. Fetching a good price for his knowledge of horses. Knew which ones to buy an' which ones best steering clear of. He fled Austria with the wind sweet in his nose after the Revolution. Fell in love with the first Roma girl he meets. My great-great-grandmother, a dark-haired beauty who could ride a horse as good as he, smoking her own clay pipe as she riding, filling it with dried oak leaves. Bought themselves a wagon home, setting off on that lonely road, looking at horses from town to town an' giving away their thinking for a handful of pennies. My family been traveling from that day on, moving from one place to the next, gathering up our skills, learning crafts that we see be most needed in the places where we stopping an' sticking for a time. Misfits, gypsy scum. Infidels. Only thing that is constant is that name calling that drives us off one piece of land to another.

My ma was a Yenish gypsy girl, light skinned, fair haired, like me, from that landlocked country they calling Switzerland. Been taunted for her "witch's blood" from when she first was walking. Seen hatred in the eyes of a child that is younger than she, a child that is smaller than she. Been stared at a thousand times, as if she smelling of something rotten. But my ma, she smells sweet as blossom.

My pa met her in a country neither of them is from, in a market on the outskirts of some shantytown. Met in a maze of cluttered stalls that my ma got herself lost in, afraid until an old 'un walks past her to piss 'gainst a wall, shouting out for her to take her eyes off him.

My pa, watching from his stall, took her hand-to-mouth gesture as shock, so he steps forward, pulling her into a metal yard, where he gets a surprise when he uncovers her laughing face. They stand an' stare with the smash of hammers all 'round them and metal sparks flying up, and my pa said that when she flicked back her varnished hair, he knew. And they been walking this tricky world side by side ever since, past all them people who wanting to see them keep on walking by.

Same with them Authorities of mine. Finally they find me that placement, and I walk on from one set of folk to another. Some man in need of a little help in his house. Gonna be my new pa, teach me how to be a proper boy, teach me how to be deserving of society, and they tell me by the looks of him he more than capable of doing that with the likes o' me. So I best be behaving, they tells me, lest I wanting what will come if I don't.

I stay low an' small. Not rising to what they calling me. And not caring where they takes me by then, 'cos I is seeking out that magic that gonna make life worth living. A magic that's gonna keep my *soori* safe. I seen what my pa done with them white crosses. Know the magic of what coming from one thing to make another. Seen how it can keep a boy alive.

Before

AUSTRIA, 1931

Her days were filled with airlessness, amassed against the sealed windows like a stale gas. The morning sunlight shone through the clear glass and cast finger-like shadows across her bed from the breeze-blown wisteria leaves outside. She lay unmoving. Seeking to remember if she had always been so, or if this was, as they explained, part of her illness. *Her* illness. You are *ill*, Lor. Still so very *ill*. That small clean click of a word. What was insanity, she wanted to ask? What was sanity? If the two were separate she could not define within her one from the other, nor a time when she had been either or. Both seemed a mere accident of holding life together. A trick of the fragile mind hidden beneath a layer of lacquered varnish, the thickness of sugared glass.

"Do you miss your father?" Dr. Itzhak would ask. "Do you read his letters?"

"Yes," she would reply.

"And your mother? Do you think of her? Do you remember her? Dream of her, still?"

"All of those things," she would tell him.

"And you still see her? She still visits you?"

"No, she no longer does that."

"And why do you think that is, Glorious?"

On these occasions she did not know what to say, what would appear sane, or insane, so she said nothing.

"I trust you to tell me if you see her again, Glorious, my dear. I trust that you will do that." And she would nod, make her promises, and, when he left, lie there bereft.

When he arrived this particular morning he said, "So Glorious, you are progressing very nicely." He held a file in his hands that he opened and studied with exaggerated interest. "I am pleased with you," he said eventually. "I wonder if you feel ready to venture outside? A short walk around the grounds?" Perhaps he was as aware as she of the staleness inside the room. "You would like that, my dear?"

"I would like that very much," she said, and shortly afterward he called for the nurse, a young girl only a few years older than Lor, who helped her dress, swapping her nightclothes for day clothes that were starched and ironed and coarse against her skin.

Then, after months of only that room, only those walls, that bed, she was led from inside to out, one small step bridging each. Surprisingly once there, it was not the grass, nor the breeze, nor the sunlight that she was first aware of, but the scent of her own skin. She could smell the sleep on it, days and nights of it, trapped between the sheets. As if time had decayed on her.

They were watching. She felt them. From behind the closed windows and doors. She blinked against the light, the arc of the sky above her, the lake that spread like a pool of spilled silver out toward the mountains, their white peaks hidden in other worlds above the clouds. She reeled beneath the space. Steadied herself. A jolt of air, dry-hot and scented with thyme.

Around her, other inmates were scattered about the immaculate lawn. She recognized some of them from the ward: the woman who was circling the wrought-iron bench, still tugging at her hair, wrenching clumps from her scabby blistered scalp. Another knelt beneath the apple tree, picking up rotten windfalls which she sniffed and discarded. They passed a man with hair the color of straw who rocked on his haunches and snarled like a dog, drooling pools of saliva into his hands. He spat at them as they passed. The nurse raised her arm in the air and immediately two men in white coats came running from the upper terrace. They dragged the man onto his feet, carted him away, his gait hunched and unsymmetrical. Long after she lost sight of them, Lor could hear his screams.

The young nurse led her down a path that cut diagonally across the lawn. She was a shy girl, less forthcoming than Lor, less likely than she, even, to light up a room. Her skin was pitted with adolescent scars, a sheen of grease across her nose. She smelled of that grease, as if she spread great quantities of lard across her bread each morning, so that at night it seeped from her pores.

They were walking toward the lake, following the path past shrubs that hid the Institution, strolling beneath overhanging trees of willow and ash that shaded them from the late morning sun. The nurse led her to the water's edge where the air smelled of shadows. To the right of them was the boathouse, which looked locked and unused. To the left was a small workshop that sat at the very edge of the walled garden beneath thick vines of wisteria that were yet to flower. Its foundations looked strong and there were flurries of intricacies in the stonework, suggesting that originally the plans for it had been for something grander: a gazebo perhaps, a summerhouse. But now it was dilapidated, discarded it seemed, with sunlight that slanted through the windows and lit up shafts of pale-gold dust. The nurse led her onward alongside the lake, following the path past the workshop, and as they did so Lor looked through a gap between stone and wood where the door was ajar and caught a glimpse of what was inside.

She stopped. Covering every surface, cluttering every crevice, were dried petals, dried leaves, pieces of fabric, stones of ochre and malachite, lake-smoothed pebbles, tinted glass, and broken china shards. Colors, everywhere. They hung across the stone walls, lined the shelves; a chink in the wall even, where a brick was missing; an open drawer; the space under the narrow metal bed with springs that sagged. And there was variety to their shade, an ordered layout that circled the entire space. Aquas, fuchsias, indigos and teals, magentas, maroons, burnt siennas, and bright vermilion reds. Lor could name them all; a row of paint cans in her mind's eye: cyans, limes, golds, olives, silvers, perus, tans. No color the same. All of them graduating from one to another with the slightest distinction.

"Come along," the nurse said softly. "Come along now." And she led her back up the path toward the Institution, back to the bleached-white walls, away from those colors.

This Day

AUSTRIA, 1944

It is at the end of the second month, the dusk is falling, and none of them can sleep for the cramps of containment.

"I used to collect. I used to collect stamps," Loslow is telling them. "I had over two thousand by the beginning of the war. They filled four leather-bound books, each of them labeled in the order of the date I acquired them. Seems futile now, but you know it gives me comfort to imagine them, sitting where I left them on the shelf in my library. I was always searching for that rare one that might make me a fortune. You know the most famous stamp in the world, the Red Magenta, came about simply through mischance. Simply because an anticipated shipment of stamps in Guiana did not arrive. The local postmaster there ordered the printing of an emergency replacement batch. There is only one of them left in the whole world. A small ship sailing on a sea of bright magenta. It sold for three hundred thousand francs. Do you collect, Jakob?" he asks.

"I am not sure," says Jakob, squeezing the stone in his hand, feeling for his box, as the line of light under his cupboard door darkens.

"Perhaps you should begin. I think it is good for the soul. Part of our makeup. Like nuts to a squirrel."

He is interrupted by the sound of Markus's shoes shuffling faster than usual across the stone slabs. "They are coming," his voice hushes outside the cupboard doors. "Be silent. They are coming over to the house."

Loslow stops talking immediately. Voices sound from the kitchen, abrupt, clipped. There is the noise of furniture scraping across the floor. When the door to the kitchen opens and boots sound on the stone flags, Cherub pushes a finger through the hole in the partition between them. Jakob feels for it in the darkness and peers through the crack beneath his door. Light spills out into the hallway. A shadow streaks across it.

The fear slips through him, immediate, sudden, like stepping over from white to black. He clenches his stone in his hand to stop from shaking, afraid that even the movement of air inside his cupboard might give him away.

"Your pictures are not straight," a voice is saying with an accent that brings dread, and Jakob listens for something recognizable in the guttural tone—the sound of honey. "Why are your pictures not straight?"

"I had not noticed," Markus's voice replies.

"How? How do you not notice a thing like this? You are too busy perhaps? You clean one window. You can clean no more?" There is no reply. "I asked if you were too busy?"

"Perhaps."

"These pictures are precious to you?"

"Not in value, but in sentiment, yes."

"So I ask again, what is it that keeps you so busy that you cannot straighten your precious pictures? Cannot clean more of your windows? With what, old man, are you so busy?"

There is no honey. No honey in that voice. The officer is moving around the floor. Jakob can hear the shifting of a picture straightened on the wall.

"It is difficult to find food. It is time consuming," Markus replies.

"Yes, that is true. But you find it?"

"Not enough."

"You have enough to feed a guest?"

"A guest?"

"Yes, a boy, a young boy?"

"There is no boy."

"That is funny. Someone said that they saw you in the yard with a boy."

"No, there is no boy."

"A mistake then."

"Yes, a mistake." There is a long silence. "Perhaps I can find you something to eat," Markus offers eventually.

"I would appreciate it. They talk of you as a brave man in the village. You fought in the Great War?"

"Yes, I did."

"So are you still as brave an old man as I have heard?" the voice is asking.

"What have you heard?" Markus's voice replies.

"Enough. You are proud to be of use to your country?"

"Yes, I am proud."

"I have heard this. Proud enough to stand up for what you believe in?"

"Yes."

There is the smack of a sound that comes suddenly and then a thud upon the floor. "So be proud, old man. Stand up for what you believe in." Silence. "Stand up. Stand up, old man."

"Please," is all they hear Markus utter. Again they hear the smack of something. "Please. Please."

Jakob squeezes his eyes shut. He waits for his cupboard door to swing open. Waits for the sound of gunshots and the hot pain that will follow. *Sich setzen.* Gypsy scum. *Sich hinsetzen!* Sit down! And behind the view of a Y-shaped tree that broke the flat of the horizon.

"Please," Markus says again, a whispered plea, hoarse, stuttered. "Please . . ."

A shadow moves across Jakob's doorway. He can just make out the black boots and the soldier's khaki coat. He is tall and broad. His bulk bulges inside his jacket. The padding is bursting at the seams. Jakob hears the rattle of the cattle trucks in his ears. He feels his brother's heel in his ribs, bare toes in the crease behind his knees.

He smells the grease of his sister's hair next to his own, feels her hot breath on his cheeks. He sees the tree on the mound. Sees the children crowded beneath it, dirt smeared and grazed. Sees the hard-set face of the officer as he lights and coaxes the flames of his fire, a man who only moments before had held his head in his hands as he wept.

But through the crack in the cupboard door there is no eagle, no white silk or aluminum wire. Jakob cannot see his face, but he knows the officer in the hallway will not smell of cologne, or carry the scent of licorice on his breath.

His sister lifts her foot from the ground, asks if the grass feels pain.

His father's voice. *Nothing wasted. Nothing futile.* The memory of his blue-stained fingers as he used to sweep back his hair.

Jakob remembers the cow, its fur damp and matted. Its wide-eyed look, long lashed and pleading. It had shifted its head, jerked it slightly upward. Only once, before it lay still, its expression one of mild surprise as the breath was stifled from it.

"*Zyli wsrod roz,*" Jakob whispers. "They lived amongst the roses. *Nie znali burz.* And they did not know of any storms."

He can hear the long, drawn-out breaths that betray the soldier's stony calm. He can smell the oil and the gasoline on his hands, the cut grass on his shoes. He listens. Hears the shift of moving fabric. A boot scuffs. Then silence. Then the grunt of effort as Markus stands, the grind of his knees as he rises.

"Come, I can find you something to eat," he says. He hears the shuffled steps on the stone flags, hears the heavy tread of the soldier following. The door to the kitchen closes again and the voices continue muted from behind the wood.

"You have earned yourself a bullet," the officer had told him, his face streaked with muddy tears as he had looked up from his fire, and Jakob had witnessed the straightening of his spine. Knew that he was no longer caught in that no-man's-land between thought and action.

Inside their cupboards, Loslow and Cherub do not utter a word. Jakob lies curled on his side, hugs his knees to his chest, inhales their scent.

"So you are on Gillum, and I on Valour," he whispers to himself. "With Malutki behind me and Eliza behind you. We are far beyond that

Ushalin World now. Far beyond them deserts of smoke and ash that eddy 'cross them Great Plains, splintering against those who stand in their path. You carry that indigo in your right saddle, a glass vas full of the night, and in your left that malachite green, what we cut from the azurite we found in them copper caves, cut and welded and ionized with fine wine. We ride fast 'cross them golden sands, till we find that crevasse, no wider than the length of you, no deeper than the height of me. An' we sleep safe in the hiding down low of there, sleep deep through that long night."

They do not get any food that evening. They have to wait until the next day. When Markus comes to them that afternoon he brings only bread.

Loslow sobs when he sees him. "My friend. My dear friend."

"Why, Markus?" Jakob hears Cherub asking, his voice tight in his throat. "Why do you hide us?"

"Because."

"Because—why?"

"Perhaps there would be no point to my life without you."

"That is it? Really?"

"Perhaps my life is not as precious as it once was," the old man whispers. "For your company, it is worth the risk."

"You are an angel," Loslow weeps.

"Only in the hell of this life. We live in a time of angels and devils, but not a single one of us is either."

"You are right," Loslow says. "War, it is mankind's illusion. Our longing for the pendulum that swings from peace to the extreme. A lust for something other than the beat of the ordinary." He is a rush of words suddenly, talking so quickly they spill out like his tears.

When Markus opens Jakob's cupboard door, Jakob sees the deep laceration across his right temple that is still bruised and inflamed, the gash on his lip, the blue wound beneath the knuckles of his hand.

"Hello, my boy," Markus says, forcing a smile.

"Why, Markus?" Jakob asks. "Why?"

"When you can hurt a man without consequence, perhaps the temptation is uncontainable." And then, "You know you cannot stay here much longer. You must get to Switzerland," he tells him. "When it is time, that is what you must try to do. You must run south and not stop until you reach the lakes. Remember that, Jakob. Be invisible and swift. You can be that?"

"Yes," says Jakob. "I can be swift," he repeats, but the thought terrifies him. Warm in his triangle cupboard, wrapped in his sheepskin coat, with faceless friends, a day passing and then another, he has come to imagine that this is the way it will always be. Day after day, in a world of sound, until . . . until . . . he doesn't know what.

He dreams of his wagon, the rattle of its wheels over rough roads, the rhythmic creaking of its axle, the occasional crack of a whip, and the wind, the wind in the leaves and the hum of flies that hung around Borromini's head; his breath soft when he walked, streaming from him when he rose to a trot. They would move from forest to field, across field to forest. Through oat and corn and walls of swaying wheat. Breathing in wood smoke as he watched his skin darken beneath the sun.

Next door everything is silent.

"Cherub?" Jakob whispers eventually in the darkness.

"Yes?"

"You ever kill a man?"

"No, I have not ever killed a man." Again they fall silent. "I imagine it would be a hard thing to do," Cherub says at last.

But Jakob does not reply. Outside there is the sound of a distant train, the rattle of it across the tracks. Once again he is transported from his cupboard to the rails. Lies on the cold cattle-truck floor again, listening to the sound of the wheels on the track. The rattle and the grind, the cradle-rock back and forth. Tuchun tuchun tuchun. Metal on metal. A hot spark. A screech of wheels twisting on a bend. Tuchun tuchun tuchun. There is no water, no food. His tongue lies like a slab of dry rock in his mouth. He drifts in a torpid haze, weak with starvation.

Asleep, he hides in dreams of color. The brightest of colors: Prussian blue, emerald green, a burning scarlet. When he wakes, everything is the color brown. Familiarity comes in the form of dust and soil on the soles of worn shoes, as the cattle trucks move on across the land. There is little light, just a sliver through a slit above his head. He feels his brother's heel in his ribs, bare toes in the crease behind his knees. He smells the grease of his sister's hair next to his own, feels her hot breath on his cheeks. The sweat crusts on their bodies. The stench of stale urine seeps into their skin. The rattle of the train rings in his ears. Nothing to do but sleep and fear. When it rains the air smells of mushrooms. When it doesn't, it smells of blood.

Tuchun tuchun tuchun, metal on metal, the cradle-rock back and forth. Tuchun, tuchun, tuchun. The rhythm of his thudding heart as he sits in the miasma of sweat and blood.

They do not stop, for two days they do not stop. Then he feels the gravity of being pushed forward, the slowing of the wheels, the sudden silence of stillness. They stop at a platform in a valley of nowhere, the doors sliding open, slamming more metal into metal as light pours into his blinded eyes. He is given only water and it is as brown as the color of his skin. Still he sips from the filthy cup his mother hands him, gulps his meager ration, and imagines the dirt that films it is from the soil of the most fertile field.

Only afterward does he notice the man opposite who is staring out at a plain of green grass, at a lone tree, shaped like a Y, that breaks the flat of the horizon. Jakob catches the rapture on his face that passes across it as if his very life depends on seeing such a tree, and not on the water that is being handed to him. Jakob watches the man's pale eyes filling with tears. The corners of his mouth quiver, and Jakob sees the almost-smile of nostalgia that moves across his lips.

"You," a guard is calling from the open door on the other side of the carriage. "Sit down. Hey, gypsy scum, look at me when I'm talking to you. *Habt ihr verstanden?* I said sit down," the guard goes on. "SIT DOWN," he yells. "*SICH HINSETZEN.* SIT DOWN." But the man doesn't sit down. He is too absorbed in the view of the tree in front of him.

The bullet hits him in the back of the head. Jakob watches him jolt forward, his temple smashing against the wall of the cattle truck before he slumps onto the floor. The blood flows from the wound, dripping down his neck as he lies, eyes open, still staring at the view of the Y-shaped tree he has died for. That and an almost-smile that was lost in nostalgia. The woman next to him sits trembling with his splattered blood on her cheeks. She makes no sound. A pool of scarlet seeps across the floor. The woman sits upright, her mouth a straight line, clenched but quivering tenuously with fury. Tears slip down her cheeks, one after the other, but they seem separate from her, an involuntary physical response that defies the strength of her jaw.

Jakob holds his screams in his throat. *Ceri pe phuv perade.* The sky falling to the earth. *Jag xalem.* He eats fire. *Thuv pilem.* Drinks smoke. *Thaj praxo.* Becomes dust.

"Jakob," his father calls. He is across from his son, several bodies away, but he moves to sit up in the tangled mess of limbs so that Jakob can see him. "I told you the story of that cochineal beetle?" In the darkness Jakob shakes his head. "You can squeeze that cochineal beetle in your fingers, pop it dead, so that its blood staining your palms," his father begins, his voice shaking. "This blood, it is the reddest dye in the world. This blood is the treasure of the Aztecs and the Incas. Been used on the robes of kings, on the lips of queens. Nothing wasted. Nothing futile." Jakob listens, closes his eyes, and lets his father's words wash over him. Nothing wasted. Nothing futile. It was his first ever train journey.

They close the metal doors, leave them in the darkness. And when, much later with the rising dawn, they open them, the first thing Jakob sees is the Y-shaped tree. And after that, the crowd of children gathered beneath it.

Long Before

AUSTRIA, 1931

L or dreamt of her mother that night for the first time. As if in doing so she might drift further into the madness Dr. Itzhak said tainted her. Vivienne was crouched down beside her feet, lacing her shoes. She caught a loop in her hand, wound it around the lace, yanked hard to form a tight bow, then trailed her long fingers down the length of Lor's shoe before moving on to tie the other. Once she had done so she returned to the first shoe, pulled at the bow, unlaced it, and began again. Lacing and relacing her daughter's shoes over and over. When Lor woke she could not envisage her mother's face. Of her features, there was only a whiteness.

She was not taken outside again until the following weekend. The insulin shots prevented it, lulled her into that strange soporific state. But the next time the young nurse came for her, Lor asked if they might once again walk down to the lake. As they had done the first time, they ambled across the grounds, past inmates who rocked and soothed themselves with the chatter of their own voices, and once again followed the path around and down to the water's edge.

When they reached the workshop Lor asked, "May I?" and the young nurse hesitated, then nodded slowly as if deciding there could be no harm.

Outside the workshop there was a stack of coarsely cut logs, set neatly in a rectangular block. They had been warmed in the sunlight and now scented the air with sycamore dust. There was an ax on a hook and a heavy garden spade resting against the wall. The wisteria vine clung to the brickwork, still empty of leaves and flowers, not yet budding. Lor wondered if when it did the flowers would cover the only window, lightening the room with a lilac hue as they had in her own house. She hovered on the shallow stoop before pushing the door wide open and stepping inside.

It was beautiful to her, the clutter, familiar. She allowed herself to walk the four walls, lifting objects here and there, examining them: a shard of green glass; a moonstone, smoothed by lapping waves; the skeleton of a leaf, so delicate she hardly dared to hold it in the palm of her hand. She moved to the center of the room, her eyes roaming from one color to the next, to the changing shift of each shade.

Behind her, the nurse fidgeted. They should go now, she said. They had stayed long enough.

"Please," Lor begged. "Just a moment longer. Just a moment."

A toolbox lay open on a table beside the bed. A pile of planed shavings scattered the floor beneath it. Someone had carved a wooden spoon, had woven limb bark into a shoe, cut and stripped a small fishing rod. Lor stood over that table, saw a silver blade beneath a handful of loose nails, felt claustrophobic with longing.

"Please," the nurse said, ill at ease. "Come now. You must come now."

But Lor could hardly hear her. She dropped down, upon the stone floor.

"I miss you," she whispered.

"Who are you talking to?" the nurse asked.

"I miss you," Lor said again.

And for the first time in months she came, still as lovely as ever, still as pale. "You are so thin, my love," her mother said. "Are they not feeding you?"

Lor rested her head in the palm of her mother's hand. It felt as if she were sinking into a tub of warm water. "I miss you so." She rocked, wept, held her own arms around herself. She could not bear to go back to the cold. "Take me from here, please. End it. End it now."

Behind her she heard the nurse's steps running back along the path, felt the space where she no longer was. They would come for her. She knew they would come soon enough.

"Please, Mother. Take me from here," she pleaded again.

"No need to end it, my darling. You can bear it," her mother said and she took up the blade from the toolbox, pulled up Lor's sleeves and slowly dragged it across her wrist, an old scar opening up as it trailed across her skin.

"There. Everything will be all right now," she whispered, as slowly she disappeared into the shadows of the room's corners. "You can bear it, where I could not. You always have. Go live amongst the roses, my love."

Lor watched the beads of blood forming on her arm. Felt the stilling calm. She sat there in the silence, more at peace than at any time over the past months, perhaps years. All that there was were the colors, nothing else: no pain, no loss, no fear. Just a room of colors, each one as simple and as beautiful as the next.

She would have stayed that way, were it not for the fact that he came as she sat upon the stone floor, aching for her mother. The boy with his shaggy clothes and defiant stare. He stood, as she had stood moments before on the threshold to the workshop, and it took a while for her to register that a shadow had been cast against the light. She lifted her head, looked up expecting to see the nurse, but instead he stood there, staring at her. His eyes were gray, not a thread of color in them. Clear as glass. They looked from her to the cluttered walls, then back again, as if he was absorbing a scene that was familiar to him, but with the startling addition that she was now in it. Once again she took in his clothes, workman's clothes that seemed too big for him, the pants folded above his ankles, the shirtsleeves folded above his wrists, loose at the seams. Her tears rolled from her chin. She felt them falling into her hands.

"So, you are crazy?" he asked eventually, looking down at her cut wrist. He did not seem surprised. His look was quizzical, thoughtful.

When she said nothing, he continued. "No matter. They saying that of me. But I knowing I not crazy. This place more crazy than I. Been here years 'nough to know it."

"These are yours?" Lor asked him of the colors in the room. He did not answer. His face seemed laid bare as if suddenly intruded upon. "I'm sorry," she said. "For being here."

He shrugged. He had not taken his gaze from her face the whole time. Eventually he came toward her, knelt first upon the floor beside the bed and then pulled from beneath it a rusted metal box. It was cluttered with strange bottles full of liquids of ochre and darkest brown, leaves and flowers that floated in jars of water. He twisted the lid off one of them, brought out a white flower, the sort she recognized growing at the sides of country roads. He moved to sit down beside her and after crushing it in the palm of his hand, he began gently to dab the juices across the cut on her wrist. She flinched slightly.

"Be still," he told her. "It'll numb that pain. Won't trouble you so much when you sleeping later."

"What is it?" she asked.

"They call it white yarrow. Soldiers used it to stop their bleeding an' to clean their dirty wounds." Afterward he pulled a handkerchief from his pocket and wrapped it around the cut, took his time to tie it tightly, glancing every so often at the door. She felt the weight of his fingers on her, felt his rough calloused skin.

"They'll come for you soon enough," he told her. "Best I'm not here. They got me working on stuff now, fixing them gardens, fences an' outdoor things. Been giving them no cause to trouble an' they got no place else to put me." He paused and looked at her again. "Them treatments gonna take the life out of you."

Then he stood, lingered on the threshold as if he was about to say something more, but in the end he turned and walked back down the path, leaving her alone again in his room of colors. She sat in the space where he had been, felt the sudden emptiness of his absence, and only then did she recognize that underneath it all, he, like her, found existence hard. That he, like her, knew the sort of sadness that did not go away. It seemed that between them, like a pool of clear water, lay the knowledge of loss.

All this, before she was discovered. Before there was the rush of thudding feet down the path, an intrusion of bodies in the tiny space, arms around her neck, too tight, heaving her up from the floor, dragging her away. She screamed for her mother, who did not come. All that was left was Dr. Itzhak's calm assertion that she was not ready, a setback in the treatment, dangerous for her own well-being, which in time they would deal with accordingly.

"Too soon, Glorious. I am sorry, it was too soon," he said, more to himself than to her. Swiftly she was dragged from outside to in, was again strapped down, this time upon a board where she was doused with iced water, felt it pouring over her face, until she was left choking, stunned with the swiftness from peace to chaos, from the brightness of colors to the gray clear sting of her own tears. She choked on bile. Then muted her screams.

"See, my dear, you are calm again now," Dr. Itzhak said when they were done, and she, too limp to respond, simply closed her eyes and let the delirium take her.

Long Before

So they packing me off to my new home, to a house in a town nothing but a short trot away from that Pro Juventute I been kept in, and though things be different here, they not better. Not better at all. My foster pa has eyes like alabaster, white lashed like an angel. But he ain't no angel. He's a *barri* man, a big 'un, with a fist that'd punch the light out o' you. Drinking all evening, and smoking brissagos, swallowing that smoke an' coughing so hard it come back up out into the air. Sitting in his big chair with his belly all hanging out around his pants, so hairy an' damp, even from where I is sitting I can smell him. All salt an' sickly sweetness.

Works in that steel factory, my *barri* man, hot an' fiery as he bends that rigid steel, singeing that rough skin o' his with sparks, so he bringing home a roaring rage, burning them singes out on me with his brissagos and his fists. I feel the pain o' that right in the *soori* of me. Like it burning all the good away inside. And still when it come to them mealtimes we thank the Lord Almighty for this stinking world he made for us. Ain't no one up in that blue heaven gonna blame me for running again, I reckon. Not God, nor Jesus who suffers all us little 'uns to come unto him. His wife stands small an' meek and sometimes

I see she feeling sorry for me, but is too afraid to go showing me so. One time, in the kitchen, when I come carrying in the coal, big heavy sackfuls that I lug 'cross that yard. Them sacks be weighing maybe fifty pounds, and sometimes I lug 'em ten miles into town.

"Bet it's been a long time since you had something sweet?" she says. Been so long I had something sweet, I've half forgotten what it tasting like. "Here," she says, and hands me a spoonful of sugar. I put that sugar in my mouth, the whole spoonful of it. Can feel it on my tongue, fizzing so sweet, half stinging, and my body all a-buzzing, like some sort of wily spell in my fingers an' my toes. And that lady, she gives me a smile that she dares not give when her *barri* man's around. Part of me is longing to put my arms around her waist, feel the warmth of her wrapping around me, soft as dough, her skin all hot an' milky scented. But I never have no courage to be doing that. And she don't either. So we stay with a good distance between us, smiling at each other. And that is like a spoonful of sugar in itself.

She come reading to me one day. Reading a book she says her pa used to read to her. About a lion, strong an' solid as a tree, who even if you rest your whole body 'gainst, will not hurt you. We sit reading by the fire, an' life not so bad to be living while her voice sounding off them pages.

We do this maybe three times before her *barri* man discovers us. Then there's a fire in his eyes as he starts asking her what she wants, reading to me, when I meant to be out in that yard. Beats me then. And beats her, and next time we see each other our faces are all bruised an' swollen and she won't be looking at me no more. Never no story of that lion. Never no spoonful o' sugar. After that, my *barri* man he puts his brisagos out on my arm more times than before, and he hits me harder, a cuffing at my ear, a cuffing at my jaw. Don't sleep so sing-song after that. Am more fearful of my life now, and wanting to hold on to it tight, 'cos I been reminded what it feels like to have a little kindness.

When my *barri* man is greasing his belt one day, I know what he has in mind, 'cos I can smell that liquor on his dirty breath, and I know I not gonna make it if I sticking around, not this time.

Remember what I been taught as a young 'un.

Te den, xa, te maren, de-nash. When you are beaten, run away. Run Away.

So I slip out small an' mute and run fast as my hungry legs gonna carry me. Get to the end of the street before I hear him shouting, his voice all a bellow an' a rage, and them neighbors come hollering to his aid, catching me like it's better for my health. But I kick an' scream, and run on down the next street an' the next an' the next one after that. Keep running till I get to the middle of that town that be all hustle 'bout me. Men in bars, dirt smeared an' hardworking. Hookers standing around showing more leg than is rightful, smelling of vanilla bean an' sweet tobacco. Feel more safe with them folk who don't talk 'bout how good for nothing I am, nor 'bout how good for something they are. They talk raw an' true 'cos they had the lies of life knocked out of them.

Get to befriend them Italian boys by the end of that long day. They standing on their scaffolding, all dust covered an' sing-songing, reminding me that there is a beauty in the dirt an' murky colored. They giving me a space upon their floor for this night and the others and I sleep softly, drowning out the past for a good few weeks.

But them Authorities be out looking for me with their beady eyes. Grabbing me in the street one day. Come out of them shadows. Hold me down too tight. And I act so crazy they think no one gonna calm the devil out of me, ranting an' raving an' pummeling my fists into the air. Show them the burns on my arms, the bruises on my back, and in the end they don't send me back to my *barri* man, and they don't send me back to that Home, neither.

Send me to a different country altogether. A place where the walls are so white they blinding me the first time I see them. Place where them corridors stink of chemicals that make your eyes sting, and toilets that stink o' shit an' piss. Place where I see women cradling babies in their arms. Only there ain't no babies. They just seeing them 'cos they can't be bearing the loss of their own. There're people in this place shouting an' hollering more loudly than I ever could, more mad than I ever seen, rocking back an' forth and laughing when there ain't nothing to laugh 'bout. Strapped down by their hands an' feet, and screaming so hard their faces are all puffed an' reddened. I am half missing my *barri* man by the time they finish with me in this place. This Institution that they calling it as if it were something white an' clean.

Who are you? them screaming women ask me, over an' over again. Who are you? And I knowing in myself who I am, but I won't be telling them. Nor them men in white coats. Keep my memories like a locket, only to be opened when I choose. Tell them I remember nothing. Look cheerful, like things of no matter. Like life's worth living.

Sometimes I drift so deep inside o' myself, all them words lose their meaning and only a silence is left that keeps my *soori* safe, like no one ever gonna be able to get to me again. Fills my head with memories. How one day, my pa gathered up them white crosses in their rows an' rows. Put a spade to the strut of every single one, pushing his foot down hard so that it dug deep into the ground, and with one shove, pulled up each an' every one of them. Clearing them away, for them new gravestones that'd be arriving, stones that'd be lasting for the end of all time.

Afterward, that mound of crosses so high it blocks out a whole lot of sky, and my pa knows he can't be leaving it to rot in the wind an' the rain. Them crosses touched the bones of all the lives he fought with. So he fetches our horse, and together they set about dragging each an' every one of them crosses from that killing field, down the lane to our *kampania*. Working in the rain that poured down. Working in the heat of that shining sun. But nothing gonna stop my pa with that task he got in hand.

He never believed in that bloody war. Not from the start to the finish. Nothing but a bewildering nightmare to him. Seeing men alive even though their legs an' arms gone whirling off, lying out in the fog with drilling guns blasting in their bleeding ears. Such a place, he told me, even the birds had left it. Only a memory of green grass 'gainst a field all muddied. Told me how he held his best friend in his arms. Held his entrails in his hands. Seeked to push them back into that black hole that had opened up in his stomach. Held him till he breathed his last, shuddering breath. Such a sight of wretchedness a terror screamed inside of my pa with not a way to make it ever hush itself. Hears it from then on, alongside the day to day, a shrieking in his head.

So, he got himself a plan. A plan for them white crosses.

Long Before

AUSTRIA, 1931

Yavy came that night and stood outside her window up at the Institution. The wind was a bluster, whistling through the crevices, and she was not sure whether it was this that stirred her, or that through a drug-induced sleep she somehow sensed him there. She turned her head and saw him behind the glass, simply standing, watching. He seemed again to be studying her with the timeless confidence of the invisible. As if he were unaware she could see him. Slowly her heavy eyelids closed again as a mist of sleep drew her under, unsure in the end whether she had really seen him at her window or simply dreamt it.

But he came the next night. And the next. Almost as a ritual. As if he were waiting for something. Finally, when she was strong enough to rise, she crept from her bed and pushed up the window, as she had that first night when he stood in the rain. She felt the chill breeze on her hands and heard him shiver.

"You are cold?" she asked him.

"No matter."

"You come to see me?" He nodded. "And they do not know it?"

"They knowing little besides their own thinking. They should watch more. Think less."

"But you risk much with it."

He shrugged and she found herself again trying to hide the scars on her arms. He glanced at them.

"Been watching crazy people come and go from this place," he said finally. "For years now. You're not one of them. Them scars 'long your arms, they'll be healing. An' one day they won't be there no more. Time changes. Nothing staying the same. You lost your balance, is all. You fell some with the loss of it."

"You do know that I see my own mother?" Lor said, surprised by the harshness of her tone. "I see her in front of me as clear as day. But you should know my mother is dead. Do you still think I am not crazy?"

"You loved your mother?" he asked. Lor nodded. "Then you are not crazy." He hesitated, seemed afraid of what he was going to say next. "Can take you from here, if you wish it," he said finally. "Been here long 'nough to know they gonna knock the life out of you if you stay."

She fell silent. What he was saying was insane. He was insane, surely, even to think it, let alone speak it.

"How? How can you?" she asked.

"I can. If you wish it."

"I am afraid of you."

He bowed his head. When he looked up, he was smiling. "Remember," he said. "Nothing staying the same. Best you sleep now. Rest yourself. You don't know it yet, but you can be trusting me."

"You are Yavy," she said.

"Yes. I am he."

And then he was gone, defiantly striding out from the shadows and out across the moonlit lawn, and she was left knowing that she alone did not have the strength either to stay or to go. That her life was broken either way, and that if he had the will for it she would go with him. The world was no longer recognizable to her. It did not matter where she was in it. She lived now too far inside herself to care.

This Day

AUSTRIA, 1944

When Jakob wakes the following morning, there are whispered discussions going on next door. Markus is there, a conversation between all three of them. He cannot make out what they are saying to one another. He stretches the stiffness from his knees, strains to catch their words, which seem to be a collection of negatives: . . . no . . . not . . . none . . . never.

When Markus brings Jakob his meal later on that day it is filled to the brim and sloshing.

"We have been talking," he tells him.

"I have been listening."

"I am afraid they will soon discover you. You have heard: they are suspicious. I cannot even clean a window in my own house. It is not safe for you all to stay here any longer, Jakob. I am going to get some help for you to cross the border. I am going to send word and we will see what comes of that. But first you must eat. You will not get there as thin as you are, so you must get stronger, you hear me?"

A hole opens up in Jakob's stomach, a fist full of dread. What is there but this cupboard? What is there but this black scented space?

Despite this, he nods, wanting to please, hearing the conviction in Markus's words.

"Now eat. It has begun. I am to strengthen you up. Day by day."

"How did you find us more food, Markus?"

"I have some things that I can sell."

"Things that are precious to you?"

"What else would be worth selling for you? You will be strong, my boy. You will be strong enough to run fast."

Jakob can remember the sheer delight of running fast. His small legs pumping up the brow of a hill, his sister beside him, racing to the very crest, where they hovered momentarily, took in the sky, before running back down over the other side. Through high grasses, both light enough for the balmy wind to pick them up, lift them in leaping bounds over mounds and ridges down the grassy slopes, running until they fell, their feet entangled as if nature had tripped them. Yes, to run fast would be good. He remembers that to do that was always good.

The next time Markus brings food, there are chunks of chopped cheese melting in the soup and slices of egg, the yolk gleaming like jewels in the murky liquid.

"Where?" Jakob asks in amazement.

"My neighbor. He has a golden goose! I will have another one for you tomorrow."

"I did not know you had a neighbor. I thought there are only fields surrounding your home."

"Everyone has a neighbor. No matter the distance between them."

The flavor fills Jakob's mouth. Never before has cheese tasted so rich, so salty. He can feel his whole head burning with the flavor of it.

"Loslow, you are happy?" he almost shouts. "You are happy for your cheese?"

"Jakob, it is like heaven has descended upon our little world. I cannot wipe the smile from my face. My cheeks are aching with it," Loslow tells him.

Jakob chews slowly, savors his mouthfuls, hears his own teeth chomping through the soft textures.

"And you, Jakob, you are happy?" Cherub asks him.

"More than. More than," he replies between mouthfuls. "My feet, they are growing, Cherub."

"Yes, Jakob. Eat up. Soon you will be as cramped as we are in our cupboards."

Afterward he slumps against his warm wooden walls and dreams of golden geese, streams of them in an empty sky.

"You have to have a vision, Jakob," Markus tells him during this time. "You have to find something to grasp onto, to feel it inside the very depths of yourself. A longing as strong as loss. We are magnificent in this way. We can rise above the very worst. Believe it, Jakob. Seek it out."

Seek it out, Jakob repeats to himself.

"See the colors. *Na spourz ne kolory*," his father whispers in his right ear. Then his mother in his left, "So you are on Gillum and I on Valour," she tells him. "With Malutki and Eliza behind. We have stepped up our pace now, left the Forest of the Light-Footed behind us, left the madness of the wind there. We are seeking out, heading for fields so vast they cover the whole land. To the farthest horizon will be the color blue, bright as the sun in our eyes."

From then onward, occasionally there is something special floating in the broth of Jakob's soup, but even if that is not so there is always more of everything: a larger bowl, more potato to gnaw and suck, more liquid to burn the lining of his chest. They eat in silence. The scrape of their wooden spoons against the china of their bowls. And afterward Loslow will ask, "You can feel your stomach swell, Jakob? Is it rotund and bursting?"

"Yes, Loslow," Jakob will reply. "I am fat with it."

"Almost fat with it."

"Yes, almost. Almost." And he will hear Loslow chuckle and imagine the smile on his face.

He thinks again of his mother at these times. How she could not cook. How every meal was as tasteless as the last, and how between the five of them there seemed an unspoken pact that this was not something to be acknowledged openly. For his mother tried so hard, worked so relentlessly to create something that resembled the food she saw being cooked on the *kampania*, the rabbit and the beef stew. No one had the heart to tell her that no matter the content of herbs and spices heaped into a dish, no matter the effort, the kneading, the rolling, the chopping, the braising or the frying, each and every meal was as bland as the last.

Only once had he found her weeping because she could not cook. She had dropped a pot, a stew of some sort, which had splattered across their wagon floor, slipping down the gaps in the wooden planks.

"It is of no matter," she had said, picking the food up from the ground: a hunk of chicken, cubes of potato, diced pieces of carrot. "No matter." But the tears that streamed from her eyes said otherwise. He knelt to help her.

"No matter, Mamo," he had repeated. "No matter at all." She had smiled weakly and they had cleaned up together in silence and afterward she had wrapped him in her apron and held her to him long enough for him to feel the warm of her through the cloth.

Long Before

AUSTRIA, 1931

In the end Yavy took her from the Institution by boat, a small wooden skiff of faded green and red. There was the echo of his hammer ricocheting down by the lake in the early and late hours of each day, the patching up of wood and iron, watertight so that the lake would not seep in through the rotting planks and drown them before they reached the far side. There was his nightly sawing of the bars that crossed her window, steady, slow. The fear of what they would do if they found him there in the night, spitting sparks out onto the lawn. When he left, Lor's head ached with watching him. On the final night there was the muffled smash of glass, before she climbed up and out of that place, touching him as he helped her down from the stone coping, the heat of him on her arms, his hands gripping her elbows, her waist.

"That what happening when you become unseen," Yavy told her. "When you become invisible they're not so careful with their watching. Not seeing what happening beneath their very eyes."

Strangely there was a space for a farewell inside her. She would have liked an ending to her time with Dr. Itzhak. But yesterday on his rounds he had inquired only politely of her health, seemed somewhat harassed and hurried. She had studied the points of his face, the corners of his mouth, always set in grim contemplation of the tasks at hand, tasks he wholeheartedly believed in, with a practiced suppression of his heart. When the parting had come, it had been fleeting and insignificant. His mind had been on other things as he had stood on the threshold of her room, nodding distractedly before closing the door as a mere afterthought behind him.

She stood now gazing back at her room. It looked strangely gray and vacant against the night dark. She took from it only a letter, one of her father's that described a walk across the greenest grasses.

Grass so green it is as if all the beginnings of everything were heaped across those rolling hills, those valleys of leaf and willow, of dandelion and anemone. And a wind, fresh and sharp, apple and salt scented.

It was all that she possessed of her old life. Like a husk, the rest of herself she discarded. Yavy gave her clothes, his clothes, which smelled of him; wood smoke and something other: grass, soil, both rain drenched and sun dried, lake water, both deep and shallow. She drew them on, too large, rolling up the cuffs and trouser hems, the scent of the outdoors upon her. Then, all too quickly, there was the rushing over the dew-drenched lawn, weak limbed, cold, afraid of looming shadows, and then the clambering down to the boathouse, the wading through icy water, the shock and the half thrill of it. She did not know where the light had gone. There seemed to be none. The sky was black. The water blacker. He helped her into the boat, which was hidden in the grasses amongst the nests of small shy warblers and reed buntings. They flew up through the darkness, twittering angrily. Then there was the breeze on her skin. She breathed it in, tasting silt and brine. The air felt full of mist, mouthfuls of it that sank into her chest, soaked into her bones. She shivered. Pulled his clothes, already dank, around her. Watched the shadow of the Institution disappear behind them as Yavy rowed out across the lake, a vast sea of tideless darkness, guided by nothing, it seemed, but his own senses. He said little. Asked at intervals if she was all right, if she was not too cold. She lied and said she was not.

Slowly the silhouettes of the mountains on the far side of the lake loomed closer, the sheer cliffs, fissured and cracked, disappearing into the dark waters. For a while he rowed alongside them, the only sound his oars cutting through the surface, and the echo against the rocks. She felt the depths beneath them, the undiscovered darkness. There were no stones in her pocket. No want of them.

Eventually they reached the river. He fought the currents as far as he could, but it was the beginning of spring and the waters were flooded, full with rain from the mountains that had been blocked by storm and snow. The current was higher, faster, thrashing in torrents over boulders and gullies. He got them to the shore, heaved the boat up onto the shingle and helped her from it.

"We best heading for the largest town," he told her.

They walked as far as she could. Sometimes it felt as if she slept as she walked, lulled to the rhythm of her own steps, weak still with months of medication and immobility. In the end he caught her as she stumbled, pulled her down into the long river grasses to sleep upon the cold earth.

"You are weary," he told her. "Best you sleep now." She lay beside him, felt the warmth of him, vaguely aware of a dawn sky bleeding out above their heads and the cry of a lone buzzard circling above.

They had not until now been together in either the confines of a room or beneath the height of a sky. Alone, she had known him from within the stark staleness of that white room, and he from a garden at winter's end, when the trees were still bare and leafless, the light low and bright enough to burn their eyes to tinder. Now they lay together amongst reeds—too tired to dream, but in the intimacy of sleep they drew the mutual loneliness from each other.

Part Four

Before

They had a suitcase with them now, old and battered, with the name alfredo lajoie painted diagonally across the front in bold white letters and a handle made of frayed rope. Inside there was a change of clothes for all of them, borrowed clothes that Alfredo's wife had ferreted together from neighbors and friends and which still smelled of the lives of the people who had once worn them. And, too, a rug to keep them warm; bread, cheese, a book, one Lor remembered Yavy had liked, that he had read and reread, scouring through the age-stained pages. She felt closer to him in the presence of something that he had touched.

Alfredo had fed them well that last night, before they had left. With a blundering kindness, as his bear-brown eyes welled, he had placed on the table before them great hunks of bread, spread thickly with pale yellow butter, the salty-sweet aroma seeping up from a small glazed dish.

"And for you, Lor," he added. "A whole pot of *pâté de lapin*."

He had picked off the lid, the scent of it wafting up, saliva spilling into all of their mouths.

"How?" Lor had asked him. "Butter, lemons, *pâté de lapin*? How?"

Alfredo had shrugged. "The pâté, my wife made you. The butter, she saved for you. The lemons, I stole."

"Go carefully," he had told her later. "Please, go carefully." He was aware that De Clomp was a place she had arrived at only to leave. It was enough that he could offer her that. In the past, the present, perhaps again one day. Clumsily he said farewell, hid his loss and trepidation for them badly. They left him holding a jar with two snails within it for his safekeeping and four badges embroidered with the letter Z that he was to burn.

The station was busy, crowded on the platform. Lor stowed her children between the coats and the warmth of shuffling bodies, avoiding anything in uniform, and moved steadily up the platform toward the middle of the train. She pulled them past the Lucky Flower Tea Stop, the smell of strong coffee and cigarettes wafting from the door as it opened and closed, slamming on its hinges. On, past the lighting attendant's office, which looked dark and unattended.

Jakob held Malutki's hand tightly. Eliza smiled, a stiff forced smile, and stared fearfully ahead. The train stood on the tracks, smoke billowing from its funnel, misting across the platform in great clouds that dispersed skyward. People vanished, then reappeared through it. They no longer looked at one another. They carried a worn, depleted look in their eyes. The scaffolding of their faces dilapidated, derelict, almost as if they had abandoned their very selves. Even the manner in which they walked had been stripped from them, and they could no longer hold their heads up high. They looked at the ground, scuttled from here to there.

"*Dokumente. Reisepass.*"

Lor heard these words being shouted behind and ahead of her, from one end of the platform to the other. "*Dokumente. Reisepass. Dokumente. Reisepass.*" She stopped, put her hand up to her chest, felt for the bulge of forged papers that Alfredo had given her, fat in her breast pocket.

"Show them only when you have to," he had told her. "I fear they are not so good as to deceive the sharpest eye."

"It is all right, Ma," Jakob assured her, and he took her hand from her chest.

"Yes, it's all right," she replied.

Ahead a milk cart was being pushed through the crowds toward them, tin jugs rattling and sloshing precious milk over onto the platform. A dog, mangy and flea infested, dipped its head and licked at the white puddles until it was kicked by hurried passing feet and disappeared yelping into the throng. The milk boy himself was young and slight, no more than seventeen years of age. He struggled with the weight of the cart, looked faintly alarmed, his face an expressive mix of nervous twitches.

A woman who had been sitting on one of the nearby benches got up and was shuffling toward him. Her face and hands were dirt smeared and she looked older than she was, but she was dressed in clothes that, though worn and faded, held a residue of finery: her skirt a velvet of darkest green; her shirt a creamy linen, intricately embroidered. Her hair was stringy and hay colored. It looked as if it had not been washed in months, and yet she had clipped it back from her face with a small silver clasp, as if somewhere within her there lay a semblance of effort still to be made. Perhaps for the baby that she held in her arms, which was swaddled in the softest wool, soiled and frayed now, but still kind against its skin. Lor watched as she dropped to her knees beside the cart, kissed the milk boy's feet, begged him for some milk.

"I cannot," he told her. "I cannot." He looked distraught, as if it was enough to navigate his cart, as if that in itself was beyond him.

"Please," she begged over and over. "For my baby, please, sir."

Then she held her tiny bundle out to him, the cloth falling aside, showing the baby's face. Its skin was black as a ripe fig. Its eyes were open, the light of them glazed with a glaucous film. A tiny hand peeked out from the swaddling, was held in a loose fist against its blue-black cheek.

"It is dead," the milk boy cried. "Your baby is dead." It had been dead for days.

The woman was not listening. "Please," she said over and over. "For my baby, please."

People stopped, were watching, someone was trying to pull her away, lifting her up from the ground with rough dismay.

"Please," the mother said again to the milk boy. "Please." And again she kissed his feet, laid her forehead upon them. In the end he gave up. His hands shook as hurriedly he reached down to give her a tin jug of milk. The woman's face broke into the sweetest of smiles, her eyes lit up with hope. She thanked him for his kindness, stood and kissed his hands again and again, stroked her child's face, whispered to it that all would be well now. All would be well. And then she shuffled back over to sit upon the bench, a faint echo of the woman she might once have been, as she rocked her baby to her, its black face to her pale one, inhaling deeply as if it was still scented with the milky sweetness of young life.

"Dear God," Lor said, and she shrank back then. Pulled her children from the track, back down the platform toward where they had first entered.

"This way, now," she told them, pulling them onward. "This way."

"*Dokumente. Reisepass,*" she heard still being shouted behind them. "*Dokumente. Dokumente.*"

They knocked against the crowd, against the tide of people walking against them, out, out, hot with despair, around the station, where they stumbled onto a street, everything shut, gates closed, doors locked, shops sealed and unwelcoming. She pulled them up the length of it to where the houses stopped at the very end of town, where the fields began, where familiar high hills of gold rolled out into the distance, and a stream rushed clear over gray-brown pebbles. She pulled them back into the edges, into the shadows where they belonged, to the very cusp of life. For they were the disappeared. The invisible. The forgotten. They belonged in the gaps, in the spaces in between other people's lives.

They waited in the undergrowth, beside the stream, still with fear, taking in their surroundings: long grasses, golden at the tips, dry earth, already cold with the clear gloaming skies above, and a field of corn, high as a wall, across the track from them. Beyond, a dense woodland of spruce trees spread across the low lying valley and out into the upper reaches of the hills.

How was it, she thought, that the world around them had not diminished? That though they themselves were duller, grayer, the color of the life around them was as bright as yesterday and tomorrow.

A constant amidst the clouds of gathering change that seemed to blacken, to expand and cast a shadow over their entire lives.

We could hide up in those woods, she thought. Hide and not be frightened when we move on. But then a while or so later, after they had waited and listened to the train lurch and heave, listened to the weight of each of the carriages locking into line as the wheels churned and built momentum away from them, a cart trundled across the earth track, pulled by a horse: a shabby creature, more mule than horse. It was stubby legged and coarse haired, staring mutely into the distance ahead, its tongue lolling from the side of its mouth, its hooves treading steady under the whip. The farmer, sallow skinned, with only a few stained teeth clinging to his retreating gums, great gaps of black space showing inside his mouth, caught sight of them from the corner of his eye and pulled his mule to a halt. He picked them up as if it were an everyday occurrence, asked no questions, took the pennies Lor gave him, shrugged his head to the back of the cart. He wiped the sweat from his brow, shifted his rubber boots, and once they had clambered in amongst the hay, the rakes, the shovels and hoes, called his mule onward.

Lor lay in the back, hidden beneath a blanket of hay, her body warm against her children's as they slept. Glimpses of the night sky appeared through gaps in the grass, the ochre haze of a low moon, gigantic above the treetops. They passed bands of wood smoke from ebbing fires, the duration of scent disclosing a village, a hamlet, a lone farmhouse. Sometimes there was no smoke, only the scent of wet grass from an empty field, already drenched with dew as the cold night set in.

There was the relief of movement again, the hope that around the next bend life might be what one longed for it to be. For this brief period in time, anything felt possible again. Death was still. Life was not. Lor heard the distant sound of church bells. Wondered how long the journey would last, how far he could take them. She had specified west, only west. When the road turned, they would alight. Malutki shifted in his sleep, dug his head deeper into the crook of her arm. She bent over him, pressed her cold palm against his cheek, and inhaled his breath. The night grew colder. She breathed out mist. Her feet and hands grew numb. Her bones ached. How old she felt. Her limbs stiff, her heart brittle.

The cart shifted over a ridge in the track. Lor started. Always now there was the steady pulse of underlying fear that they might be caught. Her grief had become a part of her now. It had coagulated and lay now set like something solid inside her.

At a crossroads, a long while later, when night was still night, but well past its zenith hour, the man pulled the mule to a halt.

"I can take you no farther than this," he said. "I'll be turning north now. You best be following the track. It leads into the village, then out up to the foot of the pass. I expect that's where you'll be heading."

Lor thanked him, saw that he half suspected their plight but would not pry, knew perhaps that it was better not to know. War had made people silent. They turned their heads away. Do not look. Do not listen. They hid inside themselves, where it was safe and dark.

She stirred Jakob first, stroked back his hair, kissed his forehead, and gave him the time to stretch, to yawn, to ask what he needed to ask to unravel the confusion of waking. He in turn did the same for Eliza, woke her with soft whispers and assurances as Lor hauled a still-sleeping Malutki into her arms, carried him down from the cart, and walked until the jolt of her steps stirred him.

"Jakob," he called as soon as his eyes opened. "Jakob."

Lor passed him over into his older brother's arms. He twisted the boy around onto his back as he walked on, Malutki's hot hands tight about his neck. They moved quickly, bleary eyed with sleep, but by now used not to question her when she embarked upon an action. How she missed the days when they would argue, when they would shout and wail and kick up a fuss. Nowadays they kept their heads low, did as they were told, seemed to know that whatever she was asking of them was something they must do.

The village was in darkness as they passed through it. The houses stood silhouetted against the clear night sky, smoke scented with fires that had long burned to embers. There was the soft bleat from grazing sheep, the clanging of a goat's bell as it dipped its head and nuzzled at damp grass, the lone coo of a dove in the eaves. But other than that, their passing roused no human from their sleep. A dog, mangy and flea bitten, followed them to the last house, a remnant of hope in its eyes that some morsel of discarded food might be dropped before him. But then it stopped in the center of the track, by the last house before the wilderness began, as if it knew that onward was not somewhere to venture. It stood there, ears pricked, smelling their scents on the wind, until they disappeared into the darkness.

"We nearly there?" Eliza asked.

"Are you tired?"

"No, not tired."

"Can you walk until you are?"

"Yes, Mamo."

They walked farther, climbed the hill up into the forest ahead, then steered off the road and followed a fire gap through the trees. Lor took Malutki from Jakob, who could carry him no longer, felt the strain of him on her back. Ahead she could see the stars through the trees.

Get to where the fire gaps cross, she told herself. Walk until you reach there.

"Ma, it is easy to die?" Jakob asked her from behind. She turned and looked at him.

"Not so easy."

"That baby was dead?"

"Yes, it was dead."

"What do you suppose it's like to die?"

"I don't know, my love. We don't, until we do so."

"Doesn't have to be the worst thing," he told her.

"No. It doesn't have to be the worst thing."

They walked on. With Jakob it seemed that always there was this pushing forward, this quest to seek out what was right. She had witnessed it in him from the very beginning. The unrelenting effort to see light where sometimes there was none.

"So I am on Gillum, and you on Valour," he said, beside her now. "With Malutki and Eliza behind."

"Yes," she told him. "We have stepped up our pace now, left the Forest of the Light-Footed behind us, left the madness of the wind there and the silent bears with their hot breath and yellow eyes that gleam in the darkness. We know what it is we have to do now. We know which paths we must follow. Which ones we must ignore."

"So our task being set, Ma?" Jakob asks.

"Yes. Our task is set. We have our seven vessels that hang strapped to our saddles. We have our indigo, our night caught in a glass jar. We have our malachite, cut from the azurite we found in the copper caves. 'Don't be afraid,' I tell you. 'We are almost safe.' The Ushalin are fearful of us now, for they know the power of what we have. They know that if they catch us, all we need do is hold a vessel up close against their sightless eyes, burn the gray of them to tinder. Scorch it and blind the blindness from them. And they know, too, that one color adds to another, that by the time we fill our seventh vas, and we will fill it, it will be the very end, because for the first time they will see the world as it is meant to be seen. They will see the green of the land, the blue of the sky, and after that they know that their God will roar. He will holler and shout and tip back his mighty head and thump his mighty fists and command them to kneel before him. And they know that this time they will not be able to do this, for the great sun in the sky, the yellow of which they have never seen before, will hold them captivated, will hold them mesmerized with wonder and that as they stand beneath its giant orb in new worship, their blind God will drown beneath the ink-black waves that roll in from the Ushalin Sea, that he will cough and choke and flail his arms, all to no avail, for the Ushalin will not rush forth to save him. They will stand back and witness his demise, and eventually he will sink down and disappear beneath the thick waves. And those flowers that withered beneath their once wan sun, and those leaves that dried up, will blossom and the Ushalin people will not, ever again, be able to heap ash over their land.

"So we move onward, heading for those saffron fields, fields so vast they cover the whole land. When we reach them all we will see from the tips of our shoes to the farthest horizon will be the color blue, a steely brightness against the light."

"I remember them, Ma," said Jakob. "I remember them so clearly. 'We best be delicate in our gathering,' Da told us. 'We best be exact, pick each stamen like we are dancing, hands steady, eyes clear.' We weren't rushing, were we, Ma? We didn't rush when we picked them saffron stamens, even though we were racing 'gainst that setting sun?"

"No, we did not rush. Your hands were steady. Your eyes were clear."

In a way, she thought, that was what they had now become. A story that they carried around with them like their tattered suitcase, telling it and retelling it over and over, in an effort to find some semblance of sense in their lives. Sometimes it felt to Lor that she could no longer differentiate between the story she was telling and the life they were now living. Both seemed as real or unreal as the other.

At length they reached a place where two fire gaps met, and there, in the cross of vertical and horizontal, sank down beneath a blanket of fallen pine needles, the light of fireflies flitting in the air around them. Jakob curled his body around Malutki, Eliza hers around his. Lor placed the rug over them, heaped leaves upon it, and by the time she herself lay down, coiling around them like a wall, they were asleep.

It was not long afterward that she heard the plane overhead, the thrum of it in the distance like some gargantuan insect. And then the advancing whistle that seemed to suck the air out from the trees as it passed above them. Lor looked up, caught the black cross beneath the wing of the Messerschmitt. It was so low she could see the oil stains on its yellow nose cone and pick out the rivets on the underside of its wing. The tops of the trees swayed and bent their heads toward the noise. She listened to the sound of the engines ebbing, disappearing into the sky, drawn up into the silence of it, until they were barely perceptible at all. The children shifted in their sleep but did not wake.

"Yavy," she whispered. Restless with the hope of him. "Yavy, where are you?"

Before

They had arrived unseen. The soldiers. They had mingled with the crowd of gypsies that was gathered in the square to hear Marli Louard give a speech about unity and to pray together for, of all things, "Peace." These people, who had already faced the gradual chiseling away of their lives. Already their names had been registered, their prints taken, fingers stained with black dye that would remind them for days afterward that they were now listed, numbered *Zigeuner*—the untouchables.

"Is that what we are, Da?" Jakob had asked.

"It's all that we ever were," Yavy had replied. "Give no matter to it."

Already they were made to wear a black triangle on a band around their arm, categorized as "asocials," alongside prostitutes, vagrants, murderers, and thieves. Already they were prohibited from entering parks and public baths, their children forbidden from attending public schools. Yavy's children knew this. What they did not know was that already camps were being built at Maxglan, Salzburg, Burgenland, Lety, and Hodonín. That there were gas chambers at Chelmo. That five thousand Roma from Lodz were being moved there. That already they had tested this gas on two hundred and fifty Romani children and that it had killed every one of them.

In the square, gathered as they were, there were men around them who did simply as the man next to them might have done. They scratched their noses, pulled down the cuffs of their sleeves, shifted their weight from one foot to another, stared upward and listened enraptured to the words of solidarity that resonated loudly from Marli Louard. It was a dishevelled looking crowd, people of all ages, young and old, listening with a bright hope in their eyes. So at first no one noticed the quiet gathering up of certain individuals. It was only when a child's scream broke through the mumbled chants of prayers that heads turned, bobbed up above the crowd to see where and why such noisy tears were being shed. And when the mother's scream echoed her child's, and the recognition that all was not well spread through the crowd, the swell of a commotion began, the sudden understanding that the man beside them was not as they were— a man head bowed in prayer—but someone to be feared, someone who with the sudden pull of a trigger had the power over who lived and who did not.

It was the crowds themselves, though, that separated Yavy from Lor, the swelling mayhem that carried her and their children one way, and he another, as if they were floating above high blue-black waves, slowly being torn apart on different currents. He fought, grabbed, and clawed with his hands to move against the tide of people coming toward him, and briefly he caught glimpses of them up ahead, but each glimpse always farther away than the last. Lor's face, her eyes frantically searching for him, as if to lock her gaze to his would defy the physical distance between them.

Lor, he called. *Lor.* Hoarsely. His voice breaking.

And then, when in one moment they were there, bright eyed— Lor's scarf ruffling in the wind, Malutki's thumb pressed against his mother's chin, Jakob, a glimpse of the sun on the crown of his head—in the next, they were gone. *Yavy. Yavy.* His name called blindly from a distance. Until he could no longer hear even that.

He went first to the *kampania*, but the soldiers were everywhere, rounding up his friends, his neighbors of the past six weeks. Already they had taken his horse, his beloved Borromini. Already they had ransacked their wagon, pulled off the door, smashed the windows. He waited until they had gone, then crept out from his hiding place beneath the steps to his wagon, set right a table, held his hand against the brow of a dying horse, hid in the shadows, then made his way back to the square, now a mess of broken chairs. He wandered the streets, asked people he thought he recognized, asked people he did not, but there was no trace of Lor or his children.

He hid for a time in the woods, on the western side of the camp, watched it daily to see if she would come. He lived off berries, washed in the stream, drank the icy water, but still she did not come.

In the end he left, for there was nothing else to be done but that. He left behind the chip in the steps that Eliza had made when she wanted to prove to him that she could chop wood as well as he; the handful of pebbles from a clear riverbed that Malutki had risked frozen feet to collect; a quilt that Lor had stitched together—too long at one end, too short at the other. The bike that Jakob had learned to ride on, wheels spinning, his arms outstretched, the closest to flying he could get without his feet leaving the ground. He left behind all of it. Their life dismantled in the time it took to turn from north to south.

He went cross-country, across field and wood. Went on foot, stole eggs and bread, following the mountain pass and then the stream where he could, the stream that he knew eventually wove from one estuary to the river, eventually to the lake. He left signs along the way, signs to show a path was safe; a white cloth tied to an overhanging branch, an arrow on an ancient trunk. In the hope that she would find him in that place of magenta and teal, of crimson and cobalt blue.

Long Before

AUSTRIA, 1932

The street ran from north to south so that at midday the sun shone down it from above, bleaching the stonework. De Clomp stood in the middle of it, facing west, always busy, always crowded, flushed faces peering through the old cross-barred windows and out onto the cobbles that had been put down one by one, hand by hand, in a week centuries back. The front door stood at street level, yet despite this a rail still jutted out alongside the building, to aid the number of drunks who stumbled out from the smoky interior. Vine leaves wove up the outer stone wall, the branches bowing over the street with the weight of inedible grapes that grew fat and purple in the summer months but that never sweetened.

By day it was a place to buy coffee and bread, a place to eat delicacies of polenta, risotto, or herb-scented salads as sunlight spilled through the windows falling onto bowls of precious sugar lumps knobbed firm by wet silver spoons. By night it was a jazzy glass-clinking club of bad wine and fast whisky shots, full of dim light and moving shadows.

As they reached the door the boy saw that the girl was afraid, was as closed as an egg. "It'll be all right," he told her. "You listen to me. It'll be all right."

Her eyes darted nervously up to his face. They were young. She just fifteen, he a year older.

"What if it is not?" she asked, still dressed in his clothes that were too big, rolled at the ankles, at the wrists, worn and still damp from the two days and the three nights that it had taken to get to De Clomp, fragments of chipped paint stuck to their skin, of faded red and green, from the wooden skiff that they had rowed upstream until they could row no more.

"It'll be all right," he said again as he tugged hard at the jarring door.

The moment they stepped over the threshold, blurry-eyed faces took them in, looked up and down the length of them suspiciously. Two musicians were cramped in the corner, under an archway, which forced the woman to stoop uncomfortably to one side. Her long hair hung loosely across her face as she played on a five-stringed harp, while the man, with a heavy unkempt beard, played on a flute, his thick fingers skipping out the notes. He stood. She sat. The melody was slow and sad.

The man behind the bar was tall and wide, the features of his face bulbous, swollen with years of holding his drink. Only his hair was thin, haphazardly wispy, windswept despite being indoors. He looked up as they approached.

"Yes?" he inquired.

"I'm looking for a job," the boy said. "An' if you have it, we're in need of a room which I'll have to be paying for with my laboring for the time being."

The man studied the boy's earnest face, glanced down briefly at the girl's attire, the damp mud stains that seeped up from around the hem of her pants. She kept looking back at the door. "Don't look so afraid," he told her. "This is a place for drunks and dreamers, sometimes for those who need somewhere to hide."

"We're not in need of nowhere to hide," the boy said brashly.

"As you like." The man paused. "The stonemasons three streets from here," he said eventually. "They are always in need of good hands. Elpie can help you with this." He nodded to an old man at the end of the bar who was seated on a high stool, smoking a pipe with one hand and in the other holding a wide-rimmed leather hat. Which he was eating. At intervals he tore at the leather with yellow tobacco-stained teeth that ground in slow cow-chew motions, his mouth slowly darkening with tannin. He wore a murky-green corduroy suit, his left leg twisted around the leg of the high wooden stool to balance himself. His right leg was missing, cut off at the thigh so that he had to wear his trouser folded up and pinned beneath his sagging buttock cheek. A pair of wooden crutches leaned against the bar beside him.

"Elpie lost a bet," Alfredo said by way of explanation.

"What was the bet?" the boy asked.

"That his hen would not lay an egg on Sunday."

"Damn hen," Elpie spoke, his voice graveled. "For four Sundays she'd not laid an egg. On the fifth I make a bet. She lays the damn egg. And so . . . my hat." He took another bite from the rim, tearing at it with his yellow teeth.

"That gonna make you sick?" the boy asked, and the old man shrugged and told him that a bet was a bet, and if he couldn't keep it he should never have made it in the first place.

"Besides," he finished. "You never eat it all at once. A little by little, day by day, until your stomach grows accustomed to it."

"Don't think him insane," Alfredo told them. "He is a hero in these parts. Won a medal for that leg. Stumbled across the enemy's camp during the war, lost his way in the mist, and held up fifteen men at gunpoint. He led every single one of them back to the allies. The air still itches where that leg used to be, isn't that so, Elpie?"

"Indeed. That in itself is enough to drive a man insane."

The musicians had picked up the tempo. Despite the instruments they had to play with, they were masterfully serenading an old Cole Porter song. The girl turned to hear it. She closed her eyes. Listened to the familiar rhythm of a tune she had not heard for a long time now. The allies of whom they spoke were not her allies. They were her enemies, or rather her country's enemies.

"How long will you be staying?" Alfredo was asking.

The girl opened her eyes.

"Awhile, perhaps," the boy told him.

"I have two rooms. The cheaper or the more expensive? The lighter or the darker?"

"The cheaper."

"And the lighter. You can pay for it when you start work." The man handed them a key that looked as if it had been forged especially with him in mind. It was heavy and ridiculously large. "The room is at the top of the house." He smiled. "And should you be in need of anything, I am Alfredo."

The girl had begun to shake, to look again nervously at the door. The boy took hold of her arm, thanked Alfredo for the room, bid farewell to the old man, and took her to a door at the side of the bar that led to the lodgings above. They climbed the three battered flights to the top floor, the boy ahead, looking back every so often to check perhaps that she was still there, that she had not turned and run from him. On the tiny landing he fumbled with the heavy key, until eventually the latch clicked and the door opened. He stepped aside for her to enter. She did so, not knowing quite how to stand, what to do with her hands, her feet, once they had stopped moving. He walked to the window, looked down onto the lamplit street, pulled across the curtains, which were worn, thin, and punctured with pinholes of light where young moths had feasted. He turned back to the girl.

They stood then in the center of the room, suddenly just the two of them. A room that wasn't filled with the sound of others screaming or the fear of intrusion. It was a room that for the time being was theirs and theirs alone. Four walls that looked out over the red-tiled rooftops and chimneys billowing with wood smoke; a mottled mirror and a narrow loose-sprung bed. They stood together in the center of this room, still for the first time in a long time, and in the silence that surrounded them there was a rawness, a self-consciousness, that had been hidden behind the noise and the chaos of before. The girl was still shivering, her thin arms wrapped around herself, the damp of the past days buried in her bones. The boy fetched the woolen rug that lay over the bed, pulled it around her.

"Don't be afraid," he whispered.

She shook her head, felt tears in her eyes.

"You do not know my name," she said finally.

"So you be telling me."

"It is Lor."

"And mine?" he asked.

She already knew it. "Yavy."

"Them tears are bright in your eyes, Lor," he said. "No matter if they spill over. Don't be thinking back," he told her. "I been long used to not thinking back. Tell me what you want of your life. What you dream of in your while-away days."

She said nothing and at length he turned and set about making a bed for himself on the floor, coiling himself into a single blanket.

"You'll sleep there?" she asked.

"Yes," he said.

"It is not too hard?"

"Not too hard."

"It is warm enough?"

"It is. Now you lie down, an' you dream of them sunflower fields we'll be finding one day. And you'll sleep soundly."

She looked at him, the earnestness with which he spoke. Was it really so simple, she wanted to ask. As simple as that? Catch a dream? Hold on to it?

She lay down upon the bed, felt the springs creaking beneath her, felt the exhaustion of days past. There was the sound of pigeons cooing in the eaves, the thrum of a distant engine. Momentarily it filled her with alarm, but, too weary now, she closed her eyes, let her tears spill from them.

Later she woke in the darkness, afraid of where she was, the familiar tremors in her chest as the space seemed to open around her. She sat up, could not still the trembling in her hands. She listened for his breathing, so soft she could barely hear it. Already the room had become a refuge without past or future, a place where it seemed they could be still for a while.

It was only later that she realized she must have slept, curling herself at the very end of her bed, faintly aware of the light flickering into the room cast by a broken moon. And again of Yavy, the slow drawn-out breath of his deep slumber.

In the morning when she woke, though, he was not there. She felt the space where he was not, was bewildered by the solid sense of it. She breathed in and tried to ward off the sudden flare of fear that she knew could take hold, then rush away, like a string unraveling on a kite. A small note, written coarsely in charcoal from the fire grate, told her he had gone out in search of food.

She walked the room, found comfort in that. Studied the crevices, the carved nooks and crannies, a hinge that caught and creaked, the dark stain on a worn square of floorboard that had once been a birth-mark on an old tree. She ran her fingers over the brass door handle, smooth as bone, the cupboard knobs that popped off easily in her hands, a patch on the wall that was shaped like a question mark. She sat on the three-legged stool, the only place they could sit other than the bed, and stared out of the window at the view which felt like something one could own.

It was not being by herself that frightened her. She had lived a good deal in herself. Locked away with her own thoughts as she sought to unravel the world around her. She did not easily understand it. Mostly other people bewildered her. It was the intrusion of them that she feared, the force with which they could impose themselves upon her.

Below, carts were being pushed toward De Clomp, laden high with wooden barrels of beer. Three men in worn demob suits unloaded them, rolling them down the street. They rumbled over the cobbles like a muffled storm. Lor listened to barrel after barrel being dropped down through the cellar hatch, and to the conversa-tion that flowed beneath the sound of everything, provincial, domes-tic, comforting in its ordinariness. She could hear Alfredo barking instructions, wondered when it was that he had his first drink of the day and how many it took for that drunken fog, the sort that she knew couldn't be hidden, to descend over him.

She was aware that dimly, already only dimly, she was looking out for the familiar faces of Dr. Itzhak, the nurse with the grease-scented skin, those she dreaded seeing. But there was a safety within the four walls she and Yavy now occupied, nestled in the rooftops with the chimneypots and the passing salt white clouds.

To the rest of the world he and she did not now exist as the people they had once been. And of who they were now, there was no official knowledge: no documents, no references. They were the disappeared. The vanished. The forgotten.

She pulled out the letter that her father had written her. It was all that there was of her past. She opened out the folded pages, held them up to her face, inhaled, seeking some remnant scent of home. But there was none, simply the must of wood and those words of his—*Grass so green, valleys of leaf and willow. And a wind, apple and salt scented.*

Yavy was not long. She heard his quick, light steps running up the stairs. Put away her letter. Put away her past. He brought with him milk, bread, cheese, seemed animated with all that was down on the streets below, his face lit up and pink with fresh air. He told her about the stores he had passed, "crammed with things I not knowing the name of," and about the crowds that they could disappear into, be as invisible as they chose.

"Don't be afraid no more," he said. "We'll be safe here awhile. No one'll find us."

Then he pulled from the pocket of his oversized coat a small book, navy blue and leather bound with gold embroidered along the spine, small enough to hold in the palm of one hand.

"Don't know what it's reading. It's written in your language," he told her. "But I thought you'd like it to run your eyes over."

She picked it up, ran her hand down the length of the spine, opened the brittle pages and smelled the musty scent of a book that had not been read in a long while. Sure enough, it was written in English, a book of old folk stories, some she knew from childhood, others she had never heard of before. There were small drawings, done by a steady hand in pen and ink, some so hazy with age they were barely a suggestion of an image, as if when she turned the page they might fade further and in time disappear altogether.

"You like it?" he asked, and for the first time she heard a nervousness in his voice.

"I like it," she assured him.

"Very much?"

"Yes, very much. Thank you for it," she said eventually, and when she looked his face was lit up with pleasure, as if she had given him something, not received it.

He told her next that Elpie had given him that job at the stonemasons' barely three streets from where they lived. They were making bricks, he told her, for a new church that was being built up above the city, with a view that showed the whole lie of the land.

"You're smiling." He grinned.

"Yes. You are proud," she said.

"Of myself?"

"Yes."

He hesitated. "You are right. Going to make us a life. A little life, an' wrap it tightly around us. That'll be good?" he asked and he seemed earnest with the question.

"Yes," she said. "That'll be good."

Long Before

"A mute," they calling me now in that Institution. But I am no mute. They knowing I can talk. Just done talking to them with their lightning that burns me, come right or wrong thing I say. Seems to make no matter to them. That first time, after I wets myself in my sleep, they strapped me down, strapped my arms an' legs so tight. Do you know what it's like to not be free in your own limbs, like you is drowning in some slurry pit? Smelling some nasty smell that makes the back of your throat gag an' choke. Chemicals floating like clouds around that white room. They say I won't feel nothing, but they lying. They never had no lightning themselves. Don't know that it burns deep, like a fire melting a hole in your insides. So I learn to stop that lightning. Say nothing. Stay ice cold inside, an' that is why they calling me, a "mute."

I watch them "patients," when they first come into this place. Laughing, crying, screaming. But alive an' bright eyed. Then, after they are carted off, locked behind them big doors, given that lightning, they return all silenced an' dead eyed.

But then them doctors deciding this silence of mine something they got to stop, and this time they laying me in a tub of water, freezing cold an' aching at my bones, and covered with a plank of wood so I can't get out. Keep me in this freezing water for an age, coaxing out the talk from me. By the time they're done, my head seeing only a gray fog and I can't be talking even if I choose to. Left with only confusion. If I talk I get the lightning, and if I don't, they drown me deep. Seek out some place in between—stay silent, lest they speak to me, and then answer with just as little as I can say. Be small an' meek, so they don't notice me with all that racket that hammers through them white walls. Stay low an' small as a mouse. Just silent enough and just loud enough for them to think I no longer crazy. Like I turned around to find my senses. And day by day, they giving me a little more freedom. No lightning rods. No icing water. No chemicals in my body that do my head something wrong. Give me odd jobs to do here an' there. See how good I am with my hands. That I know the odds an' ends of things. And I keep my head down low, stay mighty helpful, so they grow to be needing me more than I needing them.

And all the while, them Authorities begin their Education of me. To knock that gypsy stupidness out of me, they say. Teach me gentile ways of talking so that people don't just be seeing a "gypsy scum" soon as I open my mouth. First book they give me is that book of fairy tales that God wrote, and I pick out them letters, putting them together one by one, sounding them out on my tongue. That Bible's full of beautiful tales and I am famished for them once I get the hang of them words. Love the magic of that boy Jesus, with his fishes that could feed five thousand souls and that boy Moses with his parting of the waves. So my speech gets better and my reading's good, and for a while I stop knowing who I am, 'cos the voice inside of me sounds a whole lot different from the one I go speaking out loud. Slowly I am changing. A different voice outside. A voice locked inside, sinking deeper. Hidden down so low an' deep, I can barely find myself. And all the while I tell them nothing of the thoughts inside my head, of how I talk with my ma and pa, how I keep them close. How I'm working out that magic that gonna keep my *soori* alive. Remembering my pa, kneeling by the firelight, beside that mound o' white crosses that he pulled over to the fire pit, dug wide an' deep. How, one by one, he placing them in those wily hot flames, burning all of them. And all the while my ma sat weeping. Weeping an' afraid and telling him we all gonna end up in that fiery furnace of hell. But I know no devil man watching over my pa and his fire. 'Cos he knows you can't be leaving them mounds of wooden crosses to rot in the wind an' rain. Best to burn them, one by one, each with a prayer an' a nod of my pa's head.

"*Ashen Devlesa, Romale.* May you remain with God," he whispers, over an' over, a prayer for each of them crosses. Takes him eighteen days to burn all of them, eighteen days an' two thousand five hundred utterances of them prayers. That is what I remember. After I losing them. Losing all my life. All my heart.

Long Before

The next day, when Lor woke, Yavy was again already gone. Once more she looked to the room to save her, studied it with the belief that there would be safety if she accustomed herself to it. She got up. Cut herself some bread, some butter. She sat on the floor beneath the window, hugged the sunlight that fell through the nine rectangular windowpanes. She opened the book Yavy had brought her, found a crushed insect in the center page, a small mayfly, its carcass perfectly intact as if it had been flattened and dried like some cherished flower. She turned the pages, smelled them, skimmed her eyes randomly from one word to another, traced her fingers over the drawings, and felt her heart stir.

She walked from the window to the door and back again, peered down onto the cobbles, pressed her face against the glass, left her breath upon it. She walked back to the door. At the sink which clung to the wall in the far left corner she found a stain, a round swill of brown enamel where the scale had built up. She stood staring at it for a while before peeling off her clothes and running a wet cloth up and down the length of herself. Over and over again, like a penance, she washed the lake water and the days of wandering from her skin.

Afterward she washed Yavy's clothes, wringing away mud-clogged grime the color of rust and verdigris. She hung them in the sunlight, strewn across the chair, across the stool, the table. She was left standing only in her undergarments.

Again she stared down into the street, always looking, searching for what she did not want to see. It was empty but for the odd boy on a bicycle that rattled by, laden front and back with groceries. The hours trickled on as the clothes slowly dried. She was grateful for that, for the rhythmic tick-tocking of time passing. She walked from the door to the window and back again. Stared at the stain on the sink, set about cleaning it, scrubbing back and forth with a ferocity that had her arms burning. When she stopped, little had changed in its appearance. She looked down at the scars on her arms, lurid still, ran her fingers over them, heard her mother's voice.

"No, I won't swim," she said. "I shan't swim a single stroke."

Lor sat down. Took up Yavy's book, lingered over the words, again traced her fingers over them, felt them move from her mind to her mouth, whispered them. When she looked up, the sun had begun its descent. The clothes had dried. She pulled them back on, felt the warmth of the day on them. She looked back at the book. Again her heart stirred.

It was only when the shadows on the street were no more, and the sun had dropped too far behind the buildings, that Yavy returned from his first day at the stonemasons'. He carried with him a loaf of sourdough and a jar of apple jelly, sweetened with grape juice, and a handful of coins that he had earned that day.

And then again, "I bought you this," he told her, and pulled from his pocket what looked like a piece of blue cotton fabric. But when he let it drop open she saw that it was a dress. "Thought it might fit you better than them old clothes of mine," he said. Then he turned away, put his face against the wall to give her privacy.

She touched the dress first, laid the palm of her hand over the fabric. Then she stripped off his newly washed pants and the shirt and pulled the dress up and over herself, smoothed down the creases with her hands. He turned back to face her. Stared with that look of his that seemed unhurried, as if there were time enough to take her in as he wished, as if by studying her face he might know of her whole day.

"Thank you," she said. She handed him back the small pile of clothes he had lent her. "You'll be in need of these, I expect." And then, embarrassed, she turned from him. "There is nothing to cook with and I'm shamed to confess that even if there was, I wouldn't know how to use any of it. Not any of it at all."

He shrugged. "So bread and jam is what I want," he said.

They sat opposite each other on the floor in squares of light that changed from rusted yellow to a smoke blue, tore off large hunks and dipped them into the jar of apple jelly. Dusk fell.

"Them Italians singing from the scaffoldings," he told her, his eyes bright against the cement dust that filmed his face and hair. "An' everyone who hears them is grinning. Been surrounded by smiles all day. Ain't that something?"

"Yes, that is something," she agreed.

"Don't be afraid no more. This is a good place. No one will find us here. An' tomorrow you can brave them streets, buy what you need, for we have that now. We have money for that now, see."

He talked more about his day, about the cracks in the stone that it was his job to detect, how if he tapped at a fault the sound was different, a note that was flat and off-key. Because, he explained, you couldn't start work if there was a crack in the first stone, because while it might begin with one, it could move from that to the next, and slowly in time there would be a scar running right through the building, and all that hard work that people had put into it could come crashing down with the slightest shower or the most timid of passing mice.

He tried to help her clear up, but she wanted to be of use, to do something for him after he'd worked the long day.

"Let me," she insisted.

She knew how to do very little, was humiliated by this. She could feel him watching as loudly she cleared away their plates, filled up the sink and sunk her fingers into the scalding water. She had nothing to wash with, so used only her hands to scrub and clean, her fingers burning, aware that all the while he was taking her in, with a forgiveness of everything, it seemed. As if he did not care whether she was capable or incapable, sane or insane.

That night he slept again at the foot of the bed, and she could not sleep with knowing he was there. She sat up at one point, looked at his face set softly in sleep, at the outline of it upon the pillow; the curve of his nose, the slight flicker of his lashes, the blissful and stark repose of his sleeping mouth. She sat for a long while just watching him, aware that she was intruding upon something that shouldn't perhaps be witnessed by a wakeful rational soul.

The next morning, he had again already gone before she woke. Only his earnings from the day before lay on the table waiting, like a challenge for her to go out and spend. She got up, slipped on the blue cotton dress and looked at herself in the mirror. She wondered how it was possible that the vision of familiarity before her could be in a setting so utterly unfamiliar from anything she had ever known. How was it one could live a life and then live another?

She went to the window, stared down at the street. She was afraid. Certainly afraid to go out into it, yet caught, impelled by a need for practical accomplishments and, too, a sense of intrigue, a quiet desire to venture out beneath this changed sky. For too long she had stayed in the confines of a room. Now she was afraid to leave it, yet more afraid to stay, for what might become of her if she did?

In the end the longing for the outside, the scent of fresh air, gave her courage enough to open the door to their room, to climb down the stairs, her hand trailing along the walls, mold splattered like veined blue cheese, and out onto the cobbled street upon which she and Yavy had arrived only two nights ago.

For the first time in her life she found herself on a street alone. Momentarily she stood with her back to the door of the lodgings, her hand upon the brass handle. She looked upward. A clear sky. Sparrows flitting between the eaves. Her hand twisted back and forth, warming the metal, as if she might leave a part of herself safely behind so that the rest of her might move onward. Finally she dropped her hand to her side. Took one step, then another, and began to walk on down the street. The air smelled of sun-warmed bricks and the dried, salted meats that hung from giant hooks as she passed the butcher's at the end of their street. A pig's head sat on the trestle table, its mouth gaping and stuffed with a glazed green apple, the orbs of its eyes glinting as if they might still hold some semblance of life within them. The rest of it hung from the metal rack, sliced and stretched to expose its insides. The flies sat lazily in the air around it, then caught themselves on hanging fly coils, their legs scratching the air until they died of exhaustion.

Already the market stalls were rowdy, crowded with incomprehensible shouts and raucous tussles so animated they verged on aggressive. There were shelves of preserves, jars of pickles and chutneys. And flowers, battalions of them, strung up and swinging in the breeze or bursting from metal buckets: peonies, lady reds, and orchids; scents of crushed lavender wafting in bands and mingling with the stench of sewage.

She did not know this life, the exchange of it. She felt all eyes upon her suddenly, that she was something to be jeered at and locked away. She shrank back, disconcerted, stood in the shadows of terra-cotta, beside a wall of cool pink stone. For a time she could not move, afraid to stay, to linger, but more afraid to return to the void of herself in that room.

A man was standing on a table selling exotic live birds: a goldcrested finch, a bleached white dove. There was a green and yellow parrot, bobbing its head in agitation on a pole beside him, and beside that some sort of bird of prey, a kestrel perhaps, a kite?

"*Gut zu anderen,*" squawked the parrot. "Good to others—*Gute euch*—good unto you," and the crowd clapped and rummaged in their purses.

"You can make anyone believe anything if you do it with enough conviction," her mother had taught her. To act unafraid was to be unafraid. To act good was to be good.

Lor moved alongside the buildings, felt the assurance of putting one foot in front of the other. Better the movement than the static fear. She trekked the streets, walked the length of one, then another, moved from the crowds to the sparsity of the living quarters, the cluttered alleys and crowded squares of the town center to the wider, leafier suburbs, where large houses loomed behind immaculate walled gardens, and birdsong sounded in the still quiet squares. She walked until her feet throbbed. Back then, into the throng, where she felt courage enough now to linger, to seek things out.

"Come, my love," she heard her mother say. "You are well practiced in this. You know the exchange of this."

With the little money Yavy had given her she first bought things they needed and things they could afford. Clothes: a second cotton dress (she had only the one), stockings. A pot, a pan, a ceramic dish that she would learn to cook with, a wooden spoon, a knife, a whetstone. She found a teapot that reminded her painfully of an English farmhouse, blue-and-white striped with a smudged marking on the base that she could not decipher. She searched for cups to match. Failed to do that, so bought a mishmash of ones that she liked. *Not the done thing,* her mother had said, *but let's start a trend, some new fad from America.* She wanted Yavy to have wine with his dinner, because in her willingness to imitate adulthood she imagined that was the way it should be, so bought two glasses that she polished until they shone. She found a quilt for his bed on the floor, and one for her own that would brighten the room with the patchwork.

Finally she climbed the stairs back up to their lodgings in the rooftops and stood relieved, pleased with herself, in the center of the room that must now be their home, for there was no other, and listened for the Italians. They were only three streets away, and sure enough, if no carts or motorcars went trundling over the cobbles below she could indeed hear them singing their arias and their songs, reaching for their dramatic crescendos. And she smiled at the thought that he, Yavy, would hear them too.

This Day

AUSTRIA, 1944

Again his dreams have Jakob clawing at the warm earth above him. His mouth is clogged with clay, his eyes with darkness. *Pe kokala me sutem.* He sleeps on bones. *Bi jakhengo achilem.* Becomes without eyes. Again he breathes in grit and stifles his screams. Again he scratches the loose soil away until his hands are raw. He scrapes aside the stones, the splintered roots, soaked with blood, until finally his fingers feel the wind. And then, through a crack in the rubble, he catches a glimpse of the blue lapis sky.

"Jakob," he hears Cherub calling. "Jakob, you are all right?"

He has been weeping. His cheeks are wet. The sound of his sobs lingers in his ears, like the indentation of something. He does not know if it is the worst. Is it, Cherub? he wants to ask. Is it the very worst? He is back in that field, crouched down low behind the blackness of bracken, his knees upon that soft blanket of damp moss. He can hear his breath in his own ears, shallow bursts. He should run, he knows this. He should run far and fast. But he cannot bear to leave. Cannot bear to go where the scent of them will no longer reach him. He sees the tree, bone white in the moonlight, stark and stripped of all its bark. No movement around it, no wing beat or scurried dance, as if all else has fled with what has just passed. All my heart's there, he whispers into the night. All my life.

"Jakob," Cherub asks again. "You are all right?"

"Yes, Cherub," he says eventually. "I am all right."

But he is near again, that officer, the eagle and the swastika on his shoulder hand embroidered with white silk and tiny nuggets of aluminum wire. He is near with his head in his hands, clasping thick clumps of his own hair. "So you have earned yourself a bullet," he is saying, over and over, until Jakob cannot bear it anymore. Is it the worst? Is it?

His sister lifts her foot from the ground, asks if the grass feels pain.

The cow shifts its head, jerks it slightly upward. Its leg scuffs at the ground. The flies spiral upward, a black seething mass, the oilcloth glint of their wings blacking out the sky and the view beyond. Is it the worst? Is it?

"Cherub?" he asks out of the darkness.

"Yes," Cherub answers, without pause, as if all he has been doing is silently waiting for Jakob to speak. "I am here."

"You have brothers and sisters of your own?"

"I have three brothers. One older, two younger. I am the middle son."

"You know where they are?"

"No, I do not."

Jakob sits awhile in the stillness of his own waking. And then. "If I dream of dying, do I know what it is to die?"

Cherub is quiet for a moment. "What is it like?" he asks eventually. "Your dying? Is it dark?"

"Neither light nor dark."

"Cold?"

"No, not cold."

"Not so bad then. If I dream I have sucked a lemon, if I can taste the sharpness and the tang of it, who can say that I have not sucked a lemon when I wake?"

"But we know what it is to suck a lemon. In life we knowing that."

"Yes."

"An' we not know what it is to die."

"No."

Jakob is quiet awhile. He holds his feet in his hands, and wonders at the size of them. Would they be the same size as his mother's now? She had such small feet. Would he be able to place his foot heel to heel against hers and see his own toes above her own? Could she wear his shoes, he hers?

"What's it like, Cherub, your home?" he asks eventually.

"I lived in a small town in the mountains. We would fish in the summer, snow-trek in the winter."

"I've never been in an avalanche."

"Neither have I. But I have heard them. They sound like thunder, only there is no lightning to light the sky before they come, so they come without warning, out of nothing, and the sound of them continues on long enough for you to doubt that you are hearing anything at all."

"Can you survive an avalanche?"

"Yes, you can. For as long as you find a pocket of air, the coldest air."

"Yes, for as long as. And it is light in this pocket?"

"I think it would be light."

"Yes. I think that snow would be white enough to hide that dark."

Jakob imagines it, this tiny space that is not cloying with soil or rubble, but full of the lightest snow.

"Come here," she had said to him and he had done so.

She had brought him down onto the grass in front of her, and wrapped her arms tightly around him. "Tilt your face toward the sun and close your eyes," she had instructed and he had done so. "Do you see darkness?"

"No."

"Do you feel cold?"

"No." She squeezed him harder.

"Do you feel alone?"

"No."

"This is what death is. Not a place you should be afraid of." That is what she had taught him.

Jakob and Cherub remain silent until they hear the familiar shifting of Loslow waking, the theatrical drama of yawns that accompanies the stretching of limbs, the knee bones that click as they straighten.

"Loslow, tell Jakob about your cities. Loslow is a man of cities. He has lived in more of them than any man," Cherub tells him.

"Yes, for my sins." Loslow yawns again. "The countryside is more of an enigma to me. I am afraid of insects, of birds, of feathered wings. One cannot escape them. It is not something easily admitted, but I am indeed a city man in my very heart of hearts. I have lived in several. In Leningrad, where the whole flow of the river freezes over in winter. The fish are caught in the ice there, a bubble frozen above their gills. You can drive a truck across the thickness of it. The whole city gleams with a layer of frost. The stone shines."

"And Vienna?" Jakob asks, half wanting to know, half not. "You ever lived in Vienna?"

"Ah, Vienna I know best of all. Vienna is where I was born. You can hear music on every street corner, in every square. It is a city of angels."

There was no music, Jakob thinks. There was no music in Vienna for the brief time he had known it. Certainly no angels. There was a square. And there were chairs, upturned chairs, scattered and broken, as if some orchestra had been about to perform, and somehow the music had exploded the ordered layout of the open-aired auditorium. As if the time they lived in was being played out in the chaos of wrecked chairs. Wrecked chairs and the body of Marli Louard, who lay still with his head on the same stand he'd been speaking from, his shirt stained with blood that had darkened from red to eggplant. Jakob had stood alone in this square, alone for a moment only, but a moment long enough to feel an immense emptiness, a void that he felt he would never fill. There was an absence of sounds. No birdsong. No current of voices. Just a spiraling wind that brought with it a single sheet of paper tumbling across the cobbles. It spun upward and over his head.

"Jakob, please," his mother had called behind him, her face twisted with anxiety. "Come away, Jakob."

The letter caught against the leg of one of the chairs, flapped against it, the words hidden. Jakob walked toward it.

"He is not here. Come away. Please, he is not here," his mother had cried again, frantic now. She was afraid. They were all afraid. He took the letter, writing scrawled across it, folded it in his pocket, felt the weight of it there, and then did as his mother asked. Left the scattered chairs and upturned tables, that splintered space, the last place he had seen his father. Taking Eliza's cold hand, he fled.

"What is it?" she asked him as they ran. "What is it you have found?"

"Just a letter," he replied. "A letter I found in the wind."

And later he had pulled the letter from his pocket, unfolded it, tried to decipher the scrawl that swept slanting across the page.

Grass so green, as if all the beginnings of everything were heaped across those rolling hills, those valleys of leaf and willow, of dandelion and anemone.

Jakob read the words over, again and again, as if the answer to everything lay in the slanting scrawl. He longed for those hills, those valleys, that apple salted wind.

"What would we make of our lives if we were to live them over again, knowing what we knew at the very end?" The officer had asked him that, sitting as he was beside his fire. That officer with his embroidered swastika of white silk and aluminum wire. After he had wept. After he had dried his eyes. Jakob did not understand him then, wonders if he understands him now.

Long Before

Lor went to meet Yavy the following day, waited for him outside the house in which they cut the stone, waited in the stillness of late afternoon, in the heat and long shadows, when the light was at its most luminous and there was an edge to every line, a definite ending to one object against another. She stood listening to the chip and grind of the men at work. A faint cloud of chalk dust seemed to hover just above her head, along the entire street, strangely redolent, aromatic almost, as if it carried with it the scent of wild flowers that had woven their way up through the cracked rock, before a blast of dynamite sent it exploding outward into the world to become something else: a bell tower, a church, a cathedral, a field of white gravestones.

"You are here," he said, when he saw her, his face covered with a fine film, like some quarry ghost come to haunt her. He smelled of grout and pitch.

"Yes. I came to walk with you."

"I like that you did that."

"Yes."

She went again the following day, became familiar with the sound of hammer on stone. Stood by the doorway and watched the last remnants of his day. He was quick, lighter than the others, younger, too. She watched him pound in the clout nails against mortar and slate. Listened for the sound of each hit, for the musical tone within each one, a note she could find on any piano from the stones they would keep, or else the wayward tone that resonated from the damaged stones that they would discard. He pushed in the dowels, caulked seams, hoisted up lifting tackle.

He worked hard but dropped his tools as soon as the bell rang for the end of the day, stayed never a moment longer than that. He looked out for her, rushed to her with an eagerness that almost betrayed him before he reached her, stepping back to put a space between them, walking by her side as they strolled home through the maze of narrow alleyways, witnessing the packing up of stalls, the slamming down of shop shutters, the opening of bar doors, the hum of lazy evening chatter. That shift from day to evening, from work to play, when the light spun almost imperceptibly from gold to blue. Occasionally they veered off balance in their stride, brushed against the other, mortified, and yet, in those moments, aware only of the touch of the other, everything around them diminishing in sight and sound. They steadied. Walked on, let in the space once more.

They tried out their languages on each other. Wore them like clothes, changing the way they moved as they spoke. They both spoke French to each other, a smattering of German, but sometimes she used English. Sometimes he used Romani. They learned a little of each. Spattered one with another. Felt them move inside their mouths, against their tongues, their lips, like something they could taste, then swallow.

She learned that *avri* was "outside," that *adre* was "in." She learned that she was *miro*, that she was quiet. That she was *khushti*, that she was good. *Love* was the word for money. *Kamav* the word for love. *Ruv* was the wolf they ran from. She was not *dinilo*, he told her. She was not crazy. She was *rakli*, a *rinkeni rakli*, a pretty, bright-eyed, nongypsy girl.

Slowly, gently, they began a little life. It was a simple life, filled with conversations of stones and layered bricks, of the music that seeped up from the bar, already part of the past and imprinted with the memory of when it had first been listened to; of the strange food that they found in the market: cheese that was veined green and blue like a map of land and water, olives that were so sharp they stripped the moisture from their tongues; bread that they pulled apart and chewed until their jaws ached.

There was Alfredo, who talked mostly of love and wine, and a few familiar faces at the bar; Elpie, who, undeterred, was halfway through his hat; the two musicians who sang but never spoke; the men Yavy worked with. They found a corner in De Clomp that became their own, beneath a bookshelf stacked with old books, leather bound with warm browns, mahoganies, and greens, where shyly they would look for the other coiled upon a comfy chair.

For a time they hung out with the balloonists and the mystics and the opera singers who joined them in the lodgings for the season, a trickle of traveling salesmen who arrived one Sunday and left the next, who clambered up the stairs with cases of elaborate costumes or boxes of equipment that cramped the landings so that only the slimmer visitors could squeeze past. Alfredo hollered and complained, then laughed and poured out whisky shots, while Yavy and Lor listened to tales of starlit performances and flights across quilted skies. Until summer bled into autumn and the balloonists and mystics and opera singers returned to a distant place that was their home. Then once again, it was just the two of them.

Slowly Lor peeled off her past life as if it were something that could be discarded. It remained an imprint, dreamlike and only tangible in sudden moments when she was caught off guard, when a memory surfaced before it could be repressed: stirred by a bend in the road, the crown of someone's head, the gait of someone's stride, all reminiscent of another time, another place. Palpable, almost, as if she could reach out and touch the past.

When you lose something you love, darling, you live another life beside the one you are living. The life that would have been. Her mother had once told her that, staring as she did into some vacant space. "It walks only one step behind you. Like a shadow. That at times, just as when the sun is at its zenith in the sky, it can brush right up against you, overcast and blur out the life you are living altogether."

Less and less that happened to Lor now. Only sometimes would she will the past to return. "Are you there?" she would ask. "Are you close?" Only sometimes, when at night her fears seemed insurmountable. She floundered then, sought to grasp the familiar, the chaotic known, but where once there had been only solace in such a seeking, now there was trepidation at what might arise, the half-acknowledged truth that she no longer wanted to disappear. To hold stones in her pockets. Now, in the dim light of a room that was her own, with a boy who had faith enough, it seemed, to be near her, she wanted to grow old and gray.

For Yavy it seemed he had always lived this way, the ease with which he navigated himself through the day, as if the years before had been erased. There was no reference to them, ever, just a steady reassurance that they were safe, that the life they now lived was known by him. He knew how to move, to act within it.

Only with the colors did there seem to be some sort of legacy from the past. They began again gradually, like an absentminded habit. He came home from work one day with a small piece of flint, a copper hue sparring out from the very center into a dark-gray rim. He placed it on the dresser, sat down to take off his dusty shoes. Lor took it up in her own hand, ran her finger along the sharp edge, felt the warmth of him still upon it.

She looked over at him standing as he was beside the window, his face half-lit, half-shadowed. His left hand slowly undoing his laces. His right held against the pane as he stared out and over the chimneys to the sky beyond, a look in his eye that seemed wistful and full of some sweet longing. Lor turned away, felt this was not something she should bear witness to, and placed the flint in a jar for safekeeping.

A few nights later he came home holding a strip of thin parchment paper, rose colored and crumpled, that he opened out from its discarded scrunch, smoothing it with a tenderness of touch. He looked at it for a time, as if it held the answer to something, but then talked of other things: of the line upon line of bricks they had dismantled that day, of the strength of an arch that held the weight of three floors upon it.

Another time he held a piece of stained cut glass; a handful of green-colored leaves; a torn tartan cloth; later still a chipped china tile laced with flowers of celadon. Lor collected them in places, upon the shelves, upon the walls. Gradually the surfaces became cluttered, the walls covered. The light in the room transformed, accentuated, brightened. Even their voices changed within it, muffled and dimmed as if sound were being exchanged for sight.

Before

AUSTRIA, 1943

Their camp lay on the edge of the forest, set amidst a grove of maples. Sporadically the wind blew in short, sharp gusts, balmy and dusting them with leaves of rust and gold. The ground on which they slept was soft with those that had already fallen, the scent of the now buried summer still seeping up through the layered carpet. Around them towering ferns sheltered them as they slept, bowing and swaying in synchronized circles, like some troop of forest guards, while above, wide-winged birds loomed high in the branches of spruce trees, contemplating migration, before taking off into a sky rubbed with thumbs of thin cloud.

"Where do they go, Ma?" Eliza asked as she watched them. "The ones that die. Why don't they fall from that sky?"

"I don't know," Lor replied. She had only ever seen one bird fall from the air, dropping onto the ground in front of her with a dull thud. Only one. In all the years she'd walked beneath the crescent of the sky. With the very randomness of death, there must surely be many more that died with a suddenness that caught them in flight?

"If I was flying when I was alive," Jakob said. "I would want to be flying when I was dead."

Malutki sat on the ground clutching his bare feet, a halo of late sunlight catching his white-blond hair. His shoes lay beside him, the laces tucked into the worn leather sides as she had taught him to do: "A mouse's home where you must tuck in his whiskers." Taught him to do as she herself had been taught.

They had celebrated his third birthday only three days ago with blackberries from a greener field, way behind them now. He had spat them out for their bitterness, staining his lips maroon. She let her hand rest beside his, her finger to his tiny thumb, which was calloused at the knuckle where he sucked it. She tilted her palm toward him, cupped his hand and felt his skin. He was watching with deep intent a line of ants that were moving across the ground in front of him, each laden with a blade of dry scrub grass.

"They are the strongest creature on the earth, you know? For their size," she told him, but he didn't hear her. He continued to stare and draw in the soil.

Jakob got up to collect the wood she had asked him to get, the kindling first, then the thick dry sticks that would burn quickly, smokelessly. His hair was dark in contrast to Malutki's, tinted slightly at the tips with the summer sun, his gray eyes gleaming beneath an unruly fringe.

She could not bear to look at any of them for long. She could not differentiate her love from the fear of losing them. She wondered if it would ever be possible to feel one without the other again. To feel love without pain.

Jakob lit the fire from the base, his face tense with concentration. The dry sedge-grass caught alight quickly, coiling a thin line of smoke up through the sticks. He knelt and, bending his head to the fire, blew gently until the flames grew burning the cold and the damp from the wood, crackling and spitting sparks into the air. Lor watched, afraid of the fire's revealing light, but more afraid of the cold.

The sun had almost set and was turning the earth orange. In the dusky half-light everything was a contrast of light and shadows.

"You know it's only them red bits that are heaven, Ma?" Eliza said, eyes sleepy as she curled herself beside the warmth of the fire.

Lor leaned against the fallen tree behind them. It was moss covered and entwined with vines that clung to it.

"*Zyli wsrod roz,*" she whispered to herself. "We lived amongst the roses. *Nie znali burz.* And we did not know of any storms."

"Tell us more, Ma," Jakob asked.

"Yes," she replied.

"At those saffron fields, have we filled another vessel?"

"Yes, we have filled another. We are full of contentment because of it. We can hear Gillum and Valour softly chomping, happy for the oats in the fields that we've gathered for them. Happy for the rest and the shelter. As are we. And tomorrow we know which direction we are heading, following the river upward and onward, over the brow of the hill to a valley that knows we are coming and to a field of violets. The Usha-lin are far from us now, what with their crisscrossing paths, and their endless wayward missions that take them this way and that, as we pick up our pace and stretch out the distance between us. To be sure they are busy still with their Worshipping Ceremonies, but there is a hesitation before they kneel now, a subduing of their raucous laments. They are less sure than they were before, less justified. They know we are close to the completion of our task. That our vessels are nearly full."

Malutki and Eliza were asleep before she had finished, but Jakob turned around to face her.

"You'll be there, holding my hand when I die, Ma?" he asked.

"So much talk of dying?" She was afraid when he spoke of it so, afraid there was some legacy passed on from one generation to the next.

"Will you?"

"I hope to die long before you," she whispered.

He fell silent for a time. And then, "So I will be there, holding your hand?"

"You are always there, Jakob," she told him. "Even when you are not near me, I feel you there. Now hush and sleep."

He turned away with his face to the forest. She listened to his breath lengthening. "Jump your shadow, Jakob," she whispered. "You are the sun."

For a long time afterward she lay awake, listening to the sounds of the night-forest; the crack of brittle twigs breaking as they fell, the wing-swish of a passing owl. All of them rang with the threat of discovery. She watched a slug moving up the bark, oblivious to them, glistening as the low light struck its back.

When the fire began to dim she fed it with more wood, cautious, watchful, always afraid. Sometimes the fear broke through inside her, like a pebble dropped into a pool, the circles slowly expanding until there was nothing else. It drowned out the entire world of blue and green, her children's faces.

"Yavy, what are you most afraid of?" she had asked him once.

"Them dead hours," he had replied without hesitation.

"What are they?"

"When that ticking of a clock sounding out in the stillness of the day, and all that there is, is the room in which you standing, that chair, that table, that tick-tock, tick-tock. When everything is just what it is."

"So to move on?"

"To see a road ahead." He nodded. "To have a hope, always, 'round that next corner there's the possibility the country of your dreams waiting there. Sure enough that's a reason."

"Is it never just the sound of the horse's hooves, never just a wagon, a road?"

"Yes, that, too, but that road ahead always seems bright, shinning a light right down to where you are sitting."

"Always bright?" she had asked.

"Always," he told her.

It was much later when the sound of something moaning cut into her half-sleep. Something between a cry and a groan. It carried on the air, vibrating against the tree trunks around her. She could not tell where it came from. The darkness had swallowed up all direction.

She stumbled up toward the brow of the hill. Up there the trees no longer blocked out the sky. The stars spilled across the blackness, glistening like quartz. Ahead, on the edge of the hill, she could see the bulk of something lying in the long corn grasses. She stepped forward. Breathed in. Breathed out. And then she saw, with relief, that it was only a cow in labor. It lay on its side, its matted fur a chalky white, the breath steaming from its nostrils in short shallow bursts. Of its newborn calf, only the head and front legs had emerged into the night air.

On seeing her, the mother bucked, kicked out with her legs, tried to lift herself from the ground. Lor stepped back into the shadows, waited, as she had once done with a bird that had been trapped in a white room. The cow stilled. There was nothing she could do but to return to the camp. She lay listening to the muted groans that carried on into the night, until in the end she fell asleep to the twisted lullaby of it.

The dawn brought silence and a change in the wind direction that carried with it the stench of something foul. She woke with the warmth of sunlight filtering through the sparse canopy onto her face. She listened. A low persistent hum came from over the brow of the hill, a white noise, barely decipherable.

She climbed the slope to the crest where the sound was louder. The air pulsed with it. She saw the flies first, a seething cloud, the oilcloth glint of their wings blacking out the sky and the view beyond. Beneath them she saw the bulk of the mother cow, still where she had left it the night before. She moved closer, flies in her hair, in her eyes, hovering around the corners of her mouth. She leaned over its hefty form, saw the mass of insect legs crawling one on top of the other.

The cow was still alive while the flies fed off it. The calf was not. Its head and front legs still protruded from its mother as they had done the previous night. What was left of the birthing sac squirmed with flies, feeding off the blood that had seeped across the grass and darkened and dried like tar in the sun. Already the birds had pecked out its eyes. Only two dark hollows remained.

How was it possible, Lor thought, in this world of horrors, for nature to match it with one of her own? There did not seem room for the two to exist alongside each other.

The cow was barely breathing. Its fur looked damp and matted. The air rasped from its chest, heaving up and down in sporadic shudders.

Its brown, long-lashed eyes looked up at her, wide and unblinking as if it were slightly surprised by the predicament it now found itself in.

She knelt down beside it, put her hands around the calf's neck. She pulled, pushed her hands into the soft flesh that held it, tried to open up a space whereupon it might slip freely from its mother. The corn stems swayed. The wind buffeted, changed direction, wafting the stench of death over her. She retched. Moved back. The calf would not shift.

The cow would die slowly, she knew that. If she left it, the calf would gradually rot inside it. In the end she chased the flies from its face, then gathered up the edges of her skirt, and pressed it over the cow's mouth and nose, pushing her full weight down upon them. The cow's head jerked upward. Only once. A hoof scraped across the ground, left a mark upon the earth. It lay there, its eyes wide, staring into her own, blinking momentarily, until finally the breath was stifled from it and it lay still.

"Dear God," she said aloud. "Dear God."

Always bright, Yavy? Always. I cannot see it.

"Always," she heard him saying. "No matter what is happening around you, always that road ahead."

And it was then that she saw Jakob behind her, standing not ten feet away, silently watching. She stared at him, her eyes filling. But he shook his head.

"It's all right, Ma," he said. "It's all right."

"Is it?" she asked.

"Yes."

She turned once to look at the carcass of the calf and the cow, with its black tongue lolling from its mouth, its brown eyes still staring, still pleading for she knew not what now.

Then she turned and walked toward her son.

"Sit with me," she said, pulling him away from the scene. She pulled him down onto the grass in front of her and wrapped her arms tightly around him. "Tilt your face toward the sun and close your eyes," she instructed. He did as she said. "Do you see darkness?"

"No."

"Do you feel cold?"

"No."

She squeezed him harder.

"Do you feel alone?"

"No."

"This is what I think death is. Not a place you should be afraid of."

Then, Lor taking his hand in hers and pulling him to his feet, they walked back to the camp together, where he set about putting out the still-smoldering fire, kicking dust over the charred pile.

They left their home there, left behind the memory of the dead calf and cow, and took with them the dragonflies mating and the birds that flitted from the stumps and did not drop from the sky. They crossed the woods, kicking pine needles up with their steps, climbing on through mossy meadows scattered with pools of alpine bearberry and late blooms of edelweiss, then on up the hilly slopes. The ground became rockier, lichen covered and scattered with hoofprints the size of cooking pots that formed a trail they could follow.

Lor kept to a pace and the children matched it. When they grew tired they draped their shirts over the thorns of gorse bushes, made shade in which to lie down and rest their aching legs. She let them sleep during the warmest part of the day, woke them before they woke themselves. Then once again they set off.

In front of them the view stretched endlessly, the land flaming with the coming of fall, ash colored, amber and the palest of yellows, disappearing into the distant horizon after months of summer heat and fire. They walked that whole day, the shadows shortening, then lengthening as the sun reached the crest of the sky and began its descent again. They walked, full of a fragile hope that he would be there, for it was all that there was, beneath the polished dusk light, on into the blind distance.

Before

Yavy sat on the bed, listening. The light outside was navy blue. Only in the east was the sky paling where the sun rose. In the valley the mist had not yet lifted. It lingered above the lawn and over the flat fabric of the lake, pale as milk.

He could hear the creaking of the walls, the shifting of ancient stone in the six stories above him. The paint had long since peeled. The plaster had softened. The stone walls had mottled with a creamy rose-red lichen and crumbled in places. Old nails had buckled in the warped floorboards, stabbed their sharp heads into the heel of his feet. Last night he had pried them up from the shrunken wood. They had come out screaming, as if they had absorbed the cries of those who'd once stayed there.

Above him, the rest of the building loomed like an empty tomb, a gaping hole that seemed to yawn and groan. The grand stairway stretched upward from the cold-marbled hall, a chandelier vibrating from a rusty chain whenever a distant truck rattled past. At night the water thumped through the pipes like an old man's bronchial cough. Yavy found comfort in these sounds. Like the rocking of a wagon, they sent him to sleep.

The room he occupied was on the ground floor and was sparsely furnished with the discarded: chairs and tables and beds that had been abandoned by the hastily departing. It smelled of shavings from the planed slabs of old pine mixes stacked in the far corner and of the kerosene that was once used to oil down the wood.

Despite the warmer months, at night the stone seemed to leak out years of buried winters, and the temperature would become chilling. He and the others heated bricks over the fire, then took them to bed, pressing the warmth of them against their shivering bodies.

At night he dreamt of his children falling from the sky, or drifting downward into some great depth, his hand reaching out, translucent against a wall of water, unable to grasp them as they sank. He dreamt of Malutki's tiny thumb and smelled the scent of them all sleeping beside him. When he woke, the space where they were not was cold. During the day he thought of Lor, searching for memories of her in corners of the garden, in the shifting shapes of passing clouds that bruised the lawn with their blue-green shadows. Her name he could hardly bear to utter. It rested alongside his own. He could not hear one without thinking of the other. Yavy—Lor. Lor—Yavy.

He looked out through the window. The mist had seeped across the lawn, vanishing the tree trunks, so that the leaves seemed to hang eerily over the garden, burning as the summer came to an end. The whole world seemed burned to him these days. Everything was rust colored. But on the lake the water level was high, lapping over the ornate paving and up against the crumbling balustrades. There must have been a rainstorm up in the hills, he thought. Sometimes the hidden valleys muffled the sound of crashing thunder.

How much longer must they stay? he was asked daily. They were waiting for word from the other side. For men in camouflaged clothing who like him would creep out into the night, to lift the barbed wall of the border, for them to crawl from danger to safety. When they had this, it would be time to move the crowd of seventy children who lay still asleep in the early hours, on the floor of the old ballroom, once used as the Institution's dining hall. Halos of heads, lined head-to-toe: dark, fair, red, auburn, straight and curly locked. The marble slabs had long since been lifted from their foundations so that the children lay on chalky earth, as wan as their skin, smelling schoolrooms from their past, vapored memories of chalk-dusted letters scrawled across a blackboard. It saddened Yavy how quiet they all were—this crowd of gypsy children who had come to know the kind of silence that could save a life.

They had arrived in their straggling groups over the space of a week: one as large as twenty, one as small as five. Tottered in through a broken gate in the walled garden around the back of the vast house and wandered up to the ground-floor windows, where they had found their *martiya*—their angels of the night, whose signs they had followed across hills and snow passes. Found him carving wood with a knife beside a well of clear water.

"Mr. Yakov," they had pleaded. "Mr. Yakov, we are here."

And now it wasn't that they never smiled—they did, and played. The girls braided one another's hair with flowers from the garden as the boys played ball with pebbles from the lakeshore, and occasionally they sang songs from nursery classes and lullabies from bedtime slumbers. But always with the quiet guilt of the living. For every laugh, every expression of joy, seemed to trample over those whose laugh would sound no more.

Yavy could not stay with them long. He could not bear to know their faces if the outcome were to end blacker than this. He felt the weight of this responsibility in his hands. The skin there crept with a numbness.

He wandered down the corridor from his room, found Drachen in the kitchen, slumped in the worn leather chair by the fire, a frown cut between his eyebrows shaped like the number seven. He was nomadic even inside. Sleep didn't come easily to him. He snatched it when he could. He lifted his head and by the heaviness of his movements Yakov could tell he had only recently administered the morphine he took day and night. He sat, the wound in his side still infected beneath the dressing, the bullet lodged somewhere deep beneath his ribs. You could smell it from the far side of a room, sweet as a fermenting pear.

Below, in the cellar beneath the basement, a windowless warren of arched stone that ran half the length of the building, they could hear

Moreali singing. It was their hideaway should they be found, but it was an awful place. The damp there seemed to seep up through the concrete floor and rot upon the surface. Moreali loved it for the acoustics. He lit candles and closed his eyes when he sang, transporting himself from the rabbit warren of a world around him.

"Go," they had said, in the first few days of knowing him, when his relentless humming had threatened to turn them all insane. "Go, sing. It is enough. Find somewhere where you can do it." So he had. And now the songs of Rossini, Bellini, Verdi, morning after morning, came floating up through the beams and the plaster, transporting them all into pockets of his home country: the Piazza Mazzini, a tiny square hidden in the twisted streets of Castel Focognano where a fountain flowed from a bent stone tulip; a hotel in San Casciano in Val di Pesa where he'd sung from an ivy-clad balcony on the first floor; Harry's Bar in Venice, where he had stood upon a red carpet laid across the cobbles to transform the ordinary into the ornate, at a time when bingo parlors were one of the most profitable businesses in town, when porcelain-skinned prostitutes read the poems of Fóscolo, and the nights were full of ghosts that flitted past the end of the narrow streets.

"I still love and loathe that he does this," Drachen was saying as the sound drifted through the air vents. "This morning I give him until noon. I have awoken bitterly. I'm likely to be a brute of a man."

With Drachen there was little mystery, unlike Moreali, who except when he was singing was quiet and contained in voice. Yavy was grateful for this, however mournful Drachen's company could sometimes become. The older man said what he thought. Held very little within himself, and so long as one learned how quickly his moods passed, his company was quite tender.

Drachen sighed an almighty sigh and then slurped loudly from a cup of tepid coffee, made from the grains that they reused over and over again, until in the end there was just a remnant of a taste, more a memory.

"What's with your sighing, Drachen?" Yavy asked him.

"I was thinking that I was missing the sanctity of a place I could call home. I wait for this day. For a day when I can return there. And then I realized I could not picture this home I wait for. That perhaps it no longer exists. There is a longing always for a destination. A destination where this all ends. But there is no end, is there? This is now my home, as much as any other. I have lived with fear for so long, I can barely remember another way to live. Perhaps this is as it is meant. Perhaps this is living."

"Perhaps," Yavy said. "Perhaps not."

"That is the optimism of youth talking. To be young is to hope. I fear my hope is waning. At my age, I have a choice—I can choose to hope, or choose not to. You have no such choice."

"That morphine makes you morbid."

"That morphine makes me speak my mind." Drachen sighed again. "God damn it. Yakov, how can the grass outside be so dry?" His words were slightly slurred, the vowels drawn out. "When it feels like the lake is coming into the house? It is so extreme this place, too cold at night, too hot in the day. I can smell damp everywhere. I found a dead fish on the lawn yesterday. We are sinking into the lake and yet the vegetables are rotting with thirst. When will it be time? How much longer must we stay?"

Yavy did not know the answer. He, Drachen, and Moreali drew rough maps across the surface of the wooden table with chalk from the ballroom, then laid down stones for where they knew soldiers kept watch, calculated the distances between each, argued who was right and who was wrong.

Drachen's bullet wound had come from one such crossing, a few months back, when one night he had been helping three Polish Jews to cross the river. He'd waited for the whistle from the other side. But he'd been caught between the barriers when the searchlight had streaked over the river and lit them up.

That they would go at night was the only thing they all agreed upon.

"How much longer?" Drachen asked again.

"Not long," Yavy assured him. Not long, he assured himself. "They'll come soon enough." But by *they* he meant Lor, Jakob, Eliza,

Malutki. For it was they he waited for; they with whom he needed to cross that line from dark to light. He was sure they would come soon; that they would find him. He was sure she would know where to look. And until then, he believed that if *they* were no longer alive he would feel it. He tipped back his head and stared up at the tea-colored ceiling. The mist was lifting, tearing at the seams.

Long Before

AUSTRIA, 1932

"Do you hold places in your head?" Lor asked Yavy as they walked home one day from the stoneyard through the evening shadows. "Lives, perhaps, is a better word?" She had several. Lives in which to venture and linger a little while. She did not know if it was relative to the individual. Whether the fragile had fewer, the strong more. Or perhaps it was the frail who needed to hide more frequently? "Do you?" she asked him.

"I hold places in my head, yes," he told her.

"Do you wish to live in them?"

"Often."

"Now?"

"Not now," he said, and lifted his head to look at her. Briefly she felt the back of his hand against her own.

"Yes, not now," she agreed, but moved away, awkward with it. "Might we again?" she asked quietly.

"We *will* again. Truly. Sadly. When we are in need of them."

They were on the street where De Clomp stood and already they could hear the music from the corner several hundred yards away, the upbeat tempo, the blare of a swinging saxophone, the quick and nimble fingers gliding back and forth upon the keys of the old and much-played Manualo piano. They stood, not knowing quite what to say.

"They'll be dancing inside," he said.

"Can you dance?"

"Can you?"

"Yes, I can dance."

He grinned.

"You are surprised?"

"Yes."

"I am too quiet?"

"Yes."

They reached the door to their building, where the loudness within could be felt vibrating against the wood as Yavy pushed himself against it.

"Let me wash the dust from me first," he said. "Alfredo will holler if I come in looking this way."

At first, while she waited, she hovered outside the entrance, allowed herself to glimpse through the smoky windows the sinewy bodies within. They were playing Duke Ellington, and for a moment she let herself remember the parties of her past, so many parties, where she had watched the adults from some darkened corner of the garden, spinning and tapping their heels, arms linking arms, hands clasping hands, ruby and diamond clad, a stolen caress that the caresser hoped would not be seen. So much skin against skin as, decorated and luminous, they spun each other around and around. And from that place beside shrub or tree, forgotten beneath the frivolity, Lor had mimicked them, had danced as the night drew on, awkwardly with her own shadow.

She pulled open the door to De Clomp. There were several people dancing, others already leaving empty tables and empty chairs, gradually shifting them aside to make space for movement. There seemed to be no shyness in the room. The music had outstripped it, made it irrelevant beneath the rhythm. Alfredo shouted across the musty interior when he saw her. She was grateful for the sight of his familiar face, took up a stool at the bar near him and beside Elpie, who was without his hat. The old man patted her leg and grinned with the pleasure of seeing her.

"So, you are here for the bewitching hour," Alfredo said. He studied her face intently for some time.

Near them, a couple got up to dance, both of them short, as if they were together because of their height. Lor turned her head to watch them. They seemed to blink back at each other with a self-conscious reserve, but with every twist and turn their limbs moved more freely, the beat softening their shyness. Lor watched their newfound confidence, smiled at it.

"You are all misty eyed and forgetful, I see," Alfredo observed.

"She is in love," Elpie muttered.

Lor did not reply.

"You do not know it?" Alfredo asked.

She looked back at them and nodded. "I know it," she told them.

"And he, too. You know he, too, is misty eyed?"

Yavy appeared then, in the doorway to the bar, his hair and face clean, flushed with the speed with which he'd washed. She watched him seek her out amongst the crowd, saw the tension in his face slacken, as if simply seeing her reassured something inside him.

"Perhaps not that," she murmured at length. She felt afraid suddenly. She had seen the wrong turning of love.

Yavy raised his arm in the air, but then seemed to hesitate as if sensing that some sort of shift had taken place since he had left her. His look was questioning. Across the throng of dancing heads they stared at each other.

Yavy moved toward her, navigating himself with the slight shift of his shoulder, the soft force of his hand. Lor looked down, saw his shoes before she saw him. They were worn and scuffed, covered still with a film of stone dust, the stitching open at the side of his right heel.

"You need new shoes," she muttered, and looked up. He was staring at her with that look of his, defiant, timeless.

"Yes," he said.

"You need new laces."

"Yes."

He waited for her to say something else, but she could not speak. She felt stripped bare, fearful he might, in time, see the void inside her. "Please," she begged eventually. "Please."

He took her hand, pulled her up from the bar stool, held her close enough for her to smell the scent of him, still of outdoors, of wood smoke and something other: grass, soil, both rain drenched and sun dried, lake water both deep and shallow. The scent of him now had become a sort of representation of everything known. She could feel his breath in her ear, the warmth of his cheek that was almost touching hers. They stood like this for one entire song. Stayed with this slow, touching stance that seemed to her not quite dancing, not quite standing still. All she was aware of was the slightness of things between them: his shoes beside her shoes, a strand of his hair that touched her temple, his thumb against the ridge of her shoulder blade, slowly circling.

"*Me kamav tu,*" he whispered. He pushed his lips against her ear, swayed in the awkwardness of something that was to end between them as something else was to begin. "*Me kamav tu,*" he said again. In the lamplight of late evening they could have belonged anywhere.

They danced that way for only one song. When it was over Yavy took her hand, pulled her out and around to the door that led to their room. They climbed the stairs, wise with what was to take place, then stepped over the threshold and stood, ill at ease, listening to the muffled vibrations from downstairs. Outside it was raining. It had not rained for weeks. The dry top layer of sediment in the upper gardens and parks of the town was loose, caught easily in the torrents that rushed downward, bringing scents of wet soil on the wind. Their window was open, the thin drapes drifting like some half-visible ghost. Lor rushed to put her head out and hang it under the sky. The cloth on her sleeves and chest darkened and changed form, sticking to the outline of her skin. She drank the rain, as she had seen him do, felt the metal of the sky in her mouth.

"You are happy?" he asked, watching her from the center of the room.

"Yes," she whispered.

"You are no longer afraid?"

She looked back at him. "Of being found?"

"No, not of that. Of being alive."

She pulled herself back inside, stood listening to the rain. She looked down toward the rush of water in the gutters for the answer. Then she turned to face him. "I am as afraid of being alive as not being. Is there one without the other?"

"Don't be afraid," he told her.

"How not to be?"

He moved toward her, as if in this he could make it so. And somewhere in the middle of that movement there was a small and silent-enough space for him, Yavy, to draw her close. She felt the line of him against her. The bones of his pelvis, the hard plate of his chest. He did not touch his lips to hers at first, but held them a hair's breadth from hers. She felt his breath against her face. He moved closer. Kissed her. His lips cold, his breath hot. Her first. Not his.

Afterward she looked away, her face burning.

He cupped his hands about her face, kissed her eyes and the soft pulse of her temple.

"Can I?" he asked.

"Yes," she whispered.

He did not undress her. He laid out the quilt from his bed upon the floor, laid her down upon the softness of it and lifted her skirt. She felt his hands upon her, stonecutter's hands, rough and calloused. His shirt was wet now, like her own. He moved over her, bore down not the full weight of himself, but kept his arms taut, holding himself above her. Then she felt the sudden sharp cut as he broke her. She felt the wooden boards beneath the quilt. Her spine rubbed across the ridges, the skin on each knot singing. She heard the rain outside. A fountain of it pouring into the guttering. Then her name, Lor. The way he said it. An admission. He was spent quickly as if, in this act alone, his boyhood pushed through, the too eager yearning that made swift his desire. He shifted slightly to ease his weight from her. She heard his breath in her ear. She felt his heart beat against her own. Pressed him to her, wanting not to be empty of him.

It was only afterward that they saw each other naked for the first time. He undressed her, her clothes like water fern as he peeled them away. He undressed himself, hid a shyness, covered it with solicitude, as they lay side by side on the bed, one honey skinned, the other pale as milk. Her hand rested against his chest, cupped as if something undiscovered hid in her palm. Her damp face lay tilted against his jaw. He stroked the fan of her hair as they fell asleep in their room of cluttered colors.

Outside the pale light of morning rose in the east. The rain had stopped, gradually, and now there was smoke from an open brazier seeping up into the air. There was the sound of carts splashing over the wet cobbles, and later the thrum and hoot of a rushing motorcar. Swifts woke on the upper eaves and flitted off above the rooftops. The air cooled and moistened, damp with dew. Lor and Yavy slept, breathing softly, the lines of their bodies entwined, until the light woke them.

When he took her again there was a tenderness, her skin like silk, their fingers moving over each other with a lightness. He explored her with a bewildered pleasure at such freedom of time and touch. When he found courage enough to look at her, his eyes were questioning, almost sorrowful, as he took her in, a slight frown that resonated across his brow as if to see her hurt him. He moved slowly. The soft hill curve of her pelvis against his belly. The cloud of her eyes. She was trembling when it was over, lay spent and curled in lonely comprehension. Felt the cold of the wind through the open window on her damp skin, as if the husk of her old self had been discarded to reveal a new layer, startled and touched. It took time to bring words back between them. To return from touch to sound. As if in those moments before they had loved each other like a mutual suicide, all despair stripped from them, moving toward a place of light, that ended all past pain. They lay baffled by the simplicity of a biology that had bound them.

"You are my *romni*," he said at length. "My wife."

"Yes," she whispered. "Your wife."

And it was then that she, Lor, her name unfinished and barely audible, understood that to him at least she was the sort of someone who could light up a room.

This Day

AUSTRIA, 1944

A day when Jakob can feel the heat from outside brushing in beneath his cupboard door and the scent of cornflowers on the breeze. Markus gives him a small parcel. It is wrapped in a smooth sheet of cowhide and bound tightly with a leather lace.

"For you," he says. "It is a gift."

Jakob unbinds it and looks down at the contents splayed upon the sheet. There is a knife, a blade that folds in against a smooth wooden handle that has been varnished and inlaid with a line of silver either side. There is a piece of flint, a small drinking flask, a fork, an arrowhead, a long oval sharpening stone, and a round compass cased in brass.

"For the forests?" Jakob asks.

"Yes, for the forests."

"To survive?"

"Yes, for you to survive."

Markus rests a hand upon Jakob's head, keeps it there. "There is a man who goes by the name of Moreali," he says. "He crosses people over at the border. I have sent word, he knows you are coming and he will help you, Jakob."

Jakob feels the weight of Markus's hand on his head. Wants to feel it there forever.

"Help me where, Markus? This is my home."

"Always."

"I tell you, I have no other."

"You told me you are half an Englishman. Perhaps it is the half that will save you. One can have many homes, Jakob. Remember, day by day. Time changes everything. Makes everything. Undoes everything. You cannot fight it, only learn it, accept it."

"I am afraid."

"I know. I know. I am afraid also. Afraid for the loss of you."

Markus hands him the flower, indigo in color, that they had seen when he took him to look at the sky. It has been pressed and dried. "For your collection" is all he says.

Jakob holds the flower in his hand, smells it. There is a slight hint of its scent, more a memory than a reality. And that is how the past feels like to him now. As a dream, but one he will always wake from.

Even in his cupboard he can recall the stench of the cattle trucks, the memory of animal hide and dung, beneath the stench of human sweat and shit. He is inside them once again, sitting in silence, cramped upon the floor. They have stopped somewhere. He feels his brother's heel in his ribs, bare toes in the crease behind his knees. He smells the grease of his sister's hair next to his own. Night is falling. People shift in the airless space, peer through the wooden slats. Jakob can just make out the silhouettes of passing people, shuffling like silent shadows, thin as rope.

"Give me, God, two big wings," the woman next to them whispers. "That I may fly away."

When eventually the doors slide open, the sun has already risen, a white light in their eyes, blinding them.

"Out, everybody, out," the German who had shot the man for his Y-shaped tree shouts, his voice brittle in the stillness of outside. "'Raus, 'Raus, schneller. Join the back of the line. Faster, you filthy shits. Follow the man in front of you."

Jakob clambers down from the truck, his knees stiff. He wonders at the soldier's words, where they had first come from, who had first uttered them, who had followed, who had led. Eliza grips his hand. He feels his father's hand on his head, the heat of it.

"Don't be afraid, Jakob," his father says, his voice weak and wavering.

Jakob looks up. The trucks, five of them, drum in front of him, engines running. He looks past them, to the right and to the left.

"A tree with stark branches," he whispers. "Lead white, charcoal at the base where the bark is still clinging, and behind it the green of the grass."

His mother is beside him, with Malutki in her arms. Jakob grips Eliza's hand tighter and they join the line that is shuffling out across the field and up toward the Y-shaped tree. Ahead, an officer stands on a mound, staring down at them. He is a tall man, the eagle and the swastika on his shoulder hand-embroidered with white silk and decorated with aluminum wire. His skin smells of cologne, his breath of licorice. He looks right at Jakob as he passes, and what Jakob most recognizes in his eyes is a sadness that seems as anguished as his own.

Long Before

AUSTRIA, 1932

After that first night together, it was as if something had been awoken inside him, as if with the nearness of her, and the revelation that she felt as he felt, he dared to reveal himself. Yavy walked with a sense of boundlessness, with the careless delight of discovery, idiotic with the rowdy happiness that seemed to accompany first love. It spilled from his stride over into the collecting of his colors, where for the first time he would study them openly in front of her, would not hide the fascination he found in each one.

Until, one day, he brought home a rock. A rock that he carried in a wooden barrow, rattling it down the cobbled street, the sound of which she could hear before she could see. He lugged it up the stairs, stopping at each landing to collect his breath. She felt the denseness and the weight of it as he placed it down upon the wooden table. It lay there, commonplace, matte gray, and jagged in places, nothing remotely unusual to catch the eye.

"You know what it is?" he asked Lor. He had that look, that look of light about him. She shook her head, waited patiently for him to tell her. He was hardly breathing, as if these moments before were of significance, to be noted as the very beginning of something. Finally he took up his chisel and hammer, took his time to place the former in the very center of the rock before he smashed down upon it with the latter, jarring his arms with the impact, hitting once, twice, three times before he knocked against the tender grain that split the stone in two. Only then did Lor see the color at its center, sea blue and brilliant, glistening with pyrite. Yavy placed one half of it upon the windowsill where the afternoon sun rays fell across the cut plane.

"You see?" he said eventually, his voice low. "Three colors in this one stone?" He traced his finger over the place where the stone was at its darkest. "This, they calling *rang-i-ob*. Means the color of water."

Next he traced his finger along the contours of turquoise that splayed outward across the center. "This," he said, "is *rang-i-sabz*—the color green. And this," he said, stroking his finger around the third, that was tinged with streaks of violet, "is *surpar*. Means red feather. The color of fire, that deepest of flames lying at the very core."

She watched his face, the way his eyes bored into the stone, as if the secret it held within would hold the answer to whatever it was he was seeking. In these moments, it seemed to Lor that to him this was all that there was, this blue, this clear hue, unspoiled, undefined. It seemed to speak to the very depths of his soul.

"What is it?" she whispered.

He turned the stone around in his hand as if he had not heard her.

"Lapis lazuli," he said finally. "From the country they calling Afghanistan, from the valley of Sar-e Sang."

After this he began to hang about the apothecary's near the stone-yard, studying the jars, the ointments upon the highest shelves. He talked to chemists, doctors even, sought out books on minerals and pigmentation, lugged them home, studied the pages with unflinching concentration, and for hours she lost him to them. And then, when it seemed he had absorbed everything he could on the subject, when he had devoured, read and reread, questioned and requestioned, he began.

Each day, from work, he brought home his tools: hammers, chisels, stumbled in with a large metal tub full of them. To find paint in a lapis stone was delicate, he told her. It was a complexity of minerals, of sodalite and lazurite. In the best grades there was more sulfur, which shimmered violet in the stone, and in the worse grades more calcium carbonate, which dulled it gray. To make paint, all of these impurities had to go. He told her it was like making bread. For three days he lovingly kneaded a dough of finely powdered lapis resin, wax, gum, and linseed oil, his hands moving rhythmically, molding with tender deliberation. Only then did he coax out the blue. He placed the dough in a bowl of wood ash and water and began to squeeze and press for hours at a time until the silver ash slowly transformed. Then he dried it, setting it down upon the warm wooden floor, in the center of light cast through the nine-squared windowpane, and moved it as the sun moved, like a dial, until it had dried into a small powdery mound of lapis blue.

But he was not content with that first batch. Nor the next. Time and time again he set out to extract the brightness of color that he knew lay within the grayness of the stone. Obsessively, over and over, seeking out that perfect pressing until finally, in the low late light of an afternoon, when his hands were stained blue, the dye caught in his nails, in the cracks of his palms, he stepped back.

"What is it?" she asked him. "What is it?" He was pale. A sadness seemed to hang about him. It filled the room, palpable, like something she might touch. Suddenly he seemed terribly young.

"There," he whispered. "The sea. The sea, as you meant to see it."

Afterward, everything blue held within it some veneer of lazuli for her, as if it, too, had been molded and ground and soaked from rock and touched with a distant sorcery. Watching, it was as if something had alighted in him, a shy possession of sorts, an act reminiscent of something witnessed a long time ago, too long to be remembered, but engraved somehow inside him. His was a blind guide, ghost-written from the past. A passionate discourse unfolding between him and this distant memory, arcane and mysterious, like some bright star on a clear night, navigating his hand, his heart, to work its magic, to turn the dullest of stones into the most brilliant of hues. All that there was, was this blue boundary that had to be possessed first, then discovered, eventually unveiled.

Gradually their room transformed itself into a laboratory, bottles of liquids and iron salts, labels with names of chemicals she had not heard of before: potassium ferrocyanide, sodium carbonate, ammonia, citric acid, borax, gelatin. Rocks of malachite were strung up over tubs of red vinegar, the copper changing within hours from rust to green. He ground indigo leaves, pulped and dried them to a powder, mixed them with palygorskite and heated them in copal resin to a rich dark zaffre that could color a night sky at that moment of dusk to dark. He fired ochre to the almost-black of midnight. Cooked white lead to the yellow of noon. Cooked it again to the red of dusk. He soaked saffron with egg white, transformed the scarlet stamens to citron golds. Discovered the magic of salt. Mixed it with mauve-tinged azures, violet reds. Boiled roots, and thickened the dye with turpentine and alum. He found vermilion sunsets in mercury sulfide, fired them to an orange cinnabar. He ground berries to a pulp, discovered purple when he mixed the juices with acid, ultramarine when he mixed them with alkaline. He ground up malachite, found cyan and celeste, celadon and olive. Ground up madder, found crimson, ruby, and alizarin. Crushed azurite, inhaled lungfuls of deep blue, as if the air were now visible.

Then he bound these colors, set them, with gesso, plaster, linseed oil, sap from cherry trees and resin from sweet pines. He melted wax. Dabbed at his creations with paintbrushes made from fine horsehair, and swept colors across reams of white parchment paper, over and over, until he'd sought out some arcane perfection. His pigments were luminous and brilliant. They did not fade in the sun, in the wind or the rain. They lifted skies and made rich the blue-red earth.

Before

Yavy pumped a few spouts of water from the well into a tin bowl and shaved without soap. The blade snagged his skin. The well stood beneath a small alcove under the ice-clad stone arches. He remembered he had watched Lor there once. From afar, as she had looked down into the dark depths. He had watched the curve of her nose, tilted slightly upward, her dark lashes, the tendrils of hair falling haphazardly about her face.

"God help me," he was sure he heard her say. "God help me." The first words he'd ever heard her utter, before a shadow appeared through one of the stone arches and she was led away. And that was when he had decided that if not God, then he.

Back in the kitchen Drachen was staring out through the window, one hand playing with a packet of precious Gauloises.

"When I first came here in the winter, I used to dream each night of swimming in the lake waters," he said. "How deep do you think it is?"

"Deep."

"I will miss swimming in the shallows once the winter comes again. How will we bear it?"

"Of course we will bear it." Moreali flicked his hand dismissively as he pushed back a chair from the table. Even sitting he was tall. He didn't fear his height. He didn't hide it. He knew the luxury of being able to sit up straight. He stood now, moved his long limbs to stoke the fire, faltering as he did so, like some mismanaged puppet. His singing gave a balance to his frame. When he didn't sing, he mastered the art of falling down. He tripped and fell through life, but with a blitheness, always recovering himself with a smile, a sweet acceptance that the living of days was a haphazard exploration and there was to be no escaping the tumbles that came one's way.

"When winter comes we will embrace it," he said.

Drachen pulled a cigarette out from the packet of Gauloises, crumpled now, almost empty, and lit it. He inhaled deeply. The smoke seemed to disappear somewhere inside him for the air was clear on his exhale. He opened the stove door, warmed his hands against the dying embers. He smelled of the kerosene he'd doused his hair in, to kill the lice.

Yavy went to the ballroom, stood at the open door and watched the children inside. Most of them were sleeping, lulled into lethargy by the loss that washed over them the moment they woke and did not disappear until sleep found them again. He did not wake them.

The fence they would have to cross beneath that night was eight feet high, crudely alarmed with a line of hanging cans, each filled with a handful of stones. There were two barricades, lit by hurricane lamps, fifty-five yards apart. The first was guarded by Germans, the second by Swiss. Their dogs on long chains barked during the day and howled at night. The guards silenced them with bullets fired into the sky.

People went one way, cigarettes, loose tobacco, and saccharine the other. From the far side someone would whistle, and from the near those waiting would crawl to the wire. Quickly they exchanged their sacks, their stowaways, their refugees. Not a word was spoken, only a handshake, whereupon those helping retreated back again into the woods.

But before the wire, even, there was the river. It gushed or trickled depending on the density of rainfall up in the mountains. Those embarking on escape had a choice: to cross when the river was full, the sound of rushing water hiding the rattle of cans when they crawled beneath the fence, or to wait until the waters were shallow making it easier to cross over emerged rocks to the other side. People had been shot on these crossings, shot in the back, with their eyes looking up at the mountains beyond.

Yavy closed the door to the ballroom behind him. Walked back out to the garden and stared out across the lake.

"Where are you?" he whispered. Where are you? He had lost the sense of them now.

Long Before

Lor was sitting at the foot of the bed, her bare feet resting on the floor, her eyes closed. Yavy was at the head, leaning back against the wall.

"What's in them thoughts of yours?" he asked, the sound of his voice surprising her, for she had thought him asleep.

She opened her eyes. "You'll think me strange," she said.

"Tell me."

"I was thinking of mushrooms," she replied. "Truly, that is what I was thinking of. How sad it was that I did not know which mushrooms were edible, which ones were poisonous. Often, in the woods, in the meadows of England, for you walk the country pathways as a pastime there, I would think this. Why in all the years of wandering I had not striven harder to learn and recognize which ones I could pick and cook."

"I love that you fret so."

"You love it?"

"Yes. I love it. The littlest things, of such consequence to you."

"It's true. I do fret."

"Always. But not now. I can teach you 'bout them mushrooms."

"Yes, I know that of you." She thought for a while. "What happens after this?" she asked at length. "What does love become? Do you know?"

"No."

"I have seen it doesn't stay this way. That it becomes something else."

"I have seen it staying this way. I love you. It don't be feeling like a choice." He pulled her to him then, held her close. "Don't be afraid," he whispered. "Don't be afraid of this."

They were silent once more. She had sensed of late another shift within him, a fraught restlessness that manifested itself in hours of wakefulness when he would stand staring down into the dark of the street below, with that look of his that was halfway hopeful, halfway bereft.

He had found courage enough to take that first set of colors to the market. He and Lor had set them out on the three-legged stool and they had stood behind them for an entire day. Mostly people had passed without interest, bewildered perhaps by the strangeness of the wares, but in the end a local artist, Julien Biedermeier, had bought them all for more than Yavy earned in a week of stonemasonry. Julien, who was as renowned for luring pretty young girls to his attic studio as he was for his paintings of them.

"Where did you find lazuli here?" he asked, his voice soft, almost inaudible above the clatter of the market around them, but Yavy would not tell him.

After that, Yavy had sold more, if not to Julien himself, then to his friends, a rowdy group of artists who drank more than they painted, but who dreamt of colors such as those he made, and who readily bought them as quickly as he could produce them.

But it was not enough. Despite the fact that his colors could inspire the most incendiary of passions in those who found them, it was not enough. She knew that. There was a lacking, a wandering to his thoughts. Just as she had first seen him, standing that night drinking the rain, there was a look to him, an otherworldliness that seemed to separate him from the place in which he stood, so that he was never wholly there. It was that part of him which he kept hidden. He took to staring out of the window for long bouts of time, out across the chimneypots and past them as far as he could see. He would stand there as if all else had been forgotten, as if all else, other than the distant horizon, ceased to exist. What was it he looked for? She was afraid to ask.

"Please?" she pushed eventually, as they lay there on the bed. "Tell me what it is?"

He became very still. She lifted her head. His face was pained, his brow fraught as if something weighed down upon it.

Finally he spoke. "I need something from you, but I don't know how to go asking for it."

"Ask," she told him.

"That road," he said. "That road where I first come from. I need to find them old routes, to follow them seasons to the sources of those colors. But I worry it's too much to be asking of you, to live a life you not lived before. To travel with a horse, with a wagon, to be laying your head down in a different place each night?"

"You have asked," she said. "You needn't fret so. You are seeking something?"

He nodded. "I not knowing how else to find it," he said. "Most likely we'll be chased on from here in the end. If not by them, then by some other. Had that all my life. This moving on. Of no matter. Happens so much we end up needing that road anyways, longing for it like we under some spell we cannot lift."

"Then of course. We can do this. Live a gypsy life. Happily we can do it. All children have dreamt of it. Did you not know that?"

Long Before

Wonder if you knowing what ash can be used for? Can be used to bind things together, lock 'em tight, like a glue that dries thick an' hard, and this is what my pa was thinking 'bout when he burned all them wooden crosses. He sat there thinking how best he gonna turn that ash into something worthy of itself.

We watched them flames rising, spitting their fiery ashes out, lit up an' sparkling like something you'd not be putting a price to. Brightest things on earth in them moments, but come the end of that fire, we're left with a mound of ash, the dullest gray.

My pa, he comes then with all number of strange things into our *kampania*. Comes with a great hunk of rock to begin with. Grinding it down to whatever secret is held inside of it. Mixes an' kneads his mounds of ash, and his hunks of rock, and it is days later before I see what he's been up to. On the table lies the finest mound of powder I ever seen, and this mound, that come from the grayest, dullest ash, and the grayest, dullest stone, is now as bright a blue as ever I seen. And my pa stands there with his fingers all stained, as if the color has become a part of him, the dye seeping into his pores, like he is holding the sky an' the sea in his hands.

After that we packing up our horse and our wagon an' sets off on that long road again. My pa finds work as a harvester, a miner, a digger, and after he has us fed an' watered, he buys back them crops he harvested, them stones he mined. We travel onward to those saffron fields, timing it right with that blue harvest, that you best be picking before that yellow sun goes setting in that big sky. Traveling to them cactus plantations with those small cactus beetles you can crush between your fingers with a pop, staining them sweet with the brightest red. Down to the shore then, finding them sea snails that weep violet tears, tears that do not fade, that grow brighter beneath that hot sun, brighter 'gainst that gusty wind. Collect them quick after the rising o' the Dog Star, or if not then, before them first days of spring. Heading on up to them copper mines, finding rocks the size of melons, that my pa turns into green-tinged seas, and blue hues that give height to them artists' skies.

All number of smells seep from our wagon, stinging our nostrils, stinging our eyes, but not one of us is complaining 'cos we knowing this something my pa gotta do. So my ma stops her laments, and I become my pa's right hand, ready to run go get this an' go get that; a little more salt, a little more lemon, wine if we have it, my hammer, my chisel, my mortar an' my pestle. I learn the names of chemicals we not ever knew existed, strange words, hard to get our tongues around: potassium, ferrocyanide, caustic soda and sodamide, cadmium, sulfide, iron and aluminum salts.

My pa suspends hunks of orange rock over tubs of red vinegar, which we putting out under the trees, watching how the acid burns that copper metal to a green that gonna color all them artists' leaves. We chew those indigo leaves, and those woad mustard plants, crushing them to a murky yellow. Fermenting them, drying them out on the banks of some merry river as we sleep, praying it don't rain throughout the night. Come morning them leaves have changed to a dull-green clay that if we leave out beneath that burning sun is turning into the dark of midnight by day's end. Pa finds them salmon pinks in the rock lichens that grow in the damp nooks an' crannies of the earth. Finds them deep browns in cooked wild walnuts that we catch as they falling from the trees, and when he has used all them woad leaves he finds more midnight blacks in the branches of breeze blown mimosa trees.

He is stirring an' mixing and getting all his colors right, and all the while a little bit of them cross ashes gets put into his palette of paints. Like watching some magic happening before you, all them bright colors coming out of the dullest thing, like all along they'd been just waiting for someone to release them into this big bright world. Glass jars of color stack up in the back of our wagon, rattling along them roads. And in every town, and in every city, my pa is seeking out the very best painters, giving them a jar of this, and a jar of that, selling them at markets, at shops, at fancy galleries where he goes knocking on the doors. Those paints give them artists the very substance of things. They dip their brushes into the air, spreading the light of it onto bare canvases. And as we rattle around the land, I peer through them house windows, wondering if the paintings on those gray walls are the ones that hold them dead soldiers' sorrows in their skies. Life's not simple. Full of a mystery an' a magic we're not ever meant to understand. The end not always the end. The beginning not always the beginning.

Seen it with my own eyes. Seen how those colors can save a life. There was this young 'un, a wiry wreck he was, all skin an' bones under the rugs flung on top of him to keep him warm. But still he lay shivering, 'cos he got a fever buried deep and something nasty ripping through his blood.

Heard of this young 'un the day we arrived at that *kampania*. Followed a track, slipping an' sliding through the bog, mud sloshing over our wheels, that brought us to this field and this river, all beaded with frost an' silver shimmering. And lined up to face the sun, a gathering of wagons, all colored an' hand painted like our own.

We set up camp, and soon enough I could hear the hiss of them oil burners, smell that kerosene, and we'd found ourselves a place that looked good an' friendly enough to stop a while.

My pa is up before first light. Hear him shifting from his mattress below, catch the silhouette of him leaving our wagon before sleep is pulling me back. Later I hear the boil an' whistle of the kettle. Wake to light streaming through our windows.

"Where's Pa?" I ask Ma, as she standing by the hob with leaves in her hair.

"A boy's sick. They asked for him."

"They asked for Pa?"

"Yes," she tells me.

I take the buttered bread she hands me, pull on my cold boots, and out I go, running through that hard frozen grass. Smell that frost, the ice on the river, them scents of salt an' resin.

Find my pa in the last but one wagon, kneeling on the wooden floor, by a crib where the young 'un is lying, shivering still with his eyes all rolled back in his head, the whites glinting back at us. My pa's hand is resting on that young 'un's forehead, his fingers in his hair, and around him on the floor he's laying out them mounds of colors. Rubs a bit of malachite on the wrist of that boy, a bit of ochre on the other, like some strange ointment.

I watch him. Wait. Absentminded. Scoop a little bit of them colors up, one by one. Then I start streaking them 'cross the wooden walls of that wagon, streaking them in an arc, from one end to the other. Right in front of that young boy's eyes. Watching how a light film sticks to the grains, so light you barely seeing it at all. But look hard, and colors be glistening over the wood, like the haze of a rainbow.

"Pa," I says, 'cos he didn't see me come into that wagon. But my pa don't turn his head. Got a funny expression on his face, like he can't hear nothing. I step back, stay quiet an' mouse-like. Leave that rainbow arc on them walls. Go sit out front, beside the mamo and da of that sick boy, who sit pale faced and clenching their hands, chewing on a handful of nuts an' shredding the shells onto the floor. We sit like this for an age. The only movement, those nuts popping into the back of that man's mouth, and the only sound, the crunching of them nuts between his teeth. That light outside changes from blue to white, and that frost melts, by the time my pa stands up. He takes my hand like he knows I been there all this time, nods to the man and the woman on the steps, and then we are walking back to our own wagon to start unloading for our stop an' stay.

It's not 'til evening that I hear the cheering of people's voices and see a small crowd come crossing them long shadows to our wagon with their lanterns rattling. And that young 'un, he's right in the middle of that merry group, taking strong steps to get himself to us.

My ma's all smiles. My pa rises from the table inside our wagon. Comes standing in the doorway and I can hear them all thanking him, addressing him with respect, like he is something special.

My pa don't say nothing. Just stands, tall an' straight backed, taking in what they saying. When later that night them people have gone, and I ask him how he made that sick boy well again, he won't set about telling me. Eventually he gets sick of my carry-on and then he says Yavy Boy, and I know he gonna tell me something big 'cos he not using my name often. Keeps it for them important things he has to say. 'Cos he is called Yakob, and I am called Yavy right after him. Always feel a warmth inside the way my pa says my name. He speaks it soft, puts all his loving of me in the way that he says it.

"Yavy," he says this time. "Done nothing no one else can do. Them pigments I make, some got an antiseptic inside of them that gonna kill the likes of an infection. But perhaps that don't explain why a boy so sick as that can stand by sunset. Perhaps there's something else that warrants that turn around."

And he has a glint in his eye as he speaks on, like his smile is gonna widen at any moment. "I reckon he is remembering that thing we call *Apasavello*," he tells me. "What we calling the Belief. In life, in the hope of it. Ain't nothing like some rainbow arc spread out before your eyes, to be reminding you of that."

My last memory of my ma and pa. I remember hearing a noise so loud it bish-bashed the silence out of the night all around. My pa's like me, shut eyed in his sleep, with my ma cozied up beside him, her hair splayed all silky soft an' unraveled on the pillow, and her hand laid flat out on his chest 'cos she loving him even as she sleeps. Them Authorities come to take us little 'uns. Come to take my three sisters and there is nothing either Pa or I can do. My pa's up as soon as them sounds hit against the night. Standing there in his nightshirt, all undone 'gainst the dark. But those Authorities, they got my sisters by then, got them already to the door. Roughly they pull me, yanking at my arm, my shoulder sharp an' screaming in its socket. Hit my pa down when he comes stalking toward them. Hit him clean down 'cos they are *barri* men and he is slight. Still I see him get back up, and though I have a pair of heavy arms wrapped around my head, blocking out the sound from my ears, I still hear the screams of my ma as they pummeling their big fists into my pa. I ain't never heard screaming like that before. Coming from a place down deep in her belly, gravelly, like there's a big beast inside her. But ain't nothing gonna stop them Authorities taking us then. They got a task they gotta finish. To wash the gypsy out of us.

My pa got his hands over his head now. All curled up in a hedge-hog ball, trying to ward off them punches. My sisters out of the door, and I, pulled right behind them, out into that cold night in my nightshirt an' nothing else.

Trying hard to find the *dook* inside o' me. Trying so hard to see what my pa has taught me to see all my life, as them *barri* men drag me and my sisters away. 'Cos my *soori* is breaking with the last sight o' them. My ma on the ground, like she felt all the pain of the world in them last moments, her hands grasping at empty air. So weighted down with her crying, even my pa can't lift her off the ground. And my pa himself, face bleeding from them punches that didn't stop, and I can see him mouthing out my name. Yavy, he whispers. Yavy Boy.

They don't run after us, 'cos they know an' I know, them *barri* men gonna bash their skulls in if they come running to save us again. So they stay put right there on that wet earth, clinging to them footprints we pressed there before we were gone into the night. Gone their three girls. Gone their only boy. Gone. Gone.

We're pushed into a truck, and I see other faces inside that dark, sleep smeared like us. Smelling of oil an' hay, and that truck, better for the sheep, not children, who sit all weeping, scared an' missing their ma's already.

My *soori* is screaming out. Tumbling an' hammering in my chest. *Sa so sas man-Hasardem.* All my heart. *Sa so sas man-Hasardem.* All my life.

But even then, as tears spill down my sisters' faces, I hear my pa. Telling me loud an' clear what I have to find. Shouting out that *Apasavello* to me, telling me to see it, so when I close my eyes, shutting out that truck's black gloom, I see that life—sun bright. Tree bright. Sky bright. Have the whole of nature in front o' me. Seeing colors where there ain't no colors. Seeing them mounds of powder my pa made, them piles of brightness that he pulled out of the grayest stone.

Just have to find them, I keep telling myself. Keep seeking out them colors that gonna make this life worth living.

Part Five

Before

They followed the river to the lake, followed the lake to the Institution, through reeds and the nests of warblers, arriving, in the end, as Lor had left it. She could see the expanse of the building above the trees, such was its height, grand still, despite the bleached dilapidation and the crumbling stone. The mist came in swiftly, as if nature had made a sudden decision to hide the sky. Swallows that flew in across the water appeared, then vanished, then vanished and reappeared, wings beating furiously, as if they were racing the swoon of a wave. The fog spiraled in from the shore to the lawn, wrapped around them, clinging to the trees, to the grasses. The air was dank with it. They walked around to the boathouse, past collapsing balustrades and trees weighted with shriveled fruit that had refused to fall at the end of the summer and hung rotted on the branches. Around the bare vines of wisteria, to the workhouse, where at first she simply stood, lost to the ghost world of her past.

"Ma," Jakob said beside her. "We here?" She took his hand, fought to hold on to who she was now. Her past was a foreign land. She was not who she had set out to be.

"Yes, we are here," she told him.

They struggled up the path to the workhouse. It stood now like some old boat dredged up from the lake, abandoned and barnacle covered, mollusk and shell kissed. The woodpile sat much the same as it had before when she and Yavy left it, worn with wind and rain. But no one, it seemed, in all the years that had passed, had made use of his cut logs. Jakob pushed open the door, stepped inside, pulled Malutki with him. Lor hung back in the doorway with the lake behind her, looking in. Everything was as he had left it. Faded certainly. Diminished. Bleached by the sun. Layered with a film of dust. But his colors still clung stubbornly to every crevice, hung from every nail upon the stone wall. Though the edges of his leaves, his petals, his paper fragments had curled upward with time, though cobwebs had spun across the eaves, across the corners of the walls and the windows, veiling the light like a pall upon a tomb, his colors were still there.

She stepped inside, trailed her hands along the shelves, along the sills as she had done the first time she had found this space.

"Is he not here?" she asked herself. "Is he not?"

Jakob followed, watching her. "These are Da's?" he asked beside her. He held an object in his hands, a walnut that had blackened and shrunk in the years past.

"Yes, these are his."

He did as she did, caressed each object, dust on his fingertips, on the palm of his hand. They stood in the silence. She allowed time to move onward as she pushed aside the doubt that Yavy was not there. For to live hopelessly was not to live at all. He had taught her that, so she gathered her courage, as she would the pleats of her skirt, and led the way on up to the main house. They kept to the shadows and the outer fringes of the lawn. The doors to the house were open, warped from wind and rain, clinging on by loose hinges. It smelled sourer now. There was still a hint of disinfectant, but more the essence of it, as if it had for so long been washed across the floors and walls that it had become a part of the very foundations.

Though it lay abandoned, there were signs that people had been there. A scattering of food cans, some empty, some full, a stack of flour, bricks that had been heated in embers and still held some semblance of warmth inside them. They helped themselves to dried cookies, crammed them into their mouths. Lor cut open a can of beans, another of sweet peaches, the juices dribbling down their chins as they mixed mouthfuls. Tentatively they wandered from room to room, the corridors damp and bleach scented, the hallway with its grand, now dilapidated staircase that spun up to the cavity of the house above. In the old ballroom the door creaked when she opened it, the echo of it bouncing back at them from the walls. The black-and-white tiles had been ripped up from the floor. It lay now chalk scented and full of rubble. Covering it were rows and rows of tiny blankets, cut coarsely down to size, discarded now, but each laid out neatly upon the floor as if those who had slept beneath them had still made an attempt to keep a morning ritual of making their own beds. She closed the door behind her as they left, as if she might preserve the tidiness of the room.

She pumped water from the well, filled a bucket, washed her children in a patch of sunlight. Made herself practical, and hushed the words that resonated inside her head, telling her that he was not here. That either he never had been, for certainly there was no sign of him amidst the abandoned clutter, or that she was too late, that he had already left.

Eventually, as the light faded, she pulled them back down to the workhouse, where at the very least Yavy's ghost hung around them, living still in the layers of dust and leaves that had blown across the threshold.

Watching his mother, Jakob saw a calm, quiet space that made her movements lucid, seamless, one leading on from the other, as if to break the sequence would be her undoing. Slowly she made up their beds, gathered leaves, soothed her children as she had soothed them every night.

"So our vessels are full," she told them, as they lay on the floor looking up at her. "Seven vessels, seven colors. You have found a rainbow."

"A whole rainbow?" Eliza asked, her voice rising.

"Yes, the whole of it. The Ushalin still chase, with their hawkish march, the drumming of their boots across the land, the roar of their

war cries echoing back and forth, but they are halfhearted, move with
doubt. Yes, they are still bellicose and puffed up with the vision of a
future they feel is their warrant, without cause or justification, that
is theirs for the taking by the very brute force of ambition. But day
by day, step by step, the bleak horizon of their future is disintegrating
before their eyes. They can no longer hold on to the belief of it. No
longer see the clear path to their exulted ending.

"Quietly, you set out your colors upon the Walls of Monochrome,
the Boundary between light and dark, sight and blindness. One by one
you lay them out: indigo, malachite, violet, blue, saffron yellow, crimson
red, a deep Cremona. And you wait. There is nothing but that to do.
You have done the rest. Completed the task. Now all that there is, is to
watch, for the Ushalin will come. In their thousands, like a great cloud
hammering over the hills down into the valley to the lake. And you will
watch as the courage drains from them when they see the bright lights
upon the Boundary Wall. You will watch as they halt, as their horses
rear upward, and you will hear the hollering from their God, the raucous bark that cuts up from his rotund and protruding belly.

"They will appear as a manifestation of all things loud and dark,
but they will be desperate. They will be afraid. And try as they might,
they will not look away. They cannot look away. The very ruthlessness
of their inquisitive nature will be their downfall. And the light will sear
their eyes. They will be blinded to their own dark. They will turn back to
face their ashen land and find it streaked with every color, quivering and
luminous before them. They will turn this way and that, lost in a confusion, the likes of which they have never felt before. And then, when
their mighty God, roaring with contempt, unabated and still without
remorse, is sucked back into those black waves, when his clenched fists
have disappeared beneath the surface and there is no longer sight or
sound of him, the Ushalin will turn back to face you. Will fall to their
knees. Thankful for the new light in their eyes. And they will sing. Sing
with exultation. And you will have no need to fear any longer."

Only Jakob was still awake when she reached the end of the story.
Only he knew of the exultation and the reasons to no longer be afraid.
At length he stood and quietly walked around the room, picked up

first a round, lake-smoothed piece of glass and placed it inside a small wooden box with a crescent-shaped clasp that he had found hidden beneath the stack of logs at the side of the workhouse. One by one he picked up his father's colors, blew the dust from them, placed them, layer upon layer, inside the box. He collected them all, and only then did he lay himself down on his makeshift bed and, clutching his small box to him, fall asleep.

Lor lay in the darkness, the hope dimming inside her. He is not here, the voice in her head kept repeating. He is not here. Until eventually she, too, gave in to the exhaustion of the last weeks, the last months, succumbed to it wholly, and fell into the deepest of sleeps. There had been nothing else but this venture. Of their lives it was all that was left.

Much later, she woke in the night, gasping, hardly able to breathe. She stumbled from the workshop, out into the night, the cold of the ground beneath her feet. She stumbled down the path to the lake that lay like a sheen of polished glass, so flat and still was it against the frosted night sky.

"Yavy."

She called his name, felt the full force of longing for him. It rushed at her, a void expanding outward, so that it seemed she herself was skimming the water's surface, hovering above the dark depths that reached down vertiginous and endless below. She let her tears fall. She sank into the abyss where everything that was known became unknown. He was the only steadfastness in a world that was always changing, from one place to the next; he was the seam of her skin, the stitches that held her together. He was of her bones, of her heart, the only thing she could turn and recognize in the unfamiliar. The compass that she navigated her life by. Without him, who was she? She did not know.

Before

AUSTRIA, 1943

They returned from the river that night, after the first attempt to cross, all seventy children and the three of them, Drachen, Moreali, and Yavy. An attempt which ended because of the patrol planes that were circling the skies above, in search, not of them, but of something other. But as Yavy had crouched in the woods, looking out at the rushing river and the barbed wire fence beyond, he was sure he caught on the wind the faint calling of his name, out from across the still waters of the lake that shone to the distant right of them. He felt he could not move, could not take a single step farther from the Institution, crouched there as he was amongst withering ferns and thorny bracken. So it was with great relief that when Moreali said they should abandon flight that night and turn and go back, Yavy did so with an eagerness of heart. And behind him, the silent crowd of seventy children followed in his steps, trusting him, as they had first done so.

Back at the Institution he settled them once again in the ballroom, told them not to worry, that the day would come, tomorrow, or the next, when they would leave this place for white mountains. And then, tentatively, for he was afraid of what he would not find, he crept across the lawn, hugging the shadows of the privet hedges, down to the workshop.

All was silent as he moved up the path toward it. All was dark. He pushed open the door, let a faint gray light streak across the floor, as scents of dry rot stirred in the air. He peered through the dark, strained to make out what, if anything, lay within those four walls.

And then—there they were. Asleep in the place where he had prayed she would know where to find him. He sank to the ground, onto his knees, watching them in the half-light of dawn, watching them with disbelief that they were there at all.

Lor stirred in her sleep. Yavy could not bear to wake her. He waited. The light warmed, brightened.

Her eyes opened. Her lashes flickered. There was a moment's hesitation as she took him in, studied his face, his hands, down to the worn leather of his shoes. A tear slipped from her eye, ran down across the bridge of her nose. A sob resonated from inside her. Her hand reached out for his. He took it. And then she was sitting up, her arms about him, the lines of their bodies entwined. He felt the heat of her. Not a space left between them as they wept and mixed their tears.

"*Me kamav tu,*" he told her, crushing her head against his own. He heard her heart, looked down at her grazed and blistered feet.

"Yes, yes," she replied. "I love you. I love you."

This Day

AUSTRIA, 1944

And so Jakob gets stronger, fitter. His limbs do not cramp as much as they used. His stomach does not ache. He remembers the feel of grass beneath his feet, the feel of rain on his face, sunlight in his eyes. Longs for them, and in those moments the lethargy of loss is replaced by the vitality of youth. Fleetingly, his thoughts come fast and furious.

"You see," Markus tells him. "You see how miraculous we are. We can bear the unbearable. Survive the unsurvivable. You can find hope anywhere, Jakob. When I was a boy I used to find it in the snap of a slingshot. For hours my school friends and I would aim and fire at skimming stones. I dreamt of doing so all through the boredom of the classroom. Ran out with it at the sound of the bell. Even now it offers for me the very essence of happiness when I hold a catapult, to bring it up between my nose and eye, a steady hand firing out the smallest and roundest of pebbles. The sound of it in my ears as it spins through the air. The smack as it hits the center of the target."

It is as if a euphoria has taken them over. A vision of what might be. Jakob is carried upon the wave crest of their optimism. Their stories are full of a world with small bright things.

"It is so," Loslow adds, a rush of words suddenly. "We must not live under the law of limits. I once knew a man who used to hoard everything and anything. He lived at the end of my road. His garden was stacked high with old prams, ovens, burned-out farmyard machinery, great metal hunks of junk, rusting and wasting in his uncut grass. And the thing was, he was old, so old his back was bent. He walked with a stick, and barely at that. No one ever knew how he got the stuff there, how he dragged it into his yard. He could hardly even get through his own front door. You could see the trash piled up against the windows, dirty rat-filled rooms. The woman next door complained you could hear them screeching at night. He even shat in paper bags and stored them in piles outside. The place stank. Then the war started and suddenly everybody flocked to that garden, stealing his garbage as if it were jewels. They even took his bags of shit and used them as manure for their vegetable gardens. And he just watched, pink eyed and silent. And when his garden was empty, when they'd taken everything and anything, stripped his house and garden bare, he collected leaves, rusted dead leaves that crumbled with his touch. And he collected them with delight, his face a picture of pure happiness." Loslow falls silent. "I used to think this man was crazy," he says finally. "But that's not so, is it? He was just trying to make sense of a crazy world. Finding order in the chaos."

Jakob holds his box to his chest. Yes, he thinks. Scarlet leaves that fade and crumple in the hand. Flowers that bloom, then wither. Bright for a fleeting while. In the end, what is there but these?

If their days are full of a hope, though, the scales tipped upward, at night it is as if everything they have worked so hard to push away in the light hours comes at them again. As if the past were forcing its way through, and transporting them to the place that was the very ending of it all.

For Jakob always there is the tree, that lone tree, worthy of an almost-smile and the life of the man who smiled it, the vision of which comes to him in the dark, in the wind and the rain, tapping against the pane of glass outside his cupboard, as if calling to him. Always there are his brother's eyes, fleetingly hopeful, that look that cut between trust and confusion. The cattle trucks, the rattle and the grind.

He does not know if it is the very worst. Is it, Cherub? he wants
to ask. Is it the very worst? Tears sting his eyes. Spill over. So many he
cannot dry them with his hands. Hope where there is no hope. Love
where there is none. Color when all is gray.

The tree upon the brow of the hill, branches outstretched as if
in rapture, lit silver by the passing sun. He can blink his eyes and see
it there, magnificent against the steel blue sky. To begin with they
were taken deep into the forest, into the thickening trees where they
blended into the shadows and were not seen from the field. A crowd
of children sat upon damp earth, dirt smeared and grazed, sucking
their fingers, choking on their own tears, listening to the distant shouts
from their parents held back in the field, their voices already full with
the knowledge of loss.

Jakob sat with Eliza and Malutki, their hands in his hands. Grass
beneath them. The moon still white in the morning sky. They were in
a glade, surrounded by silver bark trunks, small coin-shaped shimmers
of dawn light catching where the low sun spilled through the canopy
above. The officer was building a fire, gathering the wood himself. He
was a tall man with his hand-embroidered swastika of white silk and
aluminum wire.

Jakob did not understand him, this man, whose face had been set
in an untroubled calm as he led them from the cattle trucks across the
field. He had moved with the authority of one who knew that whatever he said would be obeyed and acted upon. But now he sat crumpled, his face wet with tears that he had shed unashamedly before
them. Jakob did not understand why he seemed at intervals to clasp
his head in his hands, to tear at his own hair and mutter words that
Jakob could not understand. He was both enraged and diminished,
wayward to himself. Shouting at shadows, then shrinking in mood
and stature, venturing, it seemed, into some scene from his past. In
those moments it was as if he had absconded from the world around
him, set himself apart from what was happening up there by the tree
on the mound.

Jakob waited. That was all that was being asked of them. To sit and
wait. If nothing else, simply to be there.

Before

For the second time they set out to the river and the tall wire fence. For the second time they lifted the barbed wire border to cross into Switzerland, Yavy's birthplace. They muffled their footsteps upon soft soil. A crowd now of seventy-three children, then Jakob and Lor. Drachen and Moreali stood guard at their posts, the former on the riverbank, watching from the longer grasses, the latter behind in the woods waiting for the whistles that would sound from the other side.

The river's edge was frozen, a foot thick at the fringes but thinning as it spread out into the currents. It would crack and break easily with their weight. The children laid themselves flat and pushed their bodies out toward the meltwater. Those out front floundered to find smooth stones and rocks, slippery with river reed and moss. The older children held the hands of the younger, tried to balance themselves one against the other. To the west they could hear the dogs, barks echoing off the surrounding rocks.

Strangely though, in those moments they became children again. Certainly they were afraid, but they could not help the delight of tiptoeing from stone to stone, the thrill of the ice, the sight of the glowworms on the bosky bank amidst the ferns, shining in the dark, damp crevices. How was it that they were held more captivated by these things than the sound of barking dogs behind them, closing in, becoming louder above the rush of water? Perhaps because all they had known of dogs were wet noses that could be pressed into the crook of their arms, soft tongues that would lick pink cheeks, bringing a child to its knees. Dogs were their allies, their friends. They did not fear their bark.

Such delights to be had in water. The sliding on ice. The slip of moss-hugged rocks. All streams lead to the rivers, all rivers to the sea. As they stood with their feet in the roiling waters they touched a future ocean, the snake coil that cuts through the land, that would eventually ebb out into the sweet saline blue.

Can you swim? they asked one another. Can you?

Can skim a stone a count o' five, a count o' eight, they told one another.

Can catch the largest fish in my hands. A fish wider than a boat.

They talked big and mighty. Told tall tales, where to hear was to believe, and to speak out was to make real. Yavy hushed them. Be silent, he told them. Silent as the dark.

In the woods, Moreali waited for the whistle from the other side to signal their course ahead. Drachen guided them from the banks behind, shrunk down, his bullet wound pressing painfully into his side as he lay upon the ground. Yavy heard his low owl-hoot, instructing them to move swiftly, not to hesitate, not to flounder.

But the dogs moved closer. Then a light beam across the surface of the river, cracking the darkness. The children hid behind big boulders. They lay flat upon the ice, their woolen clothes sticking to the dryness of it. They said nothing. Hushed their white lies and their gleeful boasts.

Moreali and Drachen could do nothing but watch the horror unfolding before their very eyes, one hiding on the banks of the river behind the rocks and crannies and the other shrunk back into the woods.

The dogs did not need sound or sight. They caught the children as they reached the water, rounded them up as their tiny feet felt the cold and small mouths gaped open in shock. A dog's bark, then its bite. Finding a child, sinking teeth into the tender flesh with slow, deliberate movement, as if there was time enough for rumination. The children screamed with astonishment, then with pain, lingering on that line between belief and disbelief before they stepped over into the cold, dark well of knowing. Then all sound was shocked from them with the realization that this was the beginning of the end.

This Day

AUSTRIA, 1944

Jakob is screaming once again in his sleep.

"Jakob," Cherub shouts. He has never raised his voice before. "Jakob, wake up. Wake up. It has passed."

"It has not, Cherub," the boy tells him, his sobs raw in his chest. "It does not pass. When I run from here, it'll be a life I've not ever seen the likes of before, an' I'd rather be dying than doing without my old life. Miss it so much it stops my heart beating."

"That is true. It will not be a life you know of," said Cherub. "But there are different lives within one life. Lives that are still worth the living."

"Even with the aching of the ones you've lost? I fear they'll come haunt you."

"Would you rather not have it remembered?"

Jakob is silent. He has slipped inside himself again.

"What is it?" Cherub asks him. "Tell me?"

"I cannot. I cannot," and he is weeping now, the youngest of boys again, curled up and crying into his hands.

"Why? Why can you not tell me?"

"For the fear of it. I fear it is the very worst, Cherub. The very worst."

"And what of that?" Cherub asks. "What of the very worst? Tell me. I will be right here. I promise you, I will stay right here with you."

Jakob wrenches himself up from his triangle-shaped floor. Puts his palm against the plaster. Feels the warmth of it, the grain. The splinters beneath his feet. He breathes. Breathes in and out. And at length he finds the words. Words to describe those woods and the numbness that had replaced the fear of what was happening around them.

In those moments, all he could see was the very essence of the world: There were the woodland leaves that rustled, crimson with maple. The brightness of them, torched after the summer, flamed scarlet. A startled web that tore between the breeze blown stems and drifted out of symmetry. A bird that squawked. One that sung. A lone beetle, the color of spilled oil.

He recognized, too, that the officer who had brought them there, who was gathering sticks for his fire, could see none of this, so lost inside his own thoughts was he. Jakob watched the way he stooped as if the weight of his head might pull him to the ground. He looked as though he wished to lie down, perhaps to curl himself amidst dry leaves. To sleep. To dream himself away.

Can you see them? Jakob wanted to ask him. Can you? A line of ants was battling with a ball of termite larvae twice their size. "Strongest creatures in the world for their size," he wanted to say. "An' the cleverest. They'd collect that larvae for you if you let them. Place it safe in the shade. You could be frying it with a little oil, a little sugar. A whole meal in itself that they could give you." A mushroom had pushed up through the mulched forest floor, a shaggy ink cap that hung like a frozen fountain. "If you pick this, it turns black an' within an hour it dissolves without a trace, as if it being some illusion an' you not ever seen it at all," he wanted to tell him. Or ask him, ask him if these were things he knew.

The officer lit the fire at its base, crouched, watched the flames catch and lick at the air. Eventually he sat down, his eyes settling on them, lost to them. His hands were splattered with blood. His cuffs were soiled. His shoes stained.

"I have a mother," they heard him mutter to himself. "All men lie to their mothers." He wept then, brushed the tears away from his face with his sleeve and a roughness that verged on anger.

Malutki was gripping Jakob's arm, between his elbow and his wrist. He was gripping it still with the childlike strength that would weaken in the years to come, but that for now could hold the whole weight of himself in the grasp of his tiny fist. Jakob took his hand and waited. It was all that was being asked of him.

They came for them one by one. Two soldiers, the shadow of morning stubble on their cheeks, their eyes holding something close to contempt, something close to wretchedness, told each child that they would be taken back to their parents, who were digging a big hole beside the tree. There was the silent disappearance of one child, then another. They were too afraid to protest, too lost in bewilderment. After a time, those in the woods heard screams. Followed by the dull thudding of bone against bark. They listened to the gradual lessening of sound to silence. Were mystified.

When they came for Eliza, Malutki would not let go of her hand. A soldier began to pull the younger boy with them before the officer looked up.

"One at a time. Take them one at a time only," he barked, staring up from his crouching position beside the fire, still glazed with tears.

Eliza looked up at Jakob. Her eyes as gray as his, as light. She lifted her foot from the ground, asked him if the grass felt pain.

"No," he told her. "That grass never feels no pain."

"Not even when I am standing on it?" she asked.

"Never when you are standing on it," he told her.

"I'll tell Mamo and Da you're coming soon after."

"Yes," Jakob said. "You tell them that."

And that was the last they saw of her. She walked through the trees, her back straight, toe-to-heel upon the grass. She walked to see her mamo and her da.

Eventually the officer who had built the fire looked up.

"You are afraid also?" he asked Jakob eventually. "You know what they are doing?"

Jakob shook his head. He could see restraint somewhere behind the clenched jaw, the eyes that seemed pink, almost tender.

"You are right to be afraid," the officer said.

Jakob remembered the cow. He did not know why he thought of it now. How its death had seemed peaceful, almost grateful. He remembered his mother's calm, and the cow's wide-eyed look. He shook his head. He looked down at Malutki, knew that the two soldiers would come for him next.

"*Te na khuchos perdal cho ushalin.*" He heard his father's voice. "Jump your own shadow, my boy," he whispered. "*O ushalin shala sar o kam mangela.* You are the sun. You are the sun."

And suddenly everything else in that glade ceased to be. The tree was gone, the green of the grass, the officer, his tears, his smile that was not a smile. All that was left in that forest was a boy and his younger brother.

In that moment, Jakob, a half-blood gypsy boy of Roma and Yenish, thought that life seemed not to be life, death not death. There seemed to be the existence of neither.

Am I cold? he asked himself. Am I dark? Am I alone?

No, he answered. Can feel that yellow sun beating down sharp through them leaves, lighting up this space. Light all around us. An' I am not alone. Am side by side with our little 'un, and we're beside a man whose ma embroidered his coat with her own cotton and a little loving.

Gently he took his brother's tiny hand, pulled it close to him and uttered in his ear. "Don't be afraid, Malutki. I am right beside you," he began. "We're riding fast on our horses, holding tight to their manes with that wind whispering sweet nothings in our ears. We turn this way, turn that. Feel that wind in our hair. Off to find them right paths that'll lead us to them blue fields of yellow gold. Lead us to a place so bright we'll be blinded by the light there. *Zyli wsrod roz,* Malutki. We live amongst them roses. *Nie znali burz.* And we don't know of any storms."

He heaped it on him, all he could think of. And then he held his hand over his brother's mouth and nose as he had seen his mother do to the cow. He pressed down, held his palm there, airtight and hot, as the small boy's eyes widened. A faint spark of surprise, the stark inquisitiveness of the living. But that was all. There seemed to be no real fear, just a momentary attempt to breathe, a brief fight to live despite everything. The vein on the bridge of Malutki's nose pulsed, a fragile blue, fading as Jakob held his hand down and whispered all the while in his ear. "I love you, Malutki, I love you. *Me kamav tu. Me kamav tu.*"

What he witnessed in those final moments was the clarity of the world around him. There was the sky, always there was the sky, but the blunt edge of it was against his brother's face, the indentation of his cheek against the blue, like a photographic negative. As if the world was now inverted. Malutki's eyes were clear as pools. Alert, questioning. Full of a blameless confusion. His hand held Jakob's gently. He held it as he always did, as if they were strolling out together into the blue. And yet, throughout, Jakob saw what he always saw when Malutki looked at him. That the love the boy felt for him was certain and unwavering. He mirrored it back. Felt he had never loved him more.

And then finally, like a river loosing freshwater to a salt sea, all the life that had been, and that could still have been, slipped away to become something other, and Jakob felt the full weight of his brother in his arms, the stillness in his limbs, his unbeating heart. His little brother with his hot rabbit-mitten hands and his soft nightly snores. The vein on his nose had disappeared. The flow had ebbed. Jakob had witnessed the very end of his lessening.

"*Sa so sas man-Hasardem.* All my life. All my heart," he whispered over and over again.

When the two soldiers returned from the field, their tread sounding through the leaves, they found Malutki dead in his brother's arms. Jakob looked up, came back to the world around him. The officer was still by his fire, tending it, but in that moment he, too, lifted his head. Slowly he took in the scene before him. At first a look of bemusement flickered across his face. But then something else. He looked directly at Jakob, his eyes full of something that neither could decipher. It was not love, but rather an intimacy of one who knows what it was to kill another. We are the same, you and I, his eyes said.

"So now you are a man," he whispered quietly. "You have a secret from your mother."

And in that moment Jakob sensed the bewilderment of the past hour leaving the man whose skin smelled of cologne, whose breath of licorice. There was a visible straightening of his spine. A step back into a place of resilience. He was no longer caught in that no man's land between thought and action. He was invulnerable once more.

"That one," the officer said, pointing to Jakob. "That one you can put with his parents." And then to Jakob. "You live like a man, you can die like one. You have earned yourself a bullet."

This Day

AUSTRIA, 1944

Jakob came out of the woods alone eventually. Clutched a small wooden box in his hands. A small blue stone in his pocket. Left a small boy beneath the trees, curled into himself, sleeping not to wake. Left a small girl up by the foot of a white tree that was no longer white. She, too, sleeping not to wake. The other children lay heaped around the trunk, still now, unmoving. Quiet as the mice their parents had spent their whole lives asking them to be.

"Ma," Jakob called when he saw her. "Ma."

She was beside a mound of earth, the scent of it on the breeze, warm and damp, suffused with dew-drenched grass. She turned. Stifled her sobs, pulled him to her.

"All that we know, Jakob. Remember all that we know."

Her tears fell upon his face. They fell like warm rain. He did not wipe them away, caught them in his own eyes, tasted the brine of them on his lips, and thought of the sea snails who wept their violet tears. How he and his father would collect them after the rise of the Dog Star or before the first days of spring, diving down to the depths of a shallow reef, rising through streams of light to catch the colored tears that did not fade, that grew brighter beneath the hot sun, brighter against the gusty wind.

"Not this. Remember, not this," his mother pleaded.

His father had seen them. Had put down the spade that he held in his hands. Jakob felt the grip of him, his arms around his chest, his shoulders, the firmness of his hand upon his head. Felt the two spaces where his brother and sister were not as the three of them clung to each other.

Afterward they dug their own grave. Those without spades used their bare hands. A crowd of gypsies digging dirt. Even Jakob— a half-blood gypsy child of Roma and Yenish, small boy, barely eight, scraped back the soil, his fingers raw from the stones and roots that they struck. Some who dug fell, and were beaten until they stood. Some never stood. The sun rose in the sky behind the tree, did not stop its ascent. It was the very end of a hot summer. Its residue lay burning on the branches. The horizon lay flat as a pan, blue gold and as distant from them as it could ever be.

They were told to stop digging. Ordered to climb from the pit. All but ten, who laid themselves down, side by side, stranger to stranger, a husband beside his wife, a wife beside a mother, a mother beside a friend. There was no protest. No fight. Just the stark recognition that all was lost and that what was left to be endured was the very ending of it all.

Jakob clutched his parents' hands tightly; his father on his left, his mother on his right. Their hands trembled. Grass grew under their feet. The sun was white in the sky.

"*Nie lekaj sie*—Don't be afraid, Jakob," his father said, his voice weak and wavering.

"I am not afraid, Da. Can see a tree with high branches. Lead white its trunk, streaked with ochre, and behind, always the blue of the sky that is full of that lapis lazuli, the sound of a lullaby. Bluer than it's ever been, Da."

"Yes," his father said. "Bluer than it's ever been."

The soldiers lined up above the pit. One of them threw the stub of his cigarette to the ground. He did not tread out the fire and it singed a pale flower black. The officer with his embroidered swastika stood with his feet at the very edge of the pit. Jakob heard the first gunshot, smelled the cordite in the air. He heard the next. And the next.

"Bury me standing," a man whispered near them. "I been on my knees all my life."

And then the whack of metal against bone, the smack of a rifle butt breaking the thin skin that hung like dirty cloth. He fell. Dropped down, down until the ground caught him.

The gunshots continued, a white noise amidst the song from a lark, flitting through the flaming forest.

The three of them were the last to climb down into the pit, the last to lie side by side. Beneath them some of those already shot were not yet dead. Those who lay upon them ran the back of their hands across their cheeks, held their hands as they breathed their last breath. They lay down on top of strangers. They broke already broken bones, forced blood from already bleeding wounds—blood on skin. Skin on blood. Layer upon layer.

Once again to Jakob it seemed that life was not life, death not death. For in those final moments it was not the horror or the brutality of death that endured. All that there was in that pit, by the Y-shaped tree that reached for the soaring sky, was the sweet ache of love. For in the final moments of life, it was the last thing anyone would feel. It was the price for it.

Jakob clutched his box to him, squeezed his mother's hand, felt her eyes on him.

"*Nie konczy sie tutaj*—It does not end here, Jakob," she whispered.

She looked across at his father then. Jakob watched her smile, watched her close and open her eyes. Her blue to his gray. She had never looked so alive.

"You remember the shoes?" she asked him. "The pile of lost shoes, for a month of Sundays?"

"Yes," he said.

"Did you ever win? Did you find every pair?"

"Often we won," he told her. "Often."

His mother pressed her head against Jakob's. A shadow fell over them. Jakob looked up. There he stood above them, the officer with his embroidered swastika and his nuggets of shiny aluminum wire, his face set in calm concentration as he moved along the line, firing a single shot with each step.

"*Zyli wsrod roz,*" his mother whispered. "*Nie znali burz.*" Then suddenly she was silent, ashen skinned. The grip on Jakob's hand loosened, then broke. He felt the cold where her palm had been. She let go of him. She let go of him for the last time. Left her England and her life in his hand.

"I was there, Mamo," he wanted to tell her. "I was there. Holding your hand when you died."

On the fringes of the pit above him a bee hid in a flower. He waited, waited for his bullet that he had earned because he was now a man. His back against the damp of another, his eyes to the sky, and then suddenly he and this officer, whose skin smelled of cologne, whose breath of licorice, whose name he did not know, looked at each other. Jakob caught the indecision in his eyes. The gun that was pointing at his head quivered slightly. Jakob looked right down the barrel of it, wondered at the dark coil within. But then the officer pulled back his gun, moved on one step, and fired. Jakob felt his father jolt beside him, and from his lips exhaled a last sound. Strangled and faintly absurd, as if when death finally came it was still a surprise. As if his life itself could not let go of living. Jakob felt his father's blood on his skin, warm, gummed as sweet sap. He lay there smelling cordite, feeling the wind on his face.

Later rough soil was thrown down, piled upon them, hiding them, forgetting them. Jakob felt stones hit against him. He felt them strike his skin, his ribs, bite into the soft tissue at the side of his head. The faces he knew disappeared, bit by bit, until all that was left was layers of stones—stones on stones on stones.

And then there was silence. Time shifted, moved from the moment that was the very end, to one that was not. A moment that was indefinable. Without a name. To the rest of the world they now ceased to exist. They were as words uttered over and over until they ceased to mean anything, just a sound swirling around. They were the disappeared. The vanished. The forgotten.

Pe kokala me sutem. He slept on the bones buried beneath him. *Bi jakhengo achilem.* Became without eyes in the dark depths. Wished only to sleep and not to wake. To be as those around him. Already he had lived long enough. Already there was nothing left of him. Even the fear had withered, like desert grass. *Te merav,* he thought to himself. *Te merav.* May I die now?

It does not end here, Jakob, he heard her voice replying. *Nie konczy sie tutaj.* It does not end here. He clutched his box to him. He wept. He waited, barely able to breathe in the pocket of air in the crook of his father's right arm. He shifted his head in the airless space, crushed beneath mounds of loam and silt. He breathed in grit. He waited until the air was too stale to breathe one more breath, and then finally he pushed his arm up through the cloying earth. He scraped aside the stones, the splintered roots, soaked with blood, until his fingers felt the wind. And then, through a crack in the earth, he caught a glimpse of the blue lapis lazuli sky.

He lives.

Why, he does not know.

Why him, he cannot bear to ask.

When finally Jakob falls silent, Cherub pushes his finger through the hole in their wall. He does not take his hand away that whole night. Jakob curls himself into an exhausted sleep upon the floor, and in the morning, when he wakes, Cherub's hand is still there, the small of his index finger pushing through the hole in their partition.

Before

On the floor of the workshop Lor and Yavy had lain in each other's arms until the sun had risen and streamed in through the windows, lighting up shafts of dust pale citron. The light of it woke their children. Jakob saw his father first in the fog of his own sleep, rubbed his eyes, and sat up in the uncertainty that what he was seeing was something to be believed.

"Da," he called. "Da, have we found you?"

Yavy sat up, let the tears stream his eyes.

"This day?" Jakob asked. "This day, we have found you?"

They had rushed to him then, Jakob, Eliza, Malutki, all three of them piling from the floor onto him, breathing in his scent, the leather and the wood of him, the roughness of his stubble on their silken cheeks, taking in the sound of his voice that soothed the steps they'd walked away, erasing all the fear and doubt of the past weeks. There was laughter ringing out like it had not sounded for an age, exalted, faintly frenzied with relief.

"Da, you are more grubby than me," Jakob told him. "You smell of them trees along the way, of all those farmed soils we walked on by."

"Da, are you smaller, 'cos I am bigger?" Eliza asked him. "My feet are the size of my arm, from wrist to elbow."

They had questions, of the square, of Borromini, of the mountains they would climb tomorrow. He answered them where he could. Made up what he couldn't; Borromini he had left in a field, chomping trampled grasses with a herd of lazy cows; their wagon he left where they had left it, intact beside the bosky banks, full up and brimming with the things they owned.

"So where are we heading, Da?" Jakob asked. "What will it be like, this place 'cross them snowy mountains?"

"This place is my birth land. We calling it Switzerland. We'll be heading on up into those mountains and down into them yonder passes. Will wait there patient, in a life full of easy living, 'til it's time to head down to that salted ocean, to ride a boat 'cross them choppy waters to your mother's land. A place you knowing as England," Yavy told them. "You say it clear to yourself. You call out the name of that England."

Jakob did so. Felt the sound of it on his tongue.

"Ma, what's it like, the England?" Eliza asked her, and they watched their mother's face as she reached down deep into her past, quizzical with images she had long suppressed.

"In England," she told them, "there is the greenest grass. It is famous for its grass, and there are meadows that are awash with wildflowers and woodland paths full of bluebells and anemones."

"What are anemones?" Eliza asked.

"They are windflowers," she told her. "They open only when the wind blows."

"What else is there in the England?" Jakob asked.

"There are sandy beaches full of colored parasols and swarms of humanity. And there are shingle beaches where you'll not find a single soul, where tall white cliffs drop down into a milky ocean, and smooth round pebbles rattle onto the shore, so loud your own voices are drowned beneath the sound of them. We'll make flower chains and elderflower cordial. I'll buy you Raleigh bicycles, Vimto, Marmite, and Bird's Custard to try."

"What is custard?" they asked. "What is Vimto?"

"It is a drink full of bubbles that sing inside your nose. We'll buy a radio and dance to ritzy songs. We'll buy a painted wagon and a Welsh cob horse, whose hooves look like boots for the snow. We will ride down country lanes strewn with cowslips, sleep in woodland glades and green fields. Feel the English rain and the English wind in our hair."

"How is that rain?" they asked. "How is that wind?"

"Like apples," she told them. "Fresh and sharp."

Later, when Eliza and Malutki had fallen asleep with these pictures in their heads, half-smiles of anticipation on their lips, Yavy took something from his pocket and handed it to Jakob. "Have this," he said. Jakob looked down. A tiny stone of bright lapis lazuli lay in his palm. "From beyond the seas," his father said, stroking Jakob's bangs from his eyes with fingers that were faintly stained, that still held a memory of blue about them. "A keepsake. For all that we are," he told him.

"For all that we are," Jakob repeated.

And then, much later, when Jakob's own soft snores sounded out into a honey dusk, syrupy with shadows, and so still, it was as if the world itself were holding its breath with the portent of the night to come, when they would creep from one country to another, from war to peace, Lor and Yavy lay facing each other, side by side, hip to hip, breathing green shoots of breath onto the other.

"Is pain the price we pay for love?" she whispered to him.

"Yes," he replied simply. "Pain is the price."

She was silent for a long time. "It is worth it," she said at length. And later.

"'Long that road," he told her as a tenderness passed between them, her skin like silk, their fingers moving over each other. "Round that bend. Build a mound of shoes a month of Sundays. Dismantled to be built again. Call on that horse and wagon, toward the setting sun. Call on that horse and wagon, toward the rising sun. Eyes on that bend. Heart beating with expectation." He held her, kissed her lips, her clouded eyes, all despair stripped from them as they moved toward a place of light that ended all past pain.

"And that thing we never living without," he whispered. "That thing we call *Apasavello*. The Belief. In life, in the hope of it."

This Day

AUSTRIA, 1944

It is in the second month that the soldiers from the barn finally come to take them. There is the sound of trucks arriving, the sound of stones spitting up from the dirt track that leads from the road to the farm, the slamming of doors, metal on metal. Jakob feels the smash of them in his chest, like a stack of red bricks cracking. He hears footsteps. The cupboard door opens, the light in his eyes. He goes to scream, but the sound stops in the wreck of his chest, and he exhales precious air.

Markus is in front of him, his eyes wide with fear.

"You have to go now, Jakob, my boy. They are going to find you. They have come to look. We cannot wait any longer. Out of the back door. To the forest. And then you run south. South until you get to the border. If you wait in the woods they will find you. The man Moreali, he knows you are coming. He will cross you over to the other side. You hear? Now go."

His bony hand reaches for Jakob's, grips and pulls at it.

"You were what I held onto when life was full of loss" is the last thing Markus says to him. "Do you know that? Do you?" And that is it. That is the last of him, his gray-eyed gray-hairedness. He is the color of an old pearl. Jakob watches him go, scurrying into the kitchen, where he hears the front door slam open, loose hinges ripping from the wood like ice cracking, and the sound of breaking glass. Heavy boots sound on the stone flags, the tap of a metal sole and a shout, thick with spittle. A table is wrenched across the stone flags. Then there is a gunshot, just the one, but the sound of it reverberates in his ears over and over.

Until weak limbed, rope thin, and quivering, Jakob crawls out from the warmth of his triangle.

"Cherub," he calls. "Loslow."

The cupboard doors are open, and there, hunched in the splintered darkness, are his companions, raw and slight, with hollowed jowls, and hair that is barely distinguishable from the jaundiced pallor of their skin. Too much hollowness. Too much bone.

"Cherub," Jakob chokes, seeing him for the first time, and the image he has held for months and months, the image of this treasured man—arms splayed out above the handles of his bike, as close to flying as he can get without leaving the ground, head tipped back, a smile too wide for his face to contain—shatters. Of that image, only a shriveled emaciation remains. A sunken hole, all nose and teeth. "Cherub," Jakob cries. "What you gone and done? What you gone and done, Cherub?"

For in front of him is not the image of two men who have eaten more over the past weeks so that they might grow strong enough to run alongside him, but rather of two who have gone without. Of two who have put aside half of every meal, day by day, morsel by morsel; the husk of their bread, the pulp of their potato, the hot burning goodness of their soup, so that a small gypsy boy, who lay cramped in a triangle cupboard, who for them had become the very essence of hope, might run toward freedom.

"Go," Cherub weeps. "You must go."

Jakob reaches for him, grasps his hands. "I cannot. I cannot without you."

"We are with you, Jakob. We are very near. Always near."

"Run now," Loslow echoes. "You must run. You must not stop."

Jakob sobs.

"Please," Cherub whispers. Their hands pressed palm to palm. All the love in their fingertips. "Please, my beloved boy."

Te den, xa, te maren, de-nash, Jakob has been taught. A whispered plea. Run if you can. Always, if you can.

And so, a small wooden box clutched to his chest, a stone of lapis lazuli in his hand, Jakob, a half-blood gypsy boy of Roma and Yenish, pulls open the back door and runs out, beneath a blue sky, alone.

Spourz na kolory, he has had whispered to him all his life. See the colors, my boy. Tell me what you see.

Malachite, azurite, vermilion, mauve. Rusted ochre from a mossy bough. Steely white from the sap of the youngest tree. He runs on. Cremona orange, saffron yellow.

The sky—*Kek ceri pe phuv perade*—it has not fallen to the earth. *Kek jag xalem.* He eats no fire. *Kek thuv pilem.* Drinks no smoke. *Kek thaj praxo.* Becomes not dust.

He knows how to read the wind. He knows how to read the clouds. When to seek shelter, when not. Knows which tree to interpret the land by, knows to seek out the giant that stands wider and higher than all the others, or the tree that stands alone. Knows too that sweet is south facing, that the berries he finds will be riper on the southerly side. Knows which flowers follow the sun, which lift their heads to face the golden orb in the sky. Knows to sleep where the spider webs cling to the nooks and crannies, where the wind won't find them or him as he slumbers beneath their jewel-frosted weaves on a pillow of moss. He has grown up directing himself with the wind and the shadows. He is not afraid of them.

"*Zyli wsrod roz,*" he whispers to himself, his breath hot in his ears, his feet pounding toward the greenest grass, swift and invisible. "They lived among the roses. *Nie znali burz.* And they did not know of any storms. *Nie znali burz.* And they did not know of any storms."

BACKGROUND

The Porrajmos is the Gypsy Holocaust. It means "the Devouring." The exact number of Romani lives lost by 1945 is unknown. But figures from the U.S. Holocaust Memorial Museum Research Institute in Washington, DC, puts the number at "between a half and one-and-a-half million."

In December 8, 1938 Himmler's "Decree for Basic Regulations to Resolve the Gypsy Question as Required by the Nature of Race" marked the beginning of plans to exterminate all Sinti and Roma. In February 1939 a brief by Johannes Behrendt of the Nazi Office of Racial Hygiene stated that "all gypsies should be treated as hereditarily sick; the only solution is elimination. The aim should be the elimination without hesitation of this defective population."

A Chronology of Roma Persecution:

1933: Officials in Burgenland, Austria, call for the withdrawal of all civil rights of Roma.
1935: Marriages between gypsies and Germans are banned.
1936: The Roma are no longer given the right to vote.

1938: "Gypsy Clean-Up Week"—the start of the Porrajmos (the Gypsy Holocaust) where hundreds of Sinti and Roma throughout Germany and Austria are rounded up and incarcerated.

1940: January—the first mass genocidal action of the Holocaust takes place: 250 Romani children in Buchenwald concentration camp are used as guinea pigs to test the Zyklon-B gas crystals. There are no survivors.

August: Internment camps are built throughout Austria.

1941: 5000 Roma are sent to the Jewish ghetto of Lodz in Poland.

1942: Himmler orders the deportation of all German Roma to Auschwitz-Birkenau. At the same time all 5,000 gypsies in the Lodz ghetto are transported to Chelmo and gassed.

1943: March—1,700 Romani men, women, and children are gassed at Auschwitz-Birkenau.

In July Himmler orders that all Roma are to be killed.

1944: August 2—*Zigeunernacht* (Gypsy Night) takes place. 4,000 gypsies are dragged screaming to the gas chamber and killed.

1945: January 27—Soviet soldiers reach Auschwitz and find one Roma survivor.

The Killing Tree:

So as not to waste bullets, other methods were adopted to kill children and babies. Some were drowned. Others were picked up by their feet and swung against the trunk of a tree.

The mass murder of gypsies was not recognized at the Nuremberg trials, and not a single gypsy was called to witness. To this day only one guard has received a sentence for crimes against them.

The Nazi genocide of the gypsies was only officially acknowledged in 1982 by West German chancellor Helmut Schmidt, but even then the few gypsy survivors struggled to navigate the bureaucratic obstacles, and, unlike their Jewish counterparts, gypsies orphaned by Nazis do not qualify for reparations.

It was not until April 14, 1994, that the U.S. Holocaust Memorial held its first commemoration of gypsy victims.

* * *

In 1926, the Swiss charity Pro Juventute established the Hilfswerk für die Kinder der Landstrasse [Charity for the Children of the Country Road] with the support of the Swiss Federal Council.

As its director, Pro Juventute named the Romanist Alfred Siegfried (1890–1972) whose research focused on *"Vagantenkindern"* [children of vagrants]. He defined his task as follows:

"Whoever wants to combat vagrancy successfully has to try to explode the union of the traveling peoples, he has to rip apart the family ties. There is no other way. Chances of success are only then favorable, when the children can be totally isolated from the parents."

Between 1926 and 1973, social workers would receive a notice from either a citizen or the local police that a group of "itinerants" had arrived in the vicinity. Siegfried's people would then, accompanied by policemen, drive to the campsite of the Yenish and demand that the children be handed over. Often, resistance was met with force. The children were taken to a home for orphans. Children who escaped were caught again and sent to psychiatric clinics for evaluation. Difficult children ended up in juvenile hall, psychiatric units, or prison. Over 700 gypsy children suffered this fate.

Yenish is a term for travelers of Swiss origin. They are the third-largest population of nomadic people in Europe. They differ culturally and ethnically from the Roma. Today 35,000 *Jenische* live in Switzerland. Only about 5,000 of them live the traveler lifestyle.

The Romani are a diaspora ethnicity of Indian origin who arrived in midwest Asia, then Europe, at least one thousand years ago. They are called in the world by various names such as Romany, Roma, Zigeuner, Cigáni, or Gitano, but in their own language, Romani, they are known collectively as Romane. They live mostly in Europe and the Americas.

ACKNOWLEDGMENTS

This book is a work of fiction but in the writing of it some books were very useful to me. They were: *Stone Age,* by the Swiss Yenish writer Mariella Mehr; *Gypsies Under the Swastika, The Gypsies During the Second World War: From Race Science to the Camps,* and *The Final Chapter: Gypsies during the Second World War,* by Donald Kenrick; *A Gypsy in Auschwitz,* by Otto Rosenberg; *Travels Through the Paint Box,* by Victoria Finlay; *Bury Me Standing: The Gypsies and Their Journey,* by Isabel Fonseca; and *The Roads of the Roma: A Pen Anthology of Gypsy Writers,* by Ian Hancock.

I'm indebted to the following people: my agent, Charlotte Robertson at United Agents, for her initial faith in the few chapters I first gave her, her steadfast support, and for making it happen; my editor, Kate Parkin, for her passionate belief in this book and her discerning and heartfelt approach in all things editorial; the team at Hodder & Stoughton and Quercus US, for their delightful enthusiasm; Lindsay Clarke—my wise man in writing and the first to encourage some semblance of worth; Andrew Miller, for his gentle assurances that all would be well and for the books he gave me; Vaughan Sivell, for the early years.

Thank you to my friends, for seeing me through the murky places: Lisa Chae, Katherine Roper, Sally and Tim Palmer, Sarah and Burn Gorman, Kate Jones, Pippa Menzies, Andrew Downey, Venetia Osborne, Alex Price, Sarah Bland, Katie Skasbrook, and Alice Wyn Edwards. And to Holly Price, for her generosity and thoughtful red pen in initial chapters; Alex and Christopher Romer-Lee, for their wise council; Geraldine Thomson, for knowing what to say; Viv Blakey, for her lovely photographs; Lisa Joffe, for the inspirational talks; Lola and Mike Straw, for supporting my work; Paul Rolleman, for sharing his sunlit home; and Stephen Taylor, for listening to the stumbled early drafts and for liking them.

And lastly, but immensely, thanks to my parents, Robin and Sheila Hawdon, for a writing room with a glass roof and a view of the sky where I could finish this book, for their time and insight, their faith in my ventures, and for being there always in the dark and the light; my sister, Gemma Lee Hawdon, for writing in cafés, for swinging on vines with me, from childhood and up into the bewildering beyond, and for being the safe haven that she is to me now; and to my children, Dow and Orly, my *Apasavellos,* for their love and patience and for the day-to-day sharing of a life.

The Rainbow Hunters

In the autumn of 2014, Lindsay Hawdon embarked upon a six-month trip around the world with her two young children. The "Rainbow Hunters" traveled to seven different countries to find the origin of seven different colors, the natural pigments made by the first color-men, to raise money for the charity *War Child*. If you would like to donate please visit www.warchild.org.uk.

IN SUPPORT OF

If you would like to know more about the trip, please visit Lindsay's website at www.lindsayhawdon.com or follow her on Twitter @lindsayhawdon.

Lindsay's trip was supported in part by *Inventing Futures*, a global youth agency that works with nine- to twenty-four-year-olds who are at a transitional stage in their lives, giving them the chance to create a future full of opportunity. If you would like to know more please visit http://www.inventingfutures.org.

ABOUT THE TYPE

Typeset in Dante MT at 11.5/15 pt.

The result of collaboration between typeface artist Giovanni Mardersteig and punch-cutter Charles Malin, the Dante fonts were originally developed as hand-set punches in 1955. The fact that Dante was so easily recreated in machine-set and then digital versions is a testament to its designers' skill.

Typeset by Scribe Inc., Philadelphia, Pennsylvania.